TRACKING JUSTICE

MADDIE CASTLE BOOK TWO

L.T. RYAN

with

C.R. GRAY

LIQUID MIND MEDIA

For information contact:
contact@ltryan.com
https://LTRyan.com
https://www.instagram.com/ltryanauthor/
https://www.facebook.com/LTRyanAuthor

THE MADDIE CASTLE SERIES

For paperback purchase links, visit:
https://ltryan.com/pb

The Handler
Tracking Justice
Hunting Grounds

Receive a free copy of the Maddie Castle prequel novella:
https://liquidmind.media/maddie-castle-newsletter-signup-1/

Chapter 1

Gibberish chattered through the speakers overhead. Evelyn listened closely, trying to decipher the words as she tore open the sugar packet and dumped it in her coffee, but she couldn't make out a bit of it. She never understood that about airports. The audio from the speakers in shopping centers was discernable. Why weren't the ones in airports?

At the buzz of her phone in her pocket, Evelyn's heart skipped. Sliding it out, her shoulders drooped with disappointment. Just some promotional email. She'd hoped it was her daughter, Quinn.

Quinn had gone to college in the fall, and Evelyn missed her more than she missed carbs. They had always been close. Quinn came home most weekends and spent every holiday with Evelyn, but Quinn took her studies seriously. If her nose was in a book, Evelyn had little chance of getting in contact with her.

It was five thirty on Monday morning, though, and Evelyn hadn't heard from Quinn since Saturday morning. She knew she'd get a text or call in an hour or two. Quinn's first class started at eight. She probably wasn't even up yet.

Still, Evelyn hurried to check the next notification that came in. Another promotional email.

Why was she so worried? It was never comforting when Evelyn left town, or when Quinn was too absorbed to get in touch, but this was different. A sinking feeling in her gut.

That was silly. Everything was fine. She was sure everything was—

Two hands curved around her waist from behind.

Evelyn jolted, spilling hot coffee all over her blouse. A chuckle sounded behind her, a familiar one. Spinning to meet his gaze, laughing, Evelyn cupped a hand over her chest. "You're lucky this is iced."

Smiling, Mark dabbed her chest with a napkin from the table behind her. "I'm sorry. I thought you saw me."

She reached out for a hug, holding him tight around his shoulders. With a kiss on his cheek, and then another on his lips, embracing the stubble of each brush, the heavenly scent of his cologne and shampoo, there was no stopping her smile. Tugging back just far enough to look at him, she combed some hair behind his ear. "I would've done that if I had."

"I'll keep that in mind." Mark kissed her again, hands trailing down her lower back. "How was your flight?"

"Not bad," she said. "But I thought you weren't landing until now."

"I upgraded to first class, so we were the first to depart the plane." Releasing the embrace, Mark bent to collect Evelyn's carry-on. "I'm starving. Do you wanna get breakfast on the way home?"

"I'd kill for breakfast. Wanna stop halfway?" They lived just more than two hours from the airport. "Or do you wanna get something here?"

"Definitely not here," he said. "I do need one of those coffees, though."

"And since you spilled half mine on me"—she shot him a teasing smirk—"so do I."

* * *

EVELYN'S BACK WAS ACHING BY THE TIME SHE AND MARK MADE IT to their driveway. As much as she adored living so far from civilization, she still thought about getting a place in the city. She could afford it, but was it worth it? It wasn't like flying was a frequent part of her job description. Usually Evelyn stayed in her forest-and-farm-covered county.

Maybe a little condo would be worth it, though. It'd certainly make date night in the city more sensual if she and Mark didn't have a two-hour ride home.

With a squeeze on her knee, Mark caught Evelyn's attention. "You okay?"

"My sciatica's acting up." She shifted, trying to get comfortable. "Just can't wait to get home."

"Almost there." He lifted her hand to his lips and kissed the back. "Then I can massage it for you."

Evelyn chuckled, stretching across the center console to rest her head on his shoulder. That was what she loved about Mark. David, her late husband, had been sweet at times, but rougher around the edges. Less affectionate. Mark practically worshipped the ground Evelyn walked on.

Cresting through the foliage, the home Evelyn and Mark had built together two years ago came into view. With a sigh and a smile, Evelyn reminded herself why she loved it out here.

The home looked like a castle, mountains coated in green rolling around it in all directions. Gray stone lined every wall, accentuated with draping flowers on the dozens of windowsills. Ivy lined the turret in the corner.

It was like something from a storybook.

Except for the red Prius parked in front.

Quinn's red Prius.

"Doesn't she have school today?" Mark asked.

"I thought so." Evelyn checked her phone to be sure she hadn't forgotten about an observed holiday. She hadn't. "Maybe she's sick."

As they drove the rest of the way up the drive, Evelyn dialed Quinn's number. It went straight to voicemail.

That feeling in her gut, the maternal instinct that'd dissipated at the airport, came back tenfold. Before the blue sedan had even stopped, Evelyn burst from the passenger side door. She darted up the stairs to the porch, hurried her key into the knob, and yelled up the steps, "Quinn? Are you here, sweetie?"

Silence.

Heart hammering, Evelyn called out for her daughter again, glancing into the living room, then down the hall to the kitchen.

Still, silence.

Stomach churning, yelling, "Quinn? Why aren't you at school?" Evelyn jogged up the stairs to her daughter's bedroom. With a spin of the handle, she shoved open the door.

Tucked within the pink blankets, brown hair resting on the pillow, facing the opposite direction, Quinn lay.

"Quinn," Evelyn repeated, walking around the bed. "Sweetheart, are you feeling okay?"

Silence.

She reached out to shake her daughter's shoulder.

And her skin was ice cold.

"Quinn." Evelyn shook her bicep. "Quinn, wake up."

Silence.

Breaths hard and uneven, panic trembling her hands, Evelyn yanked the blanket down. Previously disguised by the linen, Quinn's lips were blue. Her pale flesh had the same dark, almost bruised purple undertones.

When Evelyn's fingers fell to Quinn's neck, in search of a pulse, she instead felt her daughter's unmoving cold flesh.

"Quinn!" she sobbed, shaking her from side to side. "Honey, wake up! Wake up!"

"What's the..." Mark's voice trailed off in the doorway. "Oh my god."

"Help me!" Evelyn cried, barely looking at him over her shoulder. "Call 911!"

Chapter 2

SMALL CAPS Someone once told me that Pennsylvania was Pittsburgh and Philly, with Alabama in between.

That wasn't true. Sure, we had our farmlands, and plenty of old-fashioned country folk, but amidst the mountains and rolling hills, there was wealth.

Lots of it.

For the last ten miles of my drive, all I'd seen were trees camouflaging mansions tucked deep in the early spring blooms. Most of them were so concealed by vegetation, I'd only gotten a glimpse of them as my beat-up SUV trudged up the narrow roads. There'd been one a few miles back with a massive pond in the front yard that could fit a dozen of my trailers inside it.

Unfortunately, I hadn't realized there was a mansion behind it until *after* my German Shepherd relieved herself in the bushes framing the body of water. I'd thought we were miles from civilization in the forest, so I hadn't planned on picking it up. It was fertilizer, and I was sure the bears didn't pick up theirs, either.

Then a man in a suit a few dozen yards down the road said, "You aren't leaving that there, are you?" in a particular tone, nearly giving me a heart attack.

Like there was *so* much foot traffic here.

Apologizing, I grabbed it quickly.

Now, driving twenty miles an hour and flinching at every pothole, I squinted at every break in the vegetation for a driveway. Evelyn had told me her home was hard to spot from the road, but I hadn't understood what she'd meant until that mansion with the lake. Without my GPS, which had lost service ten minutes ago, that was my only option.

The drive was pretty, at least. Something about being deep in the forest was freeing. Even if those forests were quartered off by wrought iron fences and state-of-the-art security systems.

Despite driving so slowly, I almost missed Evelyn's driveway. Then, after a sharp turn into said driveway, I almost slammed into one of those wrought iron fences, this one embossed with the letter *B* in calligraphy.

Easing off the brake, I pulled forward to the metal box. Rolling down the window, I scanned the keypad. She hadn't given me a code to get in, and the big red button on the right didn't look like a doorbell. If there was a signal out here, I'd give her a call, but there wasn't, so I couldn't, and I clicked the big red button.

It beeped.

Silence followed.

Glancing around, I half expected a convoy of guards in armored trucks to approach with guns drawn. Instead, after a few heartbeats, the gates tucked inward.

"Think that's our cue, Tempy?" I asked, reaching over to pet her ear.

She cocked her head to the side.

Laughing, I released the brake. "Let's hope so."

* * *

"EVELYN BARNES." AFTER TAKING MY JACKET, SHE EXTENDED A hand. "I hope you had a nice drive."

"No complaints." Shaking her hand—noting how smooth and well-manicured her fingernails were—I glanced around. Just standing inside this place made me feel underdressed. Made me feel weird about

Tempest at my side, too. Everything from the chandelier overhead—that probably cost more cash than I'd see in a lifetime—to the sparkling black marble underfoot screamed, *I'm better than you.*

But Evelyn's demeanor screamed the opposite.

Mascara smeared the corners of her pale blue eyes. Her graying black curls laid messily over the shoulders of her cardigan. Thick sweatpants lined her legs, the bottoms stained brown, as though she'd been wearing them for days, carelessly dragging them beneath her even when she'd been outside.

Evelyn looked like every other sorrow-filled mother I'd ever met.

Grief doesn't care about how much money you've got. It comes for us all with the same burning sword.

"I have some coffee on," she said, gesturing to the doorway behind her. "Would you like to sit and have a cup?"

"After you." Following behind her to the kitchen, I kept Tempest close.

Evelyn hardly glanced at my K9. I wasn't sure she'd even noticed Tempy, whose poor behavior had improved drastically since I'd taken her in, but I didn't trust her. It was rare that I trusted any dog wholeheartedly. They were animals, after all. But so were we.

That's also the reason I trusted few humans.

"I've got iced as well, if you'd like that better. That was all Quinn drank, and now I have gallons of iced coffee taking up all this space in my fridge and..." She gripped the backrest of the kitchen chair as she sat, as though she'd fall without it. "Anyway. Whatever you'd like, just say so."

"I'm alright. Thanks." Sitting in the chair across from her, I told Tempest to sit at my side. "And I'm so sorry for your loss."

Evelyn nodded, like that was the most she could give me.

Small talk did no good in situations like these. I was no good at it anyway.

Tugging out my notebook, I clicked my pen. "So you believe the police were incorrect about the nature of Quinn's passing?"

"I don't *believe* it," she said. "I know it."

"Why's that?"

"We were close. She didn't do drugs, she...she was a good girl. Her schoolwork mattered to her more than anything. There's no way she would've done that. Never, not in a million years."

From what I'd gathered from the police report, though vaguer than I would've expected, they didn't think it was an intentional suicide. It seemed to the cops that Quinn had overdosed accidentally.

I knew firsthand how easy it was to do that.

Firsthand knowledge also told me that people didn't like to acknowledge when their loved one was getting high.

"How old was Quinn?" I already knew the answer, but diverting her focus might help her be less defensive.

"Nineteen." Evelyn dabbed the tears in her eyes with her sleeve. "She just turned nineteen in October."

"And was she in college?"

"Yes, she was. She lived on campus, but she hated the school's library, so she came here to study. She was here most weekends, too. Her roommate snores." Evelyn chuckled. "Quinn liked having her own room a few nights each week."

I gave her a sad smile too, jotting some notes in my pad. "Can you think of anyone who may have wanted to hurt Quinn?"

"God, no. Everyone loves Quinn. She's funny, and the light of the party, and smart, and beautiful." Evelyn's lip quivered, tears bubbling over. "Was. She *was* all those things."

Despite all that sounding like a cliche, I didn't doubt it. Lots of young, beautiful, smart, lights of the party died before they got the chance to really live. One thing I did question, though, was a nineteen-year-old living on campus who always *just said no*. Most kids did drugs, whether their parents acknowledged it or not. "Does she have any close friends?"

"A few, yes," Evelyn said. "Do you want me to get a list together?"

"Please." Ripping out a page of my notebook and passing it her way, I laid a pen on her side of the table. "I just like to speak with anyone who knew her. We're all characters in a story, and the viewpoint of each one gives a clearer picture of any foggy parts, if that makes sense."

"Sure," Evelyn murmured, reaching for her phone to look up contact information.

Footsteps thumped down the hall behind Evelyn.

Tempest stood, hair on her back shooting up.

"No," I said sharply.

Growling low, too low for Evelyn to hear, Tempest tugged the lead.

I yanked it back, a quick correction that brought her attention back to me. "Sit."

Another low growl.

Giving her a firm glare, I said, "*Sit*."

With a chuff, she plopped onto her bottom.

When I looked up, a man in a suit and tie walked up behind Evelyn. He gave her a gentle kiss on the head, and she soothed at his touch. "Who's this, honey?"

"Oh, Madison Castle, that private investigator I was telling you about." Evelyn gestured between us. "Maddie, this is my husband, Mark."

"Nice to meet you." I shook his hand over the table. "I'm sorry for your loss."

"Thank you," he said, sitting beside his wife. "I'm assuming you'd like to speak with both of us, right? Get as much information as you can?"

"It makes my job easier if everyone has some input," I said. "We were just talking about Quinn's studies. She was a committed student, huh?"

"Valedictorian in high school." Tears glistened his eyes. "4.0 all first semester."

"She was gonna be a doctor." Evelyn squeezed her husband's hand atop the glass table. "Ever since she was a little girl, that's all she wanted. To save people."

"More noble than us." Mark chuckled, wiping a tear away. "She lies for a living, and I sell used cars."

Ah. A lawyer and the owner of a car dealership. No wonder they were loaded.

"That's the goal, isn't it?" I asked. "Everyone wants better for their kids than they have for themselves."

Evelyn nodded, the joy in her eyes dissipating. "Didn't think I'd have to see her buried. Or like *that*."

A chill stretched down my spine. "You found her, correct?"

Unable to hold my gaze, she turned to the tabletop, nodding in answer.

"It'd been a couple days, they said," Mark said. "We were both away for work. Evelyn had a deal she was closing in Erie, and I was at a convention in New York City. Trying to secure a new parts dealer." He nibbled his lower lip, shaking his head. "If we'd known this would happen, we would've been here, ya know?"

"There's no use in playing the 'what if' game," I said. "It doesn't help."

"Not much does." Sniffling, Evelyn grabbed a tissue from the table behind her. "Anyway, if there's anything you need, no matter the cost, you tell me."

That might make this easier. But if Evelyn was right, and Quinn had no enemies, I wasn't sure if the answers I'd have for her would be the ones she hoped for.

Now that her husband was at the table though, I needed to circle back to the elephant in the room. "I appreciate that. Mark, we were just talking about the cause of death. The reports say an accidental overdose. Do you think that's out of character for your daughter?"

He shot a quick glance at Evelyn before settling his gaze back on me. "Quinn did get caught at school with some drugs when Evelyn and I first got together—"

"She was fifteen," Evelyn snapped, releasing his hand. "She wasn't a junky, Mark. It was a little bit of pot. There were a lot of changes in her life, and she'd just lost her dad, and—"

"Ma'am." Reaching across the table, I laid my hand over her tense fist. "I'm not judging Quinn. I wouldn't judge her if she was an addict, or a stripper, or living in a hippy commune."

Evelyn's rage tempered, an unwilling smile coming to her lips.

I returned it. "I just need to understand her. If you want me to find out what happened, I need to know everything there is to know, even if those facts aren't comfortable."

Shoulders loosening, Evelyn nodded.

"A little weed is a far stretch from heroin," I said. "If she'd been using a drug like that, you would've known."

"It wasn't heroin," Evelyn said. "They said it was ecstasy."

My brows furrowed. "MDMA?"

"Yes," Evelyn said.

Odd.

While it was possible to overdose on MDMA to the point of death, it was rare. On the streets, it was called the 'hug drug.' It induced a sense of euphoria and occasionally anxiety. Some people took it and fell into intense panic attacks.

The death from an MDMA overdose involved rapid heartbeat, hyperthermia, paranoia, and even hallucinations for some. The dangers of overdose were often found at concerts and festivals, where tons of people were jammed into small spaces and could easily overheat. Users often didn't realize they were overdosing because they were too lost in the euphoria. On top of that, it was a drug people rarely used on their own, especially so for committed college students.

Alone in a mansion, a user would notice the overdose symptoms and call for help. Since it was closer to a stimulant than a downer, it wasn't the popular choice for suicide, either. Taking too many opioids meant drifting into sweet oblivion. Taking too much of a stimulant was a living nightmare anyone would want to wake from.

So why hadn't Quinn?

"Could you show me to the room you found her in?" I asked.

11

Chapter 3

"No one's been in here since the police left." Evelyn stood in the doorway, pulling her cardigan close to her body. "When they said they weren't looking into it after the autopsy, I made sure no one could disturb anything."

"Thank you." Carefully, I lifted a framed photo of Quinn from the nightstand. She was younger, wearing a cheerleader uniform, and a man stood beside her with an arm around her waist and his lips pressed to her cheek. It clearly wasn't Mark, but the pose was parental. "This your ex-husband?"

Evelyn gave a short nod.

"Do you mind if I ask what happened?"

Licking her teeth, she pulled her sweater in tighter. "He drank too much at the bar and drove off a bridge."

Gently setting it back on the dresser, I apologized again for her loss.

"Quinn wasn't like him," Evelyn insisted. "He had a problem, but Quinn didn't. She never forgave him for that. She wouldn't—"

I gave her that sad smile again. "I'm not judging anyone for anything."

Posture relaxing, she looked away.

"I don't have much yet," I said, "but it's not easy to OD on molly. That gives me reason to be suspicious, alright?"

Just a bit, her tension eased. "That's what I thought too."

"I'm gonna put everything I have into finding out what happened to Quinn." Turning to face her, I put both hands on my hips. "But maybe it's best I look around alone. It can't be easy to be in here right now."

"I'm fine."

"No disrespect, but I don't believe you are. You're grieving, so you're already easily agitated, and this is where you found her. I wanna help you, but I don't want to make you relive the worst moment of your life. So please. Just let me look around, and I'll be downstairs in a moment."

She was quiet for a few seconds, only staring at me with tears in her eyes. "Just please don't take anything without telling me. I haven't been able to go through her things yet."

"Of course."

After a short nod of understanding, she all but sprinted down the hall.

That was only part of the reason I wanted her gone.

The other part was that I knew teenagers, and there were likely things in here that Evelyn didn't need to see.

Everything looked normal at a glance. There was some clutter on the vanity in the corner. Makeup, jewelry, skin care creams. Photos hung on all the walls with pieces of scotch tape. The floor was mostly clear, aside from a sock tucked under the bed and a jacket that'd fallen off the hook in the corner. Some miscellaneous clothing spilled from the dresser drawers. It was decorated with frilly, girly things—walls pink with purple stencils of butterflies scattered about.

Just what I'd expect from a teenage girl who'd gone off to college less than a year ago.

When I rummaged through her drawers, I didn't find anything odd. Just unfolded clothes shoved inside.

I did that too. Life was too short to worry about folding laundry, wrinkles or not.

13

But I felt like I was missing something. I couldn't put my finger on what. Something just felt off.

Then I made it to the closet.

Hanging from the rack were some dresses. A shoe rack sat neatly against the wall, each shoe tucked with their matching counterpart. The shelf overtop was organized to perfection, camisoles folded into tidy piles, bras cradling one another in a row, and spare blankets bound tightly. Even the fitted spare sheet was folded into a perfect square.

Who folded fitted sheets? Everyone I knew wound them into balls, tossed them on a shelf, and said good enough.

But not Quinn.

Clothes spilled out of her dresser drawers, but her closet was tidier than a butler's. Why put so much effort into making sure this space stayed perfect when the rest of her room was cluttered and disorganized?

If I were a teenager with a mom like Evelyn, one who kept a nice home and treasured nice things, why would I keep one *single* area of my room so neat?

Because Mom might come in to tidy up the clutter. She might wash a load for me, bring it up to put it away, and see how messy my drawers were. Then she'd start sorting through it. She'd organize them for me.

Then she'd get to the closet, see it was already clean, and move on to the makeup dusted vanity in the corner.

Quinn had hidden something in here she didn't want Evelyn to see.

Flicking on the light, I craned onto my tiptoes for a better look at the top shelf. There wasn't much there, mostly spare linens, but I still leafed through it all. Once it was clear, I pulled the clothes that hung from left to right, checking in the pocket of each garment along the way. Nothing there either.

Lowering myself to a knee, I cursed beneath my breath when the pain shot up my thigh. I dropped to my ass instead. From there, I pulled out each shoe, checking in the cavern of each for a bag of drugs.

Nothing.

I was about to say my suspicion was wrong when I noted a backpack tucked in the very back behind the shoe rack.

Tugging it out, with gloved fingers, I unzipped it and peeked inside.

A lacy red thong and bra? Yeah, probably not something she wanted Mom to see.

But digging deeper, cold metal bled through the layer of nitrile. Found myself incredibly grateful for the gloves as I tugged out a set of black, furry handcuffs. She was nineteen. I had the feeling those hadn't been sterilized before she shoved them back in here.

The bag wasn't empty yet. The deeper I dug, the more I found. Another set of cuffs was next. These were furry on the inside too, but leather on the outside. The only metal was on the buckle that fastened them in place.

The things at the bottom of the bag were a bit more scandalous.

Nothing crazy, but more hardcore than the average nineteen-year-old would understand.

Staring down at Quinn's assortment, praying Evelyn wasn't gonna pop up in the doorway, I chewed my lower lip. Tempest lowered herself to her belly beside me and laid her head on my lap. Usually, I'd pet her, but considering the things I'd just touched, I decided that was a no-go.

In this room, Quinn overdosed on MDMA, the love drug. Had her collection of love toys contributed to that?

This wasn't exactly my area of expertise. Pain sucked. I wanted no part of it, whether it was paired with pleasure or not.

But I knew one thing. Partaking in sex with a sadist could be dangerous if it wasn't handled carefully. A man who enjoyed inflicting pain on the woman he was intimate with, who was nineteen and inexperienced, could be a dicey situation.

Add in the indisputable statistic that women were more likely to die at the hands of an intimate partner than anyone else, and a theory started forming.

Maybe they'd done some ecstasy together, got lost in the moment, and decided they'd try something new. Maybe it went too far.

Quinn could've had a heat stroke, or gone into cardiac arrest, and her partner wouldn't have noticed until it was too late if pain was a part of the pleasure. The recognizable signs wouldn't have been so prevalent if Quinn was tied down and lost in euphoria.

Evelyn hadn't mentioned a boyfriend, but these weren't the sorts of tools someone could use by themselves.

Once I'd tucked everything back into the bag, I put it back where I'd found it, struggled upright, and started to the door. Quinn must've had a phone, and I needed to go through it.

But my eyes caught on something on the far wall.

A photo hanging above Quinn's dresser, held up by a thumbtack.

The picture was recent, judging by Quinn's haircut.

And beside her sat a woman. A woman I knew well. I had to do a double take, because surely that couldn't be right.

But as I got closer, studying it, I was sure I had to be.

Harper.

Detective Ashley Harper.

My former best friend, who was fifty percent to blame for my failed engagement.

Quinn knew Harper.

* * *

"Did you find anything?" Evelyn asked from the foyer as I descended the stairs. "Do you need anything?"

"I think I've got what I need for now from in there." Stepping to the landing with Tempest, I decided it was best not to mention the bag I'd found. It wasn't a visual any mother wanted to hold on to. "But I do have a couple questions."

"Anything," Evelyn said.

"Where'd you find my name?" I asked.

"An old family friend. Why?"

For some reason, my belly twisted. "Ashley Harper?"

"Yeah, she used to babysit Quinn. I called her when everything happened, and she said it was odd, but it was out of her jurisdiction." Evelyn's expression was still puzzled. "Is something wrong?"

"No, I just saw a picture of her and Quinn. Thought I'd ask." I forced a smile. "Did Quinn keep in touch with Ashley?"

"They weren't best friends, but they talked. Why?"

Because Ashley knew the importance of disclosure in an investigation. Evelyn was quite concerned with Quinn's reputation. Anything she gave me was gonna come from a biased viewpoint. Ashley would tell me the facts, no matter if she liked them.

"Might bounce some ideas off her." Even if I dread looking her in the eye. "Quinn had a phone, I'm sure."

"Of course. I meant to give it to you earlier." Evelyn dug in the pocket of her cardigan and passed it to me. "I took the code off. Any other passwords you need are listed in her notes."

Quinn was considered gen Z, so likely well-aware of the risks of storing their passwords in such an accessible place. "She left them there?"

"No, I jotted them down for you. She always forgot her logins." Evelyn chuckled. "Every other day, she called me asking for her health insurance number, or how to check her balance in her savings account. Things like that."

Damn. I wondered what it'd be like to have a mom who handled all those things for me.

It backed up Evelyn's prior statement, however. They were close. Just not close enough for Evelyn to know about things Quinn did in bed.

"I understand." Giving her a smile, I started to the door. "I'm gonna do some digging. Maybe go talk to her friends. I'll get back to you when I have some more information."

"Sure. Thank you." As I grabbed the door handle, Evelyn spoke again, voice cracking, "Maddie?"

I looked at her over my shoulder.

"Do you think I'm crazy?" Her tears bubbled over again. "Everyone else does. But it doesn't add up to me. Even if she did do things I don't know about. Even if she was a typical college girl. There are still gaps that don't make sense."

No, I didn't think she was crazy. Did I think she was as close with

Quinn as she believed she was? Absolutely not. They had a good relationship, but they weren't exactly the *Gilmore Girls*.

"I agree," I said. "There are gaps. A chunk of the story's missing, but I've seen overdoses on MDMA, and they don't usually look like this. Even if she'd willingly taken the drugs, I don't believe she did them alone."

It was as if saying that lifted a world off Evelyn's shoulders. They lowered with relief.

"But there were no signs of forced entry, right?"

Evelyn shook her head.

"That tells me whoever's involved knew Quinn. She trusted them. She let them inside. That's what I'm gonna try to figure out from her phone," I said. "And I'm assuming you don't have security cameras? You would've seen something on them."

"Our system crashed right before Christmas," Evelyn said. "I kept telling myself I was gonna get it replaced, but it was the holidays, and then a work thing came up, and another came up, and—"

"And you weren't counting on something like this happening. I understand. But whatever pieces of the story we're missing, I'm gonna find."

Evelyn's eyes filled with tears again. She gave a quick nod.

"Before I start, I wanna make sure you understand something, Evelyn." Facing her, I made sure to soften my expression. "My job is finding dirt on people. And everyone has it. *Everyone* has skeletons in their closet. I'm sure Quinn had them, too. Whatever I find might mess with the image you have in your mind of your daughter. I need to make sure you understand that before I get too deep."

The tears only intensified. Evelyn didn't sob, but she did turn away to regain her composure. Eventually, she cleared her throat. "I'm a lawyer. I do the same thing for a living. And I want to know, even if it isn't pretty. Even if Quinn had a secret life I know nothing about, I want to know."

"Then I'll get to work."

Chapter 4

IT WASN'T HARD TO FIND THE BOYFRIEND. TROY AUSTIN. THEY weren't listed as "In a Relationship" on any of her social medias, but he liked every single one of her profile pictures, going all the way back to when she'd first created the account. The only time that was socially acceptable was if they were a couple, or at least seeing each other. If it'd been some random guy, she would've blocked him.

Sure enough, when I clicked through her direct messages to see if they'd exchanged any, there were hundreds. Maybe thousands. I didn't get far enough back for that, especially after finding some explicit ones I really didn't want to see more of.

Outside of the more scandalous stuff, however, were typical couple texts.

Morning, beautiful<3
Morning(:
Last night was fun. We should do it again. Are you busy Friday?
Nope, wide open. Your place or mine?
Yours prolly. There are doors, and no roommates.
Lol point taken. What time?

And plenty of others just like that.

From there, I did a deep dive on Troy Austin. He went to the same college as Quinn. A soccer champ for the school. Popular, handsome, stereotypical frat boy.

Not who I would've pictured using Quinn's assortment of toys, but judging a book by its cover wasn't wise.

Either way, one of his pictures was taken outside his fraternity, so I knew where to head next.

* * *

Tempest stayed at my side as I approached the house. I hadn't gone to college, so I didn't know much about this subculture, but the place wasn't what I expected.

For some reason, I thought there'd be beer bottles scattered about. Maybe a couch on the front lawn. Probably a bunch of drunken kids drooling over the pretty girls who walked by.

But nope.

It was fancy. The frat house looked like a luxury home. There was even a little picket fence lining the manicured grass and high green hedges.

Reaching out for the handle, someone stepped from behind those bushes. He carted an armful of books, brown eyes sunken and red. In the photos, he'd looked lively. Joyous and smiley. Like he was the happiest man alive.

After almost pummeling me with the gate, Troy eased out a deep breath. "Shit, I'm sorry. Didn't see you."

"It's alright." I extended a hand. "You're actually who I was looking for."

Confusion settling through him, he gave me a once over and shook my hand. "Yeah?"

"Troy Austin, right?" I asked.

He nodded.

"Maddie Castle. I'm a private investigator. Evelyn Barnes hired me to look into her daughter's death."

Still, he glanced me over, noticing I wasn't dressed to the nines today.

That was a rare occasion. Leggings and a hoodie. Not stylish, but were comfortable, and given the crowd who usually hired me, it helped me blend in. If I needed to run, it was easier to do so in an outfit like this than heels and a dress.

"Really?" Troy asked.

Passing him a business card, I nodded to the restaurants down the path. "Any chance we can talk?"

Looking up, expression soft and innocent, tears pearled in the corners of his eyes. This kid looked like a puppy. Was he really a sadist in disguise? "You don't think what happened to Quinn was an accident?"

"Do you?"

Nibbling his lower lip, he shook his head. "None of it makes sense to me."

"Wanna get a cup of coffee, and you can tell me why that is?"

"I'll skip my next class. Let me go set these down." He gestured to his books. "There's a coffee cart down that way. Give me, like, two minutes," he said, spinning back toward the door.

Tempest cocked her head to the side at my feet.

"What is it, Tempy?" I asked.

She stared ahead, ears up, alert.

Following her gaze to a black vehicle at the end of the street, at this distance, it was hard to make out the make and model. I could gather it was a four-door sedan, probably high-end judging by the rims. All the visible windows had tint so dark, it would've gotten them a ticket if they were pulled over. No one inside was discernable.

It was driving slowly down the road that intersected with this one. But it seemed that when I noticed it, it sped up.

In a blink, it was out of sight.

* * *

Troy gazed at the photo on the table, stroking a finger down Quinn's long brown waves. With a quiet laugh, he held it up for me to see. "I took this picture, ya know. Quinn said she hated how she looked when someone else took a picture of her, but my dad's a photographer, and I told her she was practically a model. So we went out to that lake and had this little shoot. Our first date. She said no one ever made her look so pretty."

I managed a soft smile back. "Sounds like you guys had a great relationship."

The loving look stayed, but his smile dampened. "When we were together, yeah."

"What do you mean?"

"We were sorta on and off." Tugging at a frayed piece of paper on his coffee cup, he raised a shoulder. "Quinn didn't want anything serious. That's what she said, anyway. The last month or two though, we were just on. No off. She mentioned introducing me to her mom a couple weeks ago."

"Was there a reason she didn't want to be serious?"

"It was about school. There wasn't room for distractions in her life." Troy took a sip of his coffee. "I understood. She was driven like that, ya know? She wanted to be successful. And that was cool with me, but it hurt too, I guess."

He was falling for her, and she was hesitant. If it wasn't for the fact that he agreed that she wouldn't have done this to herself, and the sincerity in his expression, I may've explored the thought of a break-up gone wrong.

I wasn't getting that gut feeling, though. Just the opposite. My gut was telling me that this kid was just that. A kid, madly in love with his college sweetheart.

"I'm sure that was tough," I said. "That's what everyone keeps telling me about Quinn. Driven, smart, focused on her studies."

"Probably the most important thing to her." Troy smiled. "She cared about other things too, but nothing came above school."

"Usually people so serious about their careers don't do party drugs. That's how Quinn died, though."

"And that's what I don't understand."

"So, Quinn didn't do drugs at all?"

Shrugging, he looked away.

Ah, so Quinn wasn't so squeaky clean.

"I'm a P.I., not a cop," I said. "I'm not trying to bust any drug dealers. I just wanna find out what happened to Quinn."

Still nervous, Troy scratched the hairline of his flowy blond waves. "She partied a little, I guess. Not all the time, but once in a while, on the weekends and stuff. Like if she got a good grade, we'd roll a little."

Rolling was the street term for getting high on MDMA.

"Just on special occasions?" I asked.

When he nodded, I gave him a look that said I wasn't sure if I believed that. "Honest, I swear. Quinn was like the mom. She'd go around with these little test strips at parties and dip them in girls' drinks to make sure no one was slipping anything in them. She wouldn't take anything unless there was enough for her to crush it up and make sure it was what she thought it was. My friends said she was weird." He laughed. "But I thought it was cute, ya know? She was just looking out for everyone. It's not like she ever tried to get anybody in trouble. She just didn't want anyone to get hurt."

A girl who carried test strips to parties. Not the kind of girl who'd overdose accidentally.

"If everyone else was partying, she stayed sober to be a designated driver. She never let the guys take girls up to their rooms if they were too drunk. Quinn wasn't, like—I don't know. Yeah, she partied sometimes, but she wasn't a party girl."

There weren't girls around like that when I was her age. But this generation wasn't like mine.

"That's why you think she wouldn't have overdosed accidentally," I said.

"I can't see it," Troy said. "I can't even see her rolling by herself."

"Any idea where she would've gotten them?"

Again, he averted my gaze.

"I'm not locking anybody up, kid," I said. "I'm just trying to figure out what happened."

"Swear you're not telling the cops?"

"On my life."

Rubbing the back of his neck, he looked at the tabletop. "She was holding onto them for me. Things were getting sketchy at the house. The dean heard students were dealing on campus. Rumor was, the cops were coming to do a search. So when she was leaving in the morning, I asked her if she could take them home with her. I didn't wanna lose my scholarship."

"How much was it?"

"Fifteen pills," he said. "Enough to overdose, I guess. But I couldn't see her taking them alone. She was cramming for a test. That's why she was going home for the weekend. Said she couldn't focus in her dorm, and she hated the library."

Hm.

It was getting harder and harder to visualize this kid killing Quinn. Even Tempest seemed to like him, which was rare. Although he was no older than twenty. She probably saw him as a kid, and Tempest *loved* kids.

"Were you planning to meet up with her that weekend?" I asked.

"No. She stayed the night at my place Friday night, and I had practice the evening she died, so I stayed on campus. We were supposed to meet up on Monday, and that's when I heard."

"You didn't think it was weird that she didn't talk to you at all over the weekend?"

"Not really. When she studied, she'd bite your head off if you interrupted her. Her phone was always on *Do not Disturb* when she had a big test coming up."

"Do you have proof you were here throughout that weekend?"

His brows furrowed. "Wait, do you think I did this?"

"I don't think so. But I like to do a thorough job."

His face told me he wasn't happy at my near accusation. "I can prove that I wasn't with her when she died. The frat house has cameras. I'll pull up the footage."

Annoyance evident, he slid out his phone and typed around for a while. Eventually, he turned the phone toward me. Sure enough, with time stamps to prove it, Troy had walked Quinn to her car, kissed her goodbye, and left in his jersey. He returned a few hours later, winded and sweaty.

"I can have my coach call you too," he said. "Except for when I was sleeping, I wasn't alone at all that weekend. I didn't walk off campus once."

All of that did check out for me. But I still didn't understand the things I'd found in Quinn's closet.

"If you could have your coach give me a call, I'd appreciate it," I said. "But I do have one more question for you."

"Which is?"

"I found a bookbag in Quinn's closet. It was full of, uh, adult toys. Do you know anything about that?"

Despite his annoyance a moment prior, his cheeks burned red. Now he didn't just look like a puppy, but a shy, embarrassed puppy. "What does that have to do with anything?"

"That stuff can get dangerous, can't it?" I asked. "If she'd been high, and you guys were using those things, then—"

"Look, that was all Quinn." Lowering his voice, he leaned over the table. "She'd read some books, and she wanted to try some stuff. It was weird, alright? She enjoyed it, but chains and whips don't excite me."

Being here made me feel old, but the fact that an eighteen-year-old knew that reference made me feel a little better. At least they still knew who Rihanna was.

"Not at all?" I asked.

"No." He wrinkled his nose. "I mean, some of it wasn't too bad, but I don't like violence. That's why I play soccer instead of hockey. And either way, I was here. Quinn was there. I've only been to her parents' house a couple times. It's confusing out there. I wouldn't even know how to drive back."

All of that was true. As long as his soccer coach corroborated his story, I had nothing to suspect him of.

"Alright. Thanks for talking to me," I said.

"I hope I helped. Just please, find out what happened to her."

Collecting his bag from the table, he stood. "And I don't know if it'd do you any good, but you might wanna talk to Chelsie."

"Chelsie Johnson?" I glanced at the notebook paper from Evelyn. "Her mom said they were close."

"Used to be," Troy said. "They had a falling out a few weeks ago. I don't know the details, and I couldn't see Chelsie hurting her, but it was messy."

"How so?"

"Screaming at each other in the middle of the cafeteria. Like I said, I don't know the details, but it might be worth looking into."

"Any idea where I can find her?"

"She doesn't live on campus, and I don't think she has classes today, but I know she'll be here tomorrow. She works at that cafe down there."

Chapter 5

"Hey, you," Alex said, voice muffled by the phone's speaker. "What're you up to?"

"Driving home from a case, what about you?" I asked.

"Same, actually. We still on for dinner next Saturday? You better not be calling to cancel."

Recently, I'd been making more of an effort in that department. The last year had been hell on my mental health. Either I pushed everyone away in the chaos, or my circumstances did. Regardless, I'd spent far too much time alone since my life imploded.

I had no family to lean on, but I did have a handful of true friends, chosen family, and I didn't want to lose them. It wasn't until I spent time with them that I realized how much I missed human connection. Almost daily, I hung out with Bentley and Grace—my next-door neighbor and childhood friend, and his daughter—and walking around the city with Alex after a nice meal made life feel normal again.

I laughed. "No, we're still on. I need your help, though."

"What with?"

"This case. You're the M.E. for surrounding counties, right?"

"Yep. Really wish our tax dollars would do something about that," she said under her breath. "Why do you ask?"

"Then you would've done the autopsy on a college girl who died in Bedford County, wouldn't you?"

A heavy sigh echoed through the speaker. "I would've. But you know the rules, Maddie. I can't discuss stuff like that with you."

"If her next of kin signs off on it, you can."

"Yeah, but—"

"I'll call you right back."

Alex didn't have time to say another word before I ended the call and dialed Evelyn. Which wasn't wise to do while driving at sixty miles an hour down the highway. But Siri did most of the work for me, so I technically wasn't violating any laws.

"Did you find something?" Evelyn answered on the first ring.

"It's still early." Although I did have a few leads, none of them were close to concrete. I couldn't relay them to Evelyn yet. "Just trying to collect all the information I can at the moment. That's why I'm calling. A friend of mine is the medical examiner who took care of Quinn. I'd like to talk to her about what she found, but she needs permission from you before—"

"What's the number?"

Knowing it by heart, I gave her Alex's cell.

"I'll handle it."

And now, I was the one who'd been hung up on.

Continuing down the highway, I expected it to be a minute before I got a call back. I also expected it to be Evelyn. Instead, it was Alex.

"Well, she's friendly." Alex's tone made it clear that Evelyn had not been. "But I've got permission. Apparently, she's faxing written consent now. So, throw it at me, Mads. What do you need?"

"Quinn Barnes. Nineteen-year-old college girl died of an accidental overdose. That match your records?"

"If memory serves, that's verbatim. Why do you ask?"

"Because I don't think that's what happened." Noting the dark clouds in the distance, I slowed the car a bit. "Were there any signs of a struggle on her body?"

"Not at all, no. She had sex recently prior to her death, but nothing there to suggest it wasn't consensual. Only trace amounts of fluid were still present. What makes you think that's not what happened?"

Considering Quinn had stayed at Troy's the night before, that wasn't a shock, and it didn't help me much.

"Because who overdoses on MDMA by themselves?"

"Heavy users? She had burns inside her nose, Maddie. She got high regularly."

"Really?"

"I mean, there weren't any other signs of addiction, but yeah. A college girl had some ecstasy, took too much. We both know how that can happen."

"Yeah, but Quinn was an honors student. She partied with her boyfriend and friends, but I don't think she was an excessive user."

"Her tox screen said she used excessively that day," Alex said. "Have you explored the possibility of suicide?"

"Who kills themselves with molly? That overdose is miserable."

"It can be, but maybe she thought the euphoria was worth it?"

"Maybe, but Quinn was smart. She carried test strips around at parties. Her plan was to be a doctor. I'm sure she knew all the possible side effects. If she wanted to die, I think she would've thought of an easier way. Opioids or sleeping pills." I paused, thinking for a moment. "Do her medical records show a history of mental health issues?"

"Nope. That's why I ruled it an accidental overdose. There wasn't a note either," Alex said. "But even so, she comes from a good family. You know how people in that tax bracket feel about reputations. As stupid as it is, there's still a stigma around depression, anxiety, and their treatment. Seeing a therapist is a joke for these people. They might not have let her get help."

If that were so, wouldn't Troy have known? I guessed friends and families weren't always aware when a loved one was struggling, especially not if Quinn was anything like her mom and wanted to keep her reputation untarnished.

But I still had that gut feeling that something was off.

"Maybe," I murmured. "I don't know. I just have a weird feeling about this. But I'm gonna see if I can run some checks on her friends and family. Can I call you back if any questions come up?"

"You know you can," Alex said. "I'm about to go through the tunnels, anyway. Bye, sweetie."

As soon as I'd ended the call, I dialed again.

Ox answered on the second ring. "You okay?"

"Nope, locked in a serial killer's basement."

"Send me your loc—"

"That was a joke." After knowing one another for almost a decade, you'd think he would've learned to detect my sarcasm by now. "Relax. Sit down. Catch your breath."

"You say that, but if you *were* locked in a serial killer's basement, you'd use that same tone to tell me."

"Nah, I'd text."

I could practically hear his eye roll. "What's going on, Maddie?"

"A case." Checking my mirrors, I merged to the right. My exit was approaching. "I was wondering if you could look some people up for me."

"Shouldn't be a problem. You have the names?"

"Evelyn Barnes, Mark Barnes, Troy Austin, and Chelsie Johnson for now. All spelled how they sound," I said.

"I'll see if I can find anything. Something you want me to look out for?"

"Not really. I just don't wanna be blindsided in this case."

"General search then. What's the case?"

I explained briefly, ending with, "It just doesn't fit together to me. It's like I'm missing something, but I can't tell what."

"Your gut's never wrong." Something about the tone he said that in gave me a warm, cozy feeling in my belly. "If something doesn't fit, keep looking until you find the missing piece."

"Thank you."

"Don't thank me. It's an excuse to get out of this damn bed." A quiet groan echoed through the speaker. "I've binged every TV show ever played in the last few weeks."

Although Ox had healed some since the shooting that had punctured his lung, he wasn't back to himself yet. He had four more weeks, minimum, before they'd clear him to return to work.

"A few more weeks, and you'll be back to your usual," I said. "Enjoy the rest while you've got time for it."

"I'll sleep when I'm dead," he grumbled.

* * *

WHEN I GOT HOME, I TOOK TEMPEST OUTSIDE FOR A FEW MINUTES. Once she finished up, I fed her, made myself a coffee, and sat on the sofa.

After confirming Evelyn's and Mark's alibis through their posts on social media, their hotel locations tagged in Eerie and New York with photos of them in the lobbies the Friday of check in, I dived into Quinn's phone.

In the modern world, seeing inside someone's phone was like a glimpse into their mind. If Quinn was depressed, there'd be some evidence of it in here.

Scrolling through her social media, full of inspirational quotes, I did have to bounce the idea around. Someone repeatedly talking about self-care and preaching about how it was impossible to fill from an empty cup could've told me that Quinn was just an upbeat, happy person.

It could also mean the opposite.

Maybe Quinn was so adamant about daily affirmations of joy and happiness because she was struggling to find it herself. My personal experiences with mental health told me that daily affirmations and manifesting happiness were trademarks of cognitive behavioral therapy. Every therapist I'd ever seen suggested them as part of a routine for trauma, anxiety, and depression.

But if Quinn was in therapy, Alex would've noticed it when checking her medical records. Was she self-maintaining her mental illnesses from articles she found online? Had she been roped into the pseudo-therapy of toxic positivity, internet culture?

Her feeds made me think it was possible.

If that were so, however, she did an excellent job of seeming like she was fine. But I supposed most people who were struggling pretended otherwise.

Something still didn't feel right, though. Maybe Quinn was depressed, maybe she was struggling, but I had a nagging feeling in the pit of my gut that said declaring this a suicide was the easy way out.

There was more to this. I didn't know how I knew it, but I did.

Flipping off her social medias, I went into her direct messages. In her texts, mostly full of daily reminders for classes, tests, and deadlines, I found Chelsie.

Their most recent conversation, dated two weeks before Quinn's death, started with Quinn.

I'm sorry that you're upset, but you'll thank me for it one day.

Go to hell.

Two minutes later, Quinn texted,

Just answer the phone. We can go talk about this.

Leave me tf alone.

This is stupid, Chels. I don't want to fight with you.

Then you shouldn't have done it.

Can we get coffee before class and talk about it?

Can you delete my number?

Seriously? You're acting like I killed your grandma.

Delete. My. Number.

Whatever, Chelsie. Let me know when you're ready to grow up.

It was far from a happy conversation, but it didn't scream *murder* to me either. Judging by Chelsie's tiny physique from her contact photo, I doubted she was physically capable of shoving pills down Quinn's throat either way.

However, maybe it would lead me to that missing piece of the puzzle. Maybe Chelsie didn't kill Quinn, but maybe she knew more about Quinn's life than Troy did. That was far from uncommon. Guys I dated never knew as much about what was going on in my life as my female friends.

That bred the question, though. Could this have been about a guy? Was that why Quinn and Troy were on and off, because he wasn't the only boy she was seeing? I'd explored the possibility of a romantic partner being the one who caused her death, and Troy didn't fit the bill. But maybe a partner she kept secret did.

Much to my disappointment, no matter how deeply I dug through all her private messages, nothing suggested she had another romantic partner. Her list of contacts, however, I found odd.

Several were only initials. KB, for instance, seemed to be from another student at her college. Their texts were things like, *Can I borrow your notes from yesterday?*

That project's due on the 13th. When do you wanna meet up to finish it?

I'm almost done with my portion. Does Friday sound good to put it together?

I dialed the number just to confirm, and sure enough, it was Kristin Barkley, Quinn's lab partner.

One was MH. Their texts were vague, like the others who were only labeled with initials.

Things like, *What time is dinner at Antonio's again?*

Do you need anything at the store?

When can I bring my car in for inspection?

Context clues should've told me who that was, but I gave it a ring to see who it was as well. Mark, Evelyn's husband, answered. While I had him on the line, I asked him a few questions about Quinn, like why she'd called him the morning of her death. He said she'd lost her key and asked where he'd put the spare, then confirmed that he didn't know her well. That wasn't surprising, since Evelyn married him when Quinn was sixteen. It wasn't like Mark was a second father to her. Just the guy her mom married after her dad died.

Quinn's texts with Evelyn were extensive. They talked on the phone regularly, half an hour to hour long conversations. Not to mention the many texts they sent throughout the day.

I have this weird rash. Should I go to the doctor? Quinn texted, with an image.

Looks like dry skin, honey. Use some lotion for a week and see if it helps.

The next day, Quinn texted, *Would it ruin my toaster if I made a grilled cheese in it?*

It might smoke and set off the alarms in your dorm.

Later that day, Quinn texted, *Will it actually ruin my whites if I wash them with colors?*

Probably won't ruin them but might make them dingy looking.

From what I could tell, they were close. Closer than I was with my mom, which wasn't saying much. Still, it brought me back to the boyfriend thing. If she hadn't told Evelyn about Troy yet, she wouldn't have told her about another boy, either.

Especially if she was getting ready to introduce Troy to her parents. She may have deleted any evidence of the previous boyfriend from her digital footprint. The last thing she would've wanted was her new boyfriend to find texts between her and the guy she kept quiet.

The best chance I had at finding out anything about a secret love affair was from her best friend.

A knock thumped at the door.

I jumped, the phone slipping from my fingertips as Tempest barreled in that direction.

Easing out a deep breath, I stood and walked that way. Glancing through the peephole, I wasn't surprised that Bentley stood on my porch in his usual. A faded pair of blue jeans, a bleach-stained T-shirt, and the sweetest smile in the world.

The second I opened the door, he said, "Dinner's done. Tacos tonight. I tried making guacamole, but the avocados weren't ripe, so I'm sorry if you break a tooth. But you've been warned."

Bentley didn't ask if I wanted dinner anymore. He just made it, told me when it was ready, and to come eat. It was inferred that I wouldn't have cooked for myself, because if he wasn't around, I'd eat an Eggo and call that dinner.

Laughing, I grabbed my jacket. "We'll be right over."

Chapter 6

As always, dinner was amazing. I didn't know how Bentley managed to cook like a five-star chef.

When we finished eating, we talked about our days. Grace had gotten her third quarter grades in—straight A's—so Bentley promised to take her rollerblading next weekend.

"I didn't realize that place was still open." Wiping my lip, I set my empty bowl of ice cream on the coffee table. "Have you been there since you moved back?"

"He hasn't, but I have," Grace said. "One of my friends had a birthday party there a couple weeks ago. It's all pretty and shiny."

"Yeah," Bentley said between chews, "I think they renovated it."

"Do you wanna come, Maddie?" Grace grinned. "It'll be fun. If Darius can get a ride out here, I can hang out with him, and you can keep Dad company."

Bentley made a noise in his throat that showed his disapproval.

Chuckling, I raised a shoulder. "Maybe. I haven't tried roller skating since I hurt my knee, but I'll give it a go. Unless something comes up with this case."

"You can use one of those walkers they have for kids," Grace said, still smirking. "And Dad'll be right there. He won't let you fall."

It was hard not to laugh.

Not so subtly, Grace had been pushing us together since she and Bentley moved in. It wasn't like she needed to, since he and I spent time together almost daily. But any time we went out to lunch together, Grace would rush in front of us and take up an entire half of the table so he and I would have to sit side by side.

I didn't mind sitting so close to him, either. Bentley and I had fallen out of touch when he'd left town for college, but more than a decade later, we fell right back into our old routine. There was nothing meaningful about us sitting next to one another or roller skating together.

But Grace was thirteen, and she liked me. Her dad hadn't dated since her mom passed. It was easy for her to see that Bentley and I were close, and she wanted a female role model. In that hormone-filled mind, it was easy to see where she wanted the two of us to end up.

That wasn't something I was ready for with anyone, let alone my best friend. It'd hardly been a year since I got out of the ten-year relationship that fundamentally changed who I was. I was still in the process of figuring out who Maddie Castle was without Lennox Taylor, without a badge, without a working body.

Bentley lost his wife when Grace was seven, and he still carried a picture of Bella in his wallet. He talked about her regularly with love in his eyes. She'd been his world, and I didn't think he was ready to let anyone else in. Bentley's focus in life was Grace.

And like me, he didn't have much else. I was his only real friend here.

Neither of us were ready for what Grace wanted us to be, and neither of us were willing to risk our friendship.

"Do you think it's gonna take that long?" Bentley asked. "I thought you said the case seemed simple."

"Yeah, when I got that call from Evelyn, I thought it would be. But now I don't know. There are so many weird components to it." I went on explaining what I'd gathered. When I got to the part about the bondage equipment in Quinn's bag, I told Grace to cover her ears.

When she didn't, we went to the kitchen and lowered our voices.

This was one nice part about being in private investigation as opposed to standard police work. As a cop, I couldn't discuss legal investigations with civilians. As a P.I., I could bounce ideas off of friends. Bentley's medical knowledge as a paramedic was helpful.

"Yeah, that is weird," Bentley murmured. "You don't have pictures from the scene, do you?"

"Actually, I do." Finding my phone in my hoodie pocket, I swiped to my emails, and showed him the photos Alex had sent me. As he flipped through them, I said, "You've been first on the scene at overdoses. Does that look normal to you?"

"If it were an opioid overdose, sure." He zoomed in on the image. "But any time I've seen someone O.D. on molly, it's a hell of a lot different than this. Usually they're at parties, hyperventilating on the edge of a couch with a bunch of friends giving them bottles of water and putting ice packs on their foreheads. But just sprawled out on the bed like this? Wearing a long-sleeved shirt? Nah, never."

"That was my thought, too. If it was an accidental overdose, why wouldn't she have done something to alleviate the symptoms?"

"Right. Weird drug to try to kill yourself with, too." Bentley handed me the phone back. "And those are some seriously high levels of MDMA. I can't see someone taking that much on purpose."

"Alex said she had burns inside her nose, but the report says she found the pills inside her stomach with her last meal," I said. "Who goes from snorting to swallowing? Even if it *was* an intentional overdose?"

"People usually stick to their method of consumption when it comes to their drugs, casual users or addicts," Bentley said. "You never would've caught my dad swallowing his stash."

"And I never snorted or injected mine." Chewing my inner lip, I tucked my phone into my pocket. "But how would you get someone to swallow a fistful of pills without leaving a mark? No way you could hide that many in food."

"Even if they crushed them, she would've tasted them," Bentley said. "But when Grace was a toddler, Bella had to physically sit on top of her while I put medicine down her throat. I felt awful when I was done with it, but if she was sick, she needed the medicine, so we did what we had to."

Valid point. My mom had done the same thing to me when I was a kid. Then she'd beat my ass for fighting her, and I swallowed the medicine without a battle from then on. "Do you think a team killed her, then?"

"Maybe," Bentley said. "Or the killer used the stuff you found in that bag."

"If she was bound, there would've been signs of a struggle."

"Not with furry, leather cuffs. Those things are made to bind someone safely. Unless she was going berserk, there wouldn't have been marks. Maybe some superficial pain, but I'm not sure if an M.E. would see anything in an autopsy."

Giving him a smile, I arched a brow. "You seem well-informed on this subject."

Bentley's cheeks reddened. "Listen, Grace wanted to read some romance novel, and the reviews said it was 'spicy.' So I read it first. It was informative." He took a gulp of his water. "And too mature for my thirteen-year-old."

I laughed. "Was it any good?"

"Not bad, actually. I didn't think werewolves were my thing, but book one hooked me. I bought the whole series."

Another laugh. "That is a valid point, though." Starting to the fridge, pain stretched up my thigh. Rubbing a hand along it, I grabbed a water. The ache rippled with each step as I walked back to the kitchen island. "I feel like I should start giving you money for how much of your food I eat."

"I'd rather share with you than dump the leftovers that sit in the fridge for a week." Bentley's eyes traveled down my body to my knee. "The pain bad today?"

"It's been worse." Taking a gulp of my water, I raised a shoulder. "We skipped our routine this morning, and I'm paying for it."

"Wanna go do some sets?" he asked. "If we skip too many days, getting back to it's gonna be a bitch."

"I'm down." I glanced at Tempest napping on the floor at Grace's feet. "Do you want me to put her in her crate while me and your dad work out?"

"Nah, she's okay." Grace reached down and gave her head a pet. "Tempy loves me. She won't hurt me."

That was true. Tempest adored Grace. Not once had she growled at her. Still, I'd bought a crate and asked Bentley if I could set it up here because we were over so often, and I didn't like not having the option. Especially when we ate. The little brat begged the entire time. She'd snatched a chip out of Bentley's hand once, she'd nicked his skin in the process, and from there on, she was in the crate or on a lead if we were eating. Hot food, at least. She didn't beg for cold stuff, like ice cream.

Celery, however, was the one cold food she would beg for. You'd think she'd want lunch meat, but nope. Celery.

Tempest was the weirdest dog I'd ever met, and I loved her to pieces.

"Alright." Starting to Bentley's third bedroom, his makeshift gym, I said, "Holler if you have any problems."

Grace ran her fingers through Tempest's fur. "You won't give me any problems, huh, Tempy?"

Bentley sprinted past me, body blocking the door to his third bedroom. "Let's do our sets outside tonight. It's nice out."

"We never work out outside."

"Well, it was cold. Now it's warming up." Side stepping so I couldn't get to the door handle, he smiled. "There's nothing like exercising as the sun sets."

Not that I disagreed. I loved burning calories outdoors. But Bentley had mentioned many times now that he wasn't a fan of it. Bugs flying in his face annoyed him, and he sweat too much.

"Uh-huh." Looking him over, I noticed his hand on the doorknob. "That all this is about? You'd just *prefer* to be outside?"

"Spring's my favorite season."

"Fall's your favorite season."

"Well, spring's *your* favorite season."

"But all our equipment's in there." I nodded behind him. "I'm not gonna do hip lifts lying flat on my back in the muddy grass."

"Let me grab what we need and meet you out there."

"What're you hiding?"

"I'm not *hiding* anything. I just wanna work out outside."

"You're a terrible liar."

"It's not a lie."

Grace laughed on the sofa behind me.

Turning, I gave her a smile. "Does he have a body in there or something? Is he secretly a serial killer?"

"Oh, yeah. A hundred and ten percent," she said. "Sorry to rat you out, Dad."

"Look at that. Now I've got an eyewitness account." Smirking, I put my hands on my hips. "Either you gotta prove her wrong or admit to what you've done."

"Show me a warrant, and you can look at whatever you want to."

"What is it?" I asked. "You were lying about where your knowledge of Quinn's recreational activities came from, huh? You've got your own set up in there, don't ya?"

Bentley laughed. "Can you just trust me?"

"I dig up secrets for a living. I trust no one."

"You trust me."

"I trust you don't have a body in there, but you're hiding something."

"I'm not *hiding* it." His smile widened. "It's a surprise. I don't want you to see it until it's ready. Alright? Is that enough for you?"

"What kind of surprise?"

"If I told you, it wouldn't be a surprise."

I let out a long, exasperated sigh. "It better not be expensive, 'cause I'm poor, and if you get me something, I feel obligated to get you something. It's bad enough that you feed me every day."

"I like feeding you every day. And no, it's not expensive, and no, I don't want anything in return." Still, he wore that sweet, boyish smile. "Please, just go outside. I'll bring out everything we need."

Looking at Grace over my shoulder, I said, "You know what this is about, don't you?"

"Yup."

"And you're not gonna tell me?"

"Nope."

Another sigh. "Fine. But now I gotta get you a surprise, damn it."

"He needs socks," Grace said. "They all have holes in them."

"And budget friendly." Walking to the door, I wagged a finger at Bentley. "Don't do this again. It makes me feel guilty."

"Just get your ass outside." That sentence sounded aggressive in black and white, but the tone of his voice made it playful, endearing. "I'll be out in a minute."

Narrowing my gaze, unable to pull down my smile, I said, "Don't tell me what to do."

Chapter 7

ALL EVENING, I PESTERED BENTLEY ABOUT HIS SURPRISE. HE wouldn't give, so I eventually accepted my defeat.

Our usual reps were followed by a walk around the block. Grace and Tempest joined us for that. By the time we made it back, it was dark, and Grace's bedtime. Considering how much I'd been on my feet today, and how swollen my knee was, I recovered in the tub with bubbles and Epsom salts. To an extent, it helped, but the pain wasn't gone.

It never was, really. I was always in some degree of pain. Maybe it was a one on the pain scale, but the last time it hit zero, I was taking opioids or drinking a few glasses of wine.

A glass of wine would've been a nice way to relax in the tub, but I hadn't had one of those in a while.

Sobriety sucked at times, but it was worth it to feel like myself. Once I'd made it through the worst of the withdrawals, it was just a matter of managing the pain in my knee. Which also sucked. But I felt like I was finding myself again, and apparently, pain was just a part of my existence now.

After my bath, I lay in bed with an ice pack on my knee, dreading the morning ahead of me, and drifted to sleep mapping out what I'd say when the inevitable came up.

* * *

AGAIN, I SKIPPED MY MORNING WORKOUT WITH BENTLEY. I HAD A lot to get done today, and I wanted to check some things off my list first. Bentley understood, saying he overslept anyway, and asked if this evening would work after dinner. I told him that sounded great.

Then I loaded Tempest into my car and got on the highway. The drive to Pittsburgh PD was longer than I'd have liked, but the traveling was a necessary part of this investigation.

I left Tempest in the car with the windows cracked and the music playing when I went inside. It was a crisp sixty degrees out—cool enough that I didn't have to worry about her overheating, but warm enough that she wouldn't freeze. I would've liked to bring her inside, but the janitors had always bitched about the fur when I'd brought Bear with me before.

The receptionist recognized me and let me pass through. After an awkward ride in the elevator with an old colleague who didn't seem to appreciate my dog fur-covered hoodie and sweatpants, I walked down the hall I hadn't stepped foot in for more than a year.

The door was open, and she sat at her desk, but I knocked anyway.

Some of us had an ounce of decency like that.

Harper looked up from the stack of paperwork on her desk, glasses falling down the bridge of her ski sloped nose. A smile wider than the curves of her voluptuous hips stretched across her face as she stood. "Hey Maddie. What're you doing here?"

I wanted to snap something about her shit-eating grin, but decided being petty wouldn't make this any easier. "I'm working a case. You knew the victim. Pretty sure you're why I'm working the case."

Smile dissipating, her shoulder slumped a bit. "Quinn Barnes."

"Yep. You have time for a few questions?"

"Yeah, of course." She gestured to the seat in front of her desk. "Anything you need, just say the word."

Lowering myself to the chair, I wasted no time. This wasn't a social call. "Evelyn said you babysat her?"

"I did, yeah." Harper reached into her desk drawer, pulled out a small

43

keepsake album, and turned it toward me. The first picture was one of Harper in her teens, just as pretty as she was now, with an elementary school aged Quinn in her lap, both smiling ear to ear. "My dad worked for Evelyn and David at their car dealership. That's how I got the gig. They were friends too. That probably helped."

"And you guys kept in touch?" I asked.

"Yeah, we did. I helped her fill out her college applications." A sad smile, looking down at the little girl in the photo. "She was the smartest kid I ever met. IQ was in the top one percent. She had her choice of colleges, she didn't wanna go Ivy League. She and Evelyn were close, and she didn't want to leave her mom."

"Were they close?" I asked. "Or is that just in the figurative sense?"

Harper shook her head. "They really were. Every moment Evelyn had off work was devoted purely to Quinn. Quinn was her whole world, and after David died, they just got closer. My mom was the one who convinced her to get back out there after David was gone because she just enveloped herself in Quinn."

"In a way that'd be concerning?" I asked. "Was she a helicopter parent? Did that push Quinn away at all?"

"No, nothing like that. Quinn was happy when her mom found Mark, but she wasn't itching to get away from her mom. They were friends, honestly. Way closer than I was with my mom. They had mani-pedi dates, went to spas on the weekends, Disney Land every year. They really were close."

I did see that in Quinn's texts, and from the array of photos she had on social media of her with her mom, but if that was so, why didn't she tell Evelyn about Troy? He wasn't the kind of guy a parent would look down upon. Not in my eyes, at least. Maybe the partying thing may not have been something Evelyn wanted for her daughter.

"Can you think of any reason she wouldn't have told Evelyn about her boyfriend, then?" I asked.

"Depends," Harper said. "Troy, Evelyn probably would've liked. But I don't think she would've been a fan of the other one."

Ah, so there *was* a second one. "Troy wasn't the only one."

"Nope. But don't ask me who he was, because she wouldn't tell me." The corners of Harper's lips fell into a frown. "I only know because I heard her talking on the phone at Evelyn's Christmas party. It was obvious she was talking to a guy, but she'd said that her and Troy weren't seeing each other anymore. I pressed, but she wouldn't tell me anything. Then she got defensive and said not to mention it again. In front of anyone."

"Did she do that with Troy?"

"Not really. She didn't tell Evelyn about him because she wasn't sure if it was gonna be serious, but with this guy, she wanted it quiet. Only a few reasons I can see somebody doing that."

"He's in a relationship," I murmured.

Unable to hold my gaze, Harper cleared her throat. "That's my best guess."

The irony was so bitter, I swore I could taste it. "Look, whatever happened between us has nothing to do with this. This whole thing is awkward enough. Let's not make it worse."

"Right. Sure," Harper said. "What else do you wanna know?"

"You've got nothing else on the other guy?"

"No. Like I said, she kept it *quiet*."

Jotting some notes in my book, I said, "What about her mental health? Do you know if she was struggling at all?"

"Definitely not. I know that people are good at hiding depression when they're going through it, but Quinn wasn't depressed. She didn't kill herself, Maddie."

I had the feeling that was the case as well, but I had to check. "How do you know?"

"Because that wasn't Quinn. Quinn kept busy, all the time. If she wasn't studying, she was with her friends. She'd call me, and we'd talk for an hour or two. I would've seen the signs. Quinn was happy. Not the fake it 'til you make it kind of happy, but truly, genuinely happy. She was excited about the future. Especially the last month or two before she passed. And you know the signs. If someone's planning to kill themselves, they aren't planning for the future. They're planning for their death. And honestly, I can't see her getting high there, let alone killing herself there, even if she was depressed. She loved Evelyn too much. There's no way in hell she would've let her mom find her like that."

A valid point, one I hadn't thought of.

The most common method of suicide for women was overdose. Often, it was out of their home where others would find them. While men would blow their brains out, not caring about who had to clean up the mess, women thought of who would find their bodies.

"Any chance she would've felt uncomfortable coming forward about her mental health?" I asked. "Would her family have made her feel crazy if she sought out help?"

"No, Evelyn put her in therapy after David died. It didn't last long, but Evelyn isn't that kind of person. She's a lawyer. She knows how trauma affects people. If something was eating at Quinn, Evelyn would've supported her getting help."

"Alex said there was no history of mental health."

"Well, she didn't have any diagnoses. It was just grief counseling. I don't know if that would show in standard medical records. But like I said, that was years ago. Quinn was doing great."

"What about drug use?" I asked. "Do you know about Quinn's consumption of MDMA?"

Harper sunk into her seat. "I know she partied sometimes, but she wasn't an addict."

"Alex found burns in her nose."

"And if she was a heavy user, there would've been more than burns. Alex let me see the records too. More than likely, she'd done a few lines the night prior at a party. But there wasn't long term damage to her septum, and there would've been if she was an addict."

Only if the use was excessive, but I saw the point she was making.

"Can you think of anyone who'd wanna hurt her?" I asked.

"Not at all. But considering she was keeping that boyfriend quiet, if he did have a girlfriend or wife, and Quinn said she was going to tell his partner or his partner found out, I'd consider them prime suspects."

Next stop then, finding boyfriend number two. "Just one more thing. You clearly think there's a case here."

"I do."

"And you haven't pushed with the local PD to investigate?"

"I did. And I was told it was out of my jurisdiction. That if I didn't mind my business, they'd file a complaint with my Sergeant. That's why I told Evelyn to call you. I think you can handle this better than a cop, anyway."

"Why's that?"

"'Cause you'll break laws to get answers." A slight shrug. "And considering the mess this all is, I think you might have to."

Not that I loved being known as the person who'd break the law to do what needed to be done, but she wasn't wrong.

Too many people got away on technicalities because they played the system. Sometimes, the good guys needed to work the system too.

"And because you're good at this," Harper said. "You woulda been a great detective. But honestly, I think you have more power to help the world than I do."

"This isn't a confession," I said, "but because you think I'm willing to break the law?"

"Because you care, and you've got nothing to lose." She paused. "That sounded like an insult. It wasn't meant to be. I'm sorry, I just meant because you're self-employed—"

"I know what you meant." Standing, I flipped my notebook shut and tucked it into my bag. "If you think of anything that might help me find out what happened to Quinn, give me a call."

"Of course." Harper followed my lead, standing as well. "But before you go, can we talk for a minute?"

"About this case?"

"No, but—"

"Then no." I started to the door.

"I just want to talk," she said, voice softening. "I know you're still angry, and you have every right to be, but you never gave me the chance to explain, and—"

Heart suddenly pounding, I whirled back around. "What is there to explain, Harper? You slept with my fiancé. You were my best friend, and *you slept with my fiancé.*"

She swallowed hard. "I did. And nothing's gonna change that or wipe it from history, but it wasn't an affair. We weren't hiding a secret romance from you. It was just one time. We had too many drinks after work, and then—"

"And then he came home and kissed me," I snapped. "Then he laid in my bed. Then you came over and sat on my couch with us. Then you took me out to get coffee. You both acted like nothing happened and made me look like an idiot."

Frowning, Harper stepped forward. "No one else knew. It wasn't office gossip or anything—"

"To me. I looked at you, and I looked at Ox, and I had no idea you'd betrayed me. You made me feel stupid for ever trusting either of you. *You* did that, Harper. You, Ox, and Alex were all I had left. I had just lost Bear, my mom died, I could barely walk, and then you betrayed me and made me feel so goddamned stupid."

A moment of silence passed, nothing but remorse shining in Harper's eyes. I considered leaving it at that, but I wanted to know how she'd respond. The glimmer of tears and the regret weren't enough. I wanted her to say something that would make me hate her less.

Eventually, she said, "It wasn't just me, Maddie. Ox did it, too. But you still visit him. You still talk to him. You gave him another chance."

"It took him getting shot for me to let him in at all."

"So, is that how it's gonna be between us?" Her eyes searched mine. "You're not gonna give a shit about me until I'm on my deathbed? There's no chance of us ever being friends again?"

"There's no chance of us being the friends we *were* again," I said. "I don't trust you anymore. I *can't* trust you anymore, just like I can't trust Ox. If it came down to it, I'd trust either of you with my life, but not my friendship."

Harper's teeth tightened to a line, as if trying to maintain her composure. "I get it. You've got walls, and you let them down for me. I hurt you, and you put them back up. But I miss you, Mads. I know it can't be like it was, but don't you miss how we used to be?"

Yeah. I did.

I missed the evenings we spent together on her deck, watching the sun set. I'd kill to travel back in time to the girls' trip Harper, Alex, and I took to California three years ago. When life was simple. When I was a twenty-something-year-old, able-bodied, joyous just to breathe and feel the warm sun on my skin.

But none of that was my reality anymore. Focusing on the past would take me nowhere. I had to learn and adjust to who I was in this rainy, pain-filled reality I was thrust into a year ago. It hadn't been long since I climbed out of the pits of addiction and depression. Lately, my focus in life had been trying to find a way to live in solidarity with the black clouds and the downpours.

I would never be the sunshine girl again, not really.

That's who Harper was. Bubbly, and fun, and excited for the next trip to Cali. A solid career that wasn't going anywhere, a comfortable, high five-figure salary, and all the things she'd ever wanted.

I didn't even know what I wanted out of life anymore. Aside from coming to terms with the fact that I had none of that—a solid career, a steady income, nor the dream life turned reality.

Harper and I were living in different worlds now.

And the truth was, I didn't wanna live in hers. I liked the gray clouds. Hated my pain, but everything else about the life I was building, the gritty fight for survival, I loved. After all, I didn't know much else.

"Yeah, Harper. I do. But you said it yourself. It'll never be like it was again." I held her gaze for a moment. "Hurts like a son of a bitch, I know, but that's something you've just gotta come to terms with. You'll get over it."

As I turned to leave, she said, "Have you? Come to terms with it?"

No. But I didn't owe her an answer.

I continued down the hallway, onto the elevator, and out to the parking garage. While I walked, I heard that conversation playing over on a loop in my mind.

Truth was, I didn't know why I'd been able to let Ox back in, but not Harper. She was right that they'd played an equal part in the damage. It felt hypocritical, even sexist, when I looked at the facts.

But as I approached my car, it became clear.

I hadn't let Ox back in. My walls still stood high. Ox just had a ladder, and he rested on its peak. Sure, he was close, but he wasn't inside, and I'd never let him in there again. Being stuck at the border of a romantic relationship with me was the equivalent of Harper being stuck at the border of our friendship.

Both were equally far from where they'd been when it all went to shit.

It wasn't hypocritical because—

The squeal of tires sounded.

I looked over my shoulder.

Just in time to see an all-black luxury vehicle with tinted windows peel tires around the bend to the next level of the parking lot.

One run-in with that car didn't mean much. Two though? Nearly a two-hour drive from where I'd seen it yesterday?

I took off in a jog—which was slow since I hadn't gotten my morning routine in—around the bend, hoping for a better glance.

But I only got a glimpse of the rear fender.

Not even enough to get a make and model, let alone a plate.

Chapter 8

Whenever I'd write out Evelyn's invoice, she was getting a twenty-five percent additional charge for all this damn travel time. Going all the way from Pittsburgh to the mountainous regions of Bedford County was a two hour drive itself, but an accident on the highway backed me up for a solid hour. It wasn't full stop traffic either, but the slow, stop and go kind. Meaning I had to constantly lift my foot off the brake and press on the gas.

My knee did not appreciate it.

Evelyn could afford the extra charge.

By the time Tempest and I made it to the college, my poor girl was shaking. After letting her relieve herself, I had to load her right back into the car.

Troy had pointed me to the coffee shop where Chelsie worked. It was a cute little place. Small, but quaint.

It was lunch by then anyway, so when I made it to the register, I got a coffee and a sandwich.

"That'll be eight forty-three," Chelsie said, passing me the coffee.

Handing her the money, I noted a bracelet around her wrist. It was simple beads tied on a rope chain. I wouldn't have thought much of it if I hadn't noticed a similar one on Quinn's wrist in a few of her social media photos. "That's a cute bracelet."

Glancing at it, a sad smile came to her lips. "Oh, thanks. My best friend made it for me in middle school."

"You still wear it?"

"I haven't in a while." Turning her wrist from side to side, she stroked a finger along the beads *C+Q=BFF*. "She just passed away, so I dug it out of my jewelry box."

"That's sweet." I gave her a smile. "Quinn Barnes?"

Face screwing up in confusion, she tilted her head. "Yeah, how'd you know?"

After finding my business card in my wallet, I held it out to her. "My name's Maddie Castle. Evelyn hired me to investigate Quinn's death. Would you be willing to answer some questions for me?"

Slowly, understanding flooded her expression. "I have a break in twenty minutes. Could we talk then?"

"Sure." I hooked a thumb toward the courtyard outside the window across the street. "I'll be out there whenever you get a minute."

TEMPEST HAD WALKED RIGHT UP TO CHELSIE WHEN SHE JOINED ME. Like she did when she greeted Grace or Darius, she wagged her tail and searched for a hand to sniff. Chelsie asked if she could pet her, and I said no. It may have been fine, but Tempest wasn't the most affectionate dog. Sometimes, with certain people, she was an angel. Others she'd happily tear an arm off.

Once she was seated at my side, gulping from the bowl of water I'd laid out for her, I took a glance over at Chelsie. Inside the café, she'd looked fine, but now that she was out here, her shoulders were slumped, gaze was distant, and voice was softer. That wasn't a sign of guilt. At work, she'd distracted herself by going through the motions. Out here, the reality of grief returned.

"So, you and Quinn knew each other since middle school?" I asked.

"Preschool. Friends ever since. She told her mom she chose this college because she didn't wanna be far from her, but she told me it was 'cause she wasn't ready to move so far from me. U-Penn was her dream school, but she came here." Tears budding in Chelsie's eyes, a moment of silence snuck in. "Now, I wish she would've."

"Why's that?"

"Because then she wouldn't be dead." Expression full of grief, she turned my way. "Evelyn told me what the police think, and they're wrong. They don't know Quinn. She wouldn't have done that, intentionally or accidentally."

So, it seemed everyone was in agreement on that much. That was rare. If Quinn had been suicidal or an addict, someone would've known. Someone would've worried for her safety.

"What makes you say that?" I asked.

"Because Quinn hated her dad for leaving her. She wouldn't have done that to the rest of us, never. She knew what it was like to grieve over losing someone to drugs. Alcohol, I guess, with her dad, but still. Quinn, she—" Tears beading over, Chelsie chomped on her lower lip to keep it from trembling, taking a moment to regain her composure. "Believe me, she wouldn't have taken too much by accident."

The tone suggested there was more to that story. I'd circle back to it. "Troy mentioned that you guys had a falling out recently. Could you tell me a little bit about that?"

"It wasn't a falling out." Chelsie rolled her eyes, raking some messy blonde hair from her face. "We just got into an argument. It was my fault, but it wasn't a huge thing."

"Can you tell me what it was about?"

Shifting on the park bench, she struggled to meet my gaze.

"Was it about a guy?" I asked.

"No." She gave me a look that said that was ridiculous. Like a boy could get between them? Not in a million years. "No, nothing like that."

"What was it like?"

Glancing me over, she noted my casual, bordering on homeless aesthetic. "Are you, like, an undercover cop?"

Ah, so it had to do with illegal activities. "No, I'm a private investigator. I don't work for any police department, and I'm not obligated to share minor crimes with them. I won't."

Her posture loosened, but she still scratched her head, discomfort evident. "I'm not smart like Quinn. She learned things really easy. It was never hard for her, but it's always been hard for me. I had some tests coming up, and I really wanna graduate, ya know? I wanna make something of my life."

Having an idea of where this was headed, I nodded with understanding.

"So I sorta got some help."

"From a doctor?"

Chelsie looked away again.

"Not from a doctor, then. Amphetamines?"

"Yeah. Some kids around here sell them. I tried them once at a party, but they didn't make me feel high, I guess. I don't know." She nibbled her lower lip. "Anyway, I was taking a lot. More than I should've. Like, I bought a whole month's worth from two people. I was using them to get through classes and work here, but then I needed them to study, too."

"And Quinn didn't approve."

"I'd been awake for, like, three days straight?" Sinking into herself, she pulled her jacket close, like she was trying to retreat from the conversation. "Quinn and I went out to eat, and she knew something was up, but it was wearing off then. I drove home, and I almost ran us off the road."

Ah. Doubted that sat well with Quinn.

"She made me pull over and drove the rest of the way. She bitched at me the whole time. Then we got to my dorm, and she found them, and dumped them down the toilet."

Good for Quinn.

"I shouldn't have gotten so mad about it. But I flipped out and then she was crying, and I was yelling. The whole thing was so stupid. Quinn kept trying to make up, but I was going through withdrawals, I guess, and I couldn't find any more. But then the withdrawals were over, and she came here while I was working. I told her I was sorry and asked if we could meet up on Saturday to talk about it. Quinn said yeah. She told me she was proud of me." Her tears trickled down her cheeks. Slapping them away, she shook her head. "I thought that we were okay again. But then she didn't show at the restaurant. I thought she was just blowing me off because she was mad still. Then Evelyn called me Sunday night."

If that had happened only a few weeks before her death, there was no way in hell that the story was as neat as the report made it sound.

"I'm never gonna get to fix that." Sniffling, Chelsie wiped her nose. "That's what hurts the most. We weren't on great terms when she died, and I'm never gonna be able to make that right."

Tempest stood and walked to Chelsie with her ears back. They said dogs were just mindless animals, but even a little shit like Tempest had sympathy in her big brown eyes as she licked Chelsie's hand.

Chelsie chuckled and reached out to pet her.

Tempest looked at me, as if to ask if it was okay.

"Good girl," I told her.

Lifting her front paws to the sides of Chelsie's lap, she leaned in to lick the tears from her cheeks. Chelsie laughed again, running her fingers through her fur.

"I'm sorry for your loss," I said. "But for what it's worth, I know what that's like. Not being able to fix a broken relationship before you lose them for good, I mean. It hurts for a while, but I think Quinn forgives you."

A sad smile. "I hope."

This was a good chunk of information, confirming questions and theories I'd been flipping between. But there was still something I'd missed. "Everybody else says Quinn had no enemies. You agree?"

"Yeah, everybody loved Quinn." Chelsie paused, face scrunching up in thought, still petting Tempest. "I don't know if this'll help, but every Thursday, between noon and dinner time, Quinn was unavailable. She didn't have classes then, and I asked her a few times what she was doing, but she'd never tell me."

That was worth noting. "Do you think it was a boyfriend?"

"Maybe?" Chelsie raised a shoulder. "She came back smelling sorta like sage or something. I don't know why she wouldn't tell me about a boyfriend, though."

Likely because she was the other woman. "Do you know why she and Troy were on and off?"

"She always said it was because she had to focus on school, but I didn't really believe it."

"What'd you think?"

"Same thing you do. A guy," Chelsie said. "But she never told me about him if he did exist. I mean, she was spending more time on campus at that time. So maybe it was about school? But I always kinda doubted it."

"Why's that?"

"Because I knew the look in her eyes when she was in love. It's a thing you pick up on with your friends, ya know? But she didn't, like, sparkle like that with Troy."

Huh. Now that made me wonder if my instincts were off about that boy. "You don't think they were good together?"

"It's not that. It's just that Troy's kinda dumb," she said. I couldn't help my laugh. Chelsie smiled. "Quinn was a genius. She got bored trying to hold conversations with him. But he's sweet, and she said he was good in bed, so she kept going back. She didn't love him, though."

"So, when did she have that loving look in her eyes?"

"It started in October, I wanna say? November was when she started disappearing on Thursdays. But it came and went, if that makes sense. Like, in sync with when she and Troy were on and off. It went away when they were together, and it came back when they broke up."

"Did she have that twinkle in her when she got back Thursday evening?"

Chelsie thought for a moment, then shook her head. "I don't think so. But her makeup was smeared sometimes. She had to fix it before we went anywhere on Thursdays."

"Like she'd been crying."

"I think so, yeah."

Still coulda been the guy who made her eyes twinkle. The men we loved were often the ones who hurt us the most. Personally, that was when I cut them off. But I'd seen my mom go back to a man who'd hurt her a thousand times.

If the guy she'd seen was in a relationship, it could've been a matter of continually hearing that he was going to leave her for Quinn, only to get in her car and know that wasn't the case. Then she'd cry the whole way home.

But did that fit the timeline?

"And it was every Thursday," I said. "Even while she was dating Troy."

"Yeah, I think so."

Hm. So not only was she likely the other woman, but also cheating on her man.

As much as that irked me, it wouldn't have any bearing on how I handled this case. I'd put all the effort I had into finding her regardless. She was a nineteen-year-old girl who made some bad relationship decisions. That didn't mean she deserved to die, nor that her death didn't deserve justice.

"Thank you, Chelsie." Standing, I instructed Tempest to join my side with a tap on my hip. She did so in a heartbeat. "You mentioned she spent a lot of time on campus when she and Troy weren't together?"

"Yeah, she did."

"Where at?"

"The library, mostly. Her roommate annoyed her when she was studying, so that was her happy place."

Interesting, because Evelyn said Quinn hated the library.

So who was lying? Evelyn, Chelsie, or Quinn?

"Can you point me that way?" I asked.

"Yeah, it's not far. Her dorm's that way if you wanna have a look there too. She wasn't there much, but maybe you'll find something." Chelsie stood too, giving me directions for a moment. Once she finished, I thanked her again. I was about to turn away when she said, "Maddie?"

"Yeah?"

"You believe me, don't you?" Her expression was soft, voice meek. "That she wouldn't have done this to herself? Because the cops acted like I was crazy when I told them they were wrong. And if somebody killed her—" A sharp breath cut her off. She took a few seconds to compose herself. "You'll find them, won't you?"

"I'm not stopping until I know exactly what happened."

Chapter 9

Something was different about leaving Tempest in the car compared to Bear. A wave of guilt rushed through me when I shut the door. Maybe because when I'd had Bear, I was leaving him in the back of my cruiser. No one was going to mess with a cop car.

My beat-up SUV, though? That was fair game.

Come to think of it, I could get her trained and certified as a service dog. I'd focused on police canines when I was a trainer, but chronic pain sufferers—AKA, me—used service dogs for all kinds of day-to-day tasks. It sure would be nice if she could grab something I dropped, so I didn't have to bend for it.

Walking into the library, I jotted a reminder in my phone to call the lead trainer who'd certified me for more information.

The library wasn't anything spectacular. Decades old red carpet lined the floors. Shelves of books framed every wall, climbing all the way to the peaks of the fifteen-foot ceiling. A few college kids were scattered around, some sitting at computers, others hunched over books at some tables. The best part about it was the smell. There was nothing in the world that smelled as good as the pages of a book.

A librarian sat at the other end of the desk at the head of the room, so that was where I went. I'd barely opened my mouth to speak when she held up a pointer finger, typing away with her free hand.

And now I remembered why I'd hated libraries when I was in school.

Sealing my lips, I waited. It was probably only a minute, but it felt like an hour before she looked up.

"What can I do for you?"

Passing her a photo of Quinn, I asked, "Does this girl look familiar?"

She tugged her glasses down to see through her bifocals. "Why do you ask?"

"Her friend says she spent a lot of time here."

The skeptical look on her face told me that wasn't what she meant. "Uh-huh."

"I'm a private investigator." I handed her a business card. "Quinn passed away two weeks ago, and her mother doesn't believe it was accidental. Her mom says she hated the library, but her best friend says she was here all the time."

Making a noise in her throat, she plucked the photo from my hand and studied it a moment longer. After a few seconds, she laid the photo on her desk and turned to the computer. "What'd you say her name was?"

I spelled it for her.

The librarian clicked and clacked on the keys for a moment, wiggling the mouse from time to time. Then she said, "Oh, yes. I remember her."

"You do?"

"She checked out *The Strange Case of Dr. Jekyll and Mr. Hyde* so often, I gave her a spare copy we were going to throw away." The librarian slid the photo across the desk. "But the friend must've been lying, because I haven't seen her in months."

"But she checked that book out all the time?"

"Six weeks in a row from December into January. The last time I saw her, I gave her that spare copy." Crossing her arms, she leaned back in her seat. "She was a smart girl. We had some good conversations."

In December, she'd been in the *off* phase with Troy. "About?"

"Books. What else?" She gestured around. "We weren't exactly friends. She was just a nice kid to talk to."

Alright, different direction then. "Did she spend a lot of time studying here?"

"Just a few times when the school year started. After that, she just stopped in for reading material."

Damn it. A dead end.

"Is there any reason you could think that'd make her mom say Quinn didn't like it here?"

"Mighta had something to do with the boy honking at her."

My face must've shown my confusion. "What do you mean?"

She nodded to a set of chairs and sofas in the far corner of the library. Sunlight shined in through the pointed stained-glass windows behind them. "About a month after school started, when she was still coming here to read, she'd sit right over there. Usually, she'd do some schoolwork at the desk, and then she'd settle in there for pleasure reading. She'd stay late too. Wasn't outta here until I was shutting the doors. But then a car would honk right outside that window, and they'd flash their high beams. She'd get a big smile and skip on out. You know what I mean. The look a young girl gets when she's in love."

Unlike the former, that was some valuable intel. "You never saw who?"

"You see those windows, don't you?" Another gesture at the stained glass. "Can't see a thing through them. I did see a car driving around this way once." She nodded to the right. "Black sedan. Something fancy. I never caught the make, but I wasn't exactly looking for it. You want me to keep an eye out for it?"

The same black sedan that I'd seen on my tail twice in the last twenty-four hours, perhaps? "That'd be great. Thank you."

"Sure."

Starting to the door, I made another note in my pad.

I didn't know much, but I could confirm one thing. There'd been another guy in Quinn's life, and she'd kept him secret. Now I needed to do a deep dive through every file in her phone. Last night, I'd looked at a fair bit of it, but I needed to search any and everything I could find going all the way back to November.

Somewhere, there had to be a hint at who this guy was. No one was *that* good at hiding.

"One more thing," the librarian said.

Holding the door handle, I looked at her over my shoulder.

"Check the book."

"What book?"

"Her copy of *Jekyll and Hyde*," she said. "She annotated. You can find out a lot about someone from the notes they leave in margins. Robert Louis Stevenson wrote a lot of books. There's gotta be some reason that one resonated with her."

* * *

From there, I headed to Quinn's dorm. The roommate let me in, saying I could look around. Like everyone else, she mentioned being jarred by Quinn's death. She didn't even know Quinn did drugs.

She also told me they weren't close. They didn't hate one another, but they were in different cliques. The roommate's green hair, nose piercings, and gauged ears told me that much. According to her, they'd only shared the room at bedtime. She'd never been to Quinn's parents' home, nor did she have any idea where it was. Even so, she showed me timestamped photos of her at parties the Saturday Quinn died.

They were concerning because the hundred-pound girl standing before me was perched in a headstand on top of a keg at eleven a.m.

Still, she said I could look at whatever I wanted, but Evelyn had already collected Quinn's belongings, so there wasn't much to take note of. I still checked under the bed and in her dressers, not finding much.

At that point, I let Tempest out of the car again, let her do her business, and fed her some kibble. While she chomped away at my feet, I sat on a park bench, diving deeper into Quinn's phone.

The girl had a thousand classes, all scheduled into a time management app. It was a fancy one, the kind that had a geolocation for every activity. She had reminders set for each activity, whether it was a class, a test, yoga, study time, class reading, pleasure reading, or a date with Troy. Quinn even scheduled in her naps and bedtime.

I'd kill to have that level of organization in my life.

But like Chelsie had said, every Thursday since November was blocked out from one p.m. to four p.m.

And there was no geolocation.

In fact, I went into her phone's history for a daily breakdown of her location. Fun fact, almost every phone had one of those. With the right password, someone's entire schedule was available anywhere in the world. So long as the settings were correct, Quinn would've known if someone had hacked into her account to see where she was.

So why had her location been turned off between one and four p.m. every Thursday? Did she share her location with her friends or Evelyn as a safety measure? It wasn't uncommon. At this very moment, Alex had my location, and I had hers. It was common practice for women. A year ago, when a serial killer had wreaked havoc across mine and neighboring counties, every woman I knew utilized it.

But why would Quinn have shut hers off during that time block?

Did she trust this boyfriend enough for that?

I didn't care how well I knew a man. I didn't care if I was out with Bentley, who I'd known since childhood and trusted with my whole existence. There was no man I'd shut off my location for, especially if I was having an affair with him.

If Quinn weren't so cautious, I could see her doing that to keep their relationship safeguarded. But Quinn was the girl who carried test strips at parties to check other girls' drinks.

No, it had to be deeper than that.

Sighing, I laid the phone on my lap.

Tempest panted up at me, a smile across her lips, tongue flopped to the side of her mouth.

"What do you think, Tempy?" I rubbed her ear. "I'm missing something, aren't I?"

She stopped panting.

"You know what it is?"

Her tail wagged.

"Well, tell me then. What is it?"

Jumping up, she put a paw on each side of my hips. After she lapped my cheeks for a moment, I chuckled. "Down."

She got back onto all fours, then plopped onto her butt when I told her to sit.

Picking up the phone again, I scrolled to Quinn's social media. Last night, I'd scoured it, but maybe there was a missing piece hidden somewhere in there.

After a few scrolls through her photos, I found it.

It was from Quinn's high school graduation. Still wearing her cap and gown, holding her diploma in one hand, keys dangled from her pinky in the other. The smile across her lips was wider than the forests she'd grown up in.

Behind her was a brand new, red, sparkly 2022 Toyota Prius.

That was the kind of car that had a GPS in it.

It stored data, like where it'd been driven every Thursday.

Heart skipping, I slid my phone from my pocket and dialed Evelyn's number. She answered on the second ring. "Did you find something?"

"I've gathered a lot." Standing, I tapped my hip for Tempest to join my side. She did. "But I need something from you."

"Anything."

"Quinn's car. Can I take a look at it?"

"I'll meet you at the house in twenty minutes."

Chapter 10

When I arrived, Evelyn asked about what I'd gathered. I didn't give her much. Was it my place to tell her about a boyfriend, or boyfriends, that Quinn had kept from her? Did she want to know that her daughter may've been the other woman to a possibly married man? Did she want to know that Quinn wasn't the squeaky clean kid she thought her daughter was? Although parts of what I'd gathered I was certain were true, I didn't have much proof. Other aspects were speculation. I wasn't sure what was or wasn't relevant to Quinn's death yet.

What I did know were some bitter pills, and I needed to figure out a way to candy coat them before I fed them to Evelyn.

Tempest sat outside the car, and Evelyn sat in the passenger seat. For the last twenty minutes, I'd been googling how to pull up the history on this damn car's computer. It wasn't like I was illiterate when it came to tech, but the operating systems in vehicles were different than those on computers and cell phones.

After cussing under my breath when I clicked the icon that read *GPS options*—only displaying ways to customize the formatting and configuration of the screen display—Evelyn said, "Are you trying to find her map's history?"

"That's the goal."

"May I?" Evelyn asked.

"Please." I gestured to it. As Evelyn fiddled around, I said, "You're familiar with this sorta thing?"

"Yeah, David was no good with electronics. He was a mechanic. Got so mad when everything started going digital." Evelyn gave a half smile as she clicked away. "He ran the dealership, but when a little old lady brought her car in because she couldn't figure out how to work the radio, I guided him through it. I minored in computer science in college. My mom told me that was stupid."

"Mine didn't think computers were gonna take off either, and I was a kid in the nineties. How wrong she was."

"It's the way of the times now." She kept clicking around on the dash. "This system is frustrating though, isn't it?"

I huffed in answer.

"Can I ask why you need her driving history?"

"Because I can't figure out what she did on Thursdays."

Evelyn furrowed her brows. "She was in class."

"Not on Thursdays between one and four," I said. "Quinn tracked every moment of her life in a scheduling app. Every Thursday was blacked out from one to four."

"But she told me she was in school. We talked on her hour off for lunch every day." Confusion still shined in her eyes for a minute. Hoping Evelyn would put two and two together on her own, I stayed quiet. "She was lying."

"I think so."

Slowly, Evelyn's gaze fell. A moment of silence passed. If the circumstances were different, I'd tell her to get back to figuring out that address. The sooner I had information, the sooner I'd be able to figure out what happened.

But those few sentences seemed to cut Evelyn's heart out. Quinn was the Rory to her Lorelai. This was the moment she realized things weren't so black and white.

"Do you know if she lied to me about anything else?" Evelyn asked, resuming her clicks on the dashboard. Her face was blank now, how I imagined she'd look in a courtroom, defending someone she knew to be guilty. "That why you keep telling me that you're still early and don't have much yet?"

"I don't have much *proof* yet," I said. "But I don't think Quinn ever lied to hurt you. She was just a typical kid. There were things she didn't want you to be ashamed of her for."

"I hired you to give me that information, Madison." Still, she didn't meet my gaze. "I appreciate you protecting my feelings, but I want to know anything and everything that I don't already know about my daughter."

Ugh.

I was no good with feelings.

But I'd do my best to make it sting the least.

"Quinn had an on and off again boy in her life," I said. "They weren't exclusive, but they cared about one another. I believe she didn't tell you about him because you'd think she was out of his league. He's a sweet kid, but he's only in college because of a sports scholarship. Not very bright."

"You don't believe he's connected to her death?" she asked.

"He has an alibi. He couldn't have hurt her. I don't think he has the balls for that anyway."

"Is that all?"

Onto the pill that might lodge in her throat on the way down. "Quinn did use drugs recreationally. Not in excess, from the accounts her friends have given me, but she wasn't a hundred percent clean and serene."

Another moment of silence. "I knew that."

Now, I gave her the look. "You could've told me so."

"I didn't want you to put less effort into finding out what happened." She gave me a side eyed glance. "I told the police I knew she'd taken things at parties, and that was when they told me there was nothing more worth investigating."

Understandable on Evelyn's part. "I meant what I said. Whether Quinn was an addict, or a sex worker, or a hippy living in a commune, I'll work just as hard to find out what happened."

That got a faint smile out of Evelyn.

"Is there anything else you haven't told me? Because if there is and I have to dig to find it, it's on your dime. Makes my job harder, but hey, I don't mind a bigger check."

"No!" Evelyn seemed to catch my teasing tone, and her smile grew. "You?"

"Just another hunch."

"Which is?"

The bitterest of all the pills. "I believe she had another boyfriend, and she told no one about him. And I don't see why she wouldn't tell her best friend unless the guy was..."

Evelyn looked confused, then her mouth opened in disbelief. "You think she was seeing a married man?"

"It's a theory. That's why I'm still digging." Spring wind blowing in from the open door, fluttering hair into my face, I tucked it behind my ear. "I could be way off. That's the part I'm too early to say anything for certain on."

"But if she was," Evelyn said, voice trembling, "and his wife found out, that could be a lead."

"Could be. Three things I've seen people get killed over the most are drugs, sex, and money."

"And you don't think it's about the drugs that showed up in her tox screen?"

"No. The boyfriend gave her those to hold onto. He was worried about the dean cracking down on drug use on campus. Quinn took them so they weren't in his room when it got searched."

Evelyn's jaw tightened. "You're sure he had no part in this?"

"Aside from that, I'm certain."

Still tense, she turned back to the screen. "No one would've killed her over money, either. I sent money to her account every week, but it wasn't much. If it was a mugging gone wrong, maybe I could see that, but to have come inside our home?"

"When there were no signs of breaking and entering, I can't see it. Even if it was a robbery, they wouldn't have shoved pills down her throat and staged it as an accidental OD."

Evelyn expelled a deep breath in response, then looked puzzled at the screen. "That's odd."

With a glance at it, I agreed.

On Thursday, the week of her death, Quinn had been an hour away in a little town. It was smack dab between Westmoreland and Bedford County in Somerset. Not far from my place.

The odd part was the town.

It wasn't known for fostering rich college girls like Quinn. It was the sort of place you didn't walk through alone, and you drove through with the windows up and your doors locked.

What was Quinn doing there?

"Doesn't look familiar to you?" I asked.

"Not at all," Evelyn murmured. "I've driven through a few times, but I've never stopped. Certainly never took Quinn."

Looking between the coordinates and my phone, I searched for the address. Service was trash out here, but it loaded after a moment, showing a nondescript apartment building.

Didn't seem like the sorta place a guy who drove a luxury vehicle lived, to say the least.

"I'll check it out," I said. "Some friends might be able to help me figure out who lives there. I can cross reference the names with anyone associated with Quinn."

"By check it out, do you mean watch it?" she asked. "Because I can find everyone who lives in this place too, but there are ways to not leave a paper trail."

"Are you asking if I'll stake it out?"

"Do you do that?"

"I do. But it's the same hourly rate."

"I already told you. Money is no issue."

"That's where I'll be tonight, then."

"I appreciate it. Anything else you need here?"

"There is." Shifting in my seat to face her better, I said, "I visited Quinn's dorm. Her roommate said you'd already taken her things."

"They're in boxes in the basement. I assumed that wouldn't help you much because she was found here."

"I agree. Probably wouldn't get much from it. But I was hoping to find her copy of *Jekyll and Hyde*. Do you know where that is?"

"The book?" she asked. I nodded. "I remember seeing it when I was packing her things. She loved that book. David used to read it to her when she was little. When we moved in here, she lost his copy and was heartbroken over it. I can go find her new copy."

"Perfect." Standing from the vehicle, I tossed my phone into my bag. "And mind if I take a look at her room again?"

"That's no problem. Can I ask why?"

"Just feel like I missed something. Another look might help."

WHILE EVELYN SEARCHED THE BASEMENT, I SNOOPED AROUND Quinn's room. It looked just as it had yesterday. Like Evelyn said, this room hadn't been touched by anyone aside from the cops, and me.

But something didn't feel right.

I couldn't put my finger on what, but when I'd stood in this room yesterday, I'd known there was something I overlooked. Finding Harper's picture threw me off. Maybe my head hadn't been on right, and something important slipped right past me.

This time, I was using every resource available to me.

There was a valuable one at my feet.

Holding out Quinn's sweater, the one she'd left on the kitchen island downstairs the day of her death, I told Tempest, "Article search."

She'd gotten good at this.

She dropped her nose to the ground and sniffed away. She went to the bed first and lay beside it.

Although the police had collected Quinn's blankets as evidence, I was sure her skin cells were still on the mattress. That wasn't what I was looking for.

"Leave it," I said. "Article search."

Tempest resumed sniffing. She went to the closet this time. Pawing at the door, she looked up at me. As if to say, *Something smells like her in here, Mom.*

I wasn't surprised when she lay beside the bookbag either. There were plenty of skin cells on those belongings.

"Leave it," I told her. She stood back up. Again, I held out the shirt. Once she'd gotten her whiff, I said, "Article search."

Tempest went back to sniffing.

Beside Quinn's vanity, Tempest lay flat again, signaling me.

Ready to sigh and call it quits, having known Quinn's skin cells would be on her makeup, I walked that way. But Tempy wasn't angled toward the vanity. She wasn't angled toward the jacket that draped the back of the seat either.

Tempy faced the wall.

Holding the wall for stability, growling at the pain in my knee as I squatted, I paid close attention. I didn't want to move anything because positioning was important. The very angle the chair was facing could've told me something.

But there, hardly visible on the mahogany floors, were a handful of crimson droplets, turning brown in some places.

Blood.

Certainly something I'd missed, and not something I'd seen in the police report. It wasn't much, but it could've meant something. The fact that the local police hadn't noticed it told me a little something about how thorough they were.

"Good girl, Tempy." Roughing up her scruff, I grabbed my phone to snap a picture. Tempy blinked at the camera flash. I chuckled an apology as I straightened.

That was what I was missing.

My eyes locked on a dent in the wall, hidden by the curtains. Some drywall dust speckled the hardwoods, also disguised by the curtains. The dent wasn't huge, hardly larger than a half dollar. The spindle on the back of the vanity matched it perfectly.

That vanity chair was on wheels. The range of motion would've made impacts mild should it bump into something. These walls weren't cheap, either. I imagined it'd take some *oomph* to put a hole in one.

Stepping back, I examined the space, trying to get an image in my mind of how that chair would've wound up banged against the wall.

The vanity was tucked into the corner. The chair sat neatly in the center.

If Quinn had been sitting there, speaking to someone, and they grabbed either armrest, they could've pushed her backwards into the wall. It would've caged her in place. If the person who'd done so was bigger than Quinn, she couldn't have gotten out.

It could've been the other boyfriend. Quinn liked it rough in the bedroom. My original theory may've been right. Maybe they'd gotten high, decided to embrace the euphoria with their bodies, and everything went wrong.

That still didn't explain why Quinn had taken so many.

Leaning down, I snapped another photo.

And as I did, my breath fogged the glass. Like a child using the rear door in a car as an easel on a long drive, six words painted a picture in the condensation on the window.

Im srry Mom
I love u

Chapter 11

"If your supervisor isn't out here in the next minute, I'll file a lawsuit, and every single one of you will lose your jobs." Evelyn hunched over the front desk of the local police department. She was two seconds from flames shooting out of her orifices. "We've already been waiting for—"

"Five minutes," I said, tone calm. "We've been here for five minutes, Evelyn."

Her scowl turned on me.

I got it. She had every right to be pissed. The things I'd found at the scene should've been caught sooner.

But we were here now, and I knew cops. I'd been one.

As understanding as I'd always attempted to be with a heartbroken mother, the fact of the matter was, the ones who came in sweet as honey always walked out happier than those who came in spewing vinegar. Public servants or not, no one liked being yelled at.

Gesturing to a few chairs in the waiting area and guiding Evelyn in that direction, I relayed that experience. To which she snapped, "I'm an attorney. I know how to talk to cops, thanks."

I shut up after that, but after a few minutes of silence, her stiff posture softened.

When the lead detective stepped into the waiting area wearing a badge that said J. Fitz, I stood first. Also stepped in front of Evelyn. She may've been versed on interactions with officers, but I spoke their language in a way she couldn't.

Fitz was an older gentleman, pushing sixty. Despite his burly body, he had kind brown eyes and an inviting smile. It was rare to hold on to that after being in this line of work for so long, but I guessed around here in the wealthy countryside, he didn't see the worst of the worst often.

"Maddie Castle." Offering my hand, I said, "Evelyn hired me to—"

"I know who you are." His smile was genuine, handshake firm. "You put a bullet in the Country Killer."

Fighting my cringe at the memory, I returned his expression. "Didn't hit him where I was trying to."

"Hey, ya hit him somewhere. More than anyone else managed. Thanks for your service."

"Don't mention it." *Seriously, don't.*

"Why'd you get into private investigation?" he asked. "You make any real money there?"

"Money's good when it's good. Fluctuates." Glancing at my knee, I raised a shoulder. "But the rest is a long story."

"I'd love to buy you a beer sometime and hear it."

"Maybe a cup of coffee."

"Better on your liver, they say."

"That's what they tell me. But this isn't a social call, Detective."

Fitz looked behind me. Pulling in a deep breath, he forced his expression to soften. "Hello, Mrs. Barnes."

She gave him a tight-lipped smile, apparently deciding I could handle this better than she could after all.

"Evelyn hired me to do some digging." Unlocking my phone, I tilted the screen toward him. "Looks like something you might wanna see as well."

Lifting his glasses up his nose, he studied the photos. He spent a few moments flicking through them, then zooming in and zooming out. "Hm."

"Not what I'd expect to see at the scene of an accidental overdose."

"Well, none of it's exactly condemning, is it, Miss Castle?"

"You don't find the blood suspicious? Or the message?"

Frowning, he handed me my phone. "It's just a few droplets. Coulda been a paper cut."

Fair enough. That could've been true. "What about the writing on the window?"

Another short glance at Evelyn behind me. "When you take that much ecstasy, it isn't ecstasy that you feel. She was probably hallucinating and didn't know how to get out of the room."

Uh, no.

Not that I was proud, but I'd done a fair bit of experimenting with substances, especially in my younger years. I'd taken five hits of acid at once. Yes, I tripped *hard*. No, I would not recommend it. Yes, it was absolute hell. Probably the worst decision of my life.

But I hadn't seen dragons flying through the sky and purple elephants in my living room. I could walk fine. Certainly fine enough to make it to the door. Back then, I didn't have a cell phone, but if I'd felt like I was dying, I would've gone to the landline to call for help.

Of course I'd done some odd things that night, like staring at the ceiling fan spinning for an hour straight, but even when the trip turned bad, I could still see just fine. If it was needed, I would've been able to write my mom a note.

"No disrespect sir, but I don't think that's the case here," I said. "Even with those high quantities of MDMA coursing through her, if she needed to talk to her mom, I believe she would've."

After another half glance past me, he said, "Mrs. Barnes, would you mind waiting out here for a moment?"

"Yes, I would."

Sliding a card of his own from his pocket, he said to me, "Then you give me a call when you get a moment, Miss Castle."

"Are you f—"

"It's alright, Evelyn." Cutting her off before she finished the word that started with F and I imagined rhymed with *truck*, was my best shot at keeping a positive rapport with Fitz. "It'll just be a few minutes."

She gave me a look that said, *I'm writing your checks.*

I returned it with one that said, *And we're on the same team. I have no doubts in my mind that someone else is responsible for Quinn's death.*

Still, Evelyn snapped, "Fine. I'll be here."

* * *

"You think that was her suicide note?" As hard as I was trying to be respectful with Fitz, I was sure my tone came off condescending. "That doesn't make sense. If Quinn had tried to kill herself, why wouldn't she just grab a pen and paper?"

"Because she was tweaking."

"You don't *tweak* on MDMA, Detective." It wasn't intentional, but damn. Was he this dumb? "You roll. How much experience do you have in narcotics?"

"Less than you, apparently." He leaned back in his chair. "Either way, kid, Quinn was high out of her mind."

"True, she was. And if you dug deeper into the reports, or if you talked to her friends, you'd know that she typically snorted those drugs, and in regular doses. But she swallowed them that day. All of them. Why?"

"Slower release to a more peaceful death."

"There's nothing peaceful about dying on a drug like that." It took everything I had not to grit my teeth. "Do you know what the overdose is like?"

"Not personally, but—"

"Tachycardia. Heart attack. Sweating profusely, rapidly increasing body temperature. In some cases, with *massive* dosages, it can cause painful bleeding through the eyes and nose. Her brain would've felt like it was exploding. Her chest would've hurt, and she would've been more paranoid than a drug dealer with a cop behind them on the highway."

Fitz laughed quietly at that.

I didn't return it. "Quinn Barnes did not kill herself."

"Hey, you said it yourself. Those are rare cases," he said. "Which brings me back to accidental overdose."

"Even with that message on the window." Tucking my arms against my chest, I glared down at him. "Even with that hole in the wall."

"I've seen kids on drugs rip chandeliers off ceilings. I'm sure you have too."

"At parties, sure, but this isn't a drug someone takes by themselves."

"Unless they're regular users, and the autopsy confirmed she was one." Still, he frowned up at me. "I'm sorry, Miss Castle, but this case is closed. Frankly, I think you should have Evelyn cut your check and move onto something with substance. 'Cause this one doesn't have any."

No matter how hard I tried to understand, I couldn't believe this. All the signs pointed to a bigger picture. There were so many things about this case that didn't add up, and he wrongfully debunked each one with his limited knowledge of drugs.

But should I be surprised?

No. I knew how law enforcement looked at people who had a history with substances. People like me, even like Quinn, who only used casually, were nothing to some so-called public servants.

I could bitch about the hypocrisy. How he'd offered to buy me a beer but denied all the evidence of a young girl's murder simply because she used drugs just as dangerous as alcohol, but that'd get me nowhere.

"Or milk Evelyn until you get a bigger check. But no, Castle, I ain't reopening the case."

Nope. Wasn't gonna hold my tongue after that.

"I'm not *milking* Evelyn," I snapped. "There's substantial evidence that says Quinn's death was an intentional homicide. Evidence that you're choosing to ignore. But ya know what, Fitz, that's fine. Go back to writing tickets to farmers whose cows escaped their pens and moms speeding on their way to soccer practice in their minivans. I'll worry about the son of a bitch who shoved a fistful of pills down a nineteen-year-old girl's throat. When I find him, I'll call."

I flung the door open, and I didn't give a damn when it banged off the wall.

The look on my face must've concerned her, because Evelyn stood quickly as I made it into the waiting area. She opened her mouth to speak, I cut in before she had the chance. "Let's talk outside."

* * *

ONCE WE MADE IT TO EVELYN'S CAR, I EXPLAINED WHAT DETECTIVE Fitz had said, throwing in some colorful language along the way. Most of the time, I did my best to disguise my potty mouth, but men like him pissed me right the hell off.

"I don't understand it." Forcing my tight jaw to soften, I snorted a laugh. "Both detectives I'd talked to in Pittsburgh agree that something doesn't fit. I don't know if he's just an idiot, but he's not gonna help us."

The reaction I expected from Evelyn wasn't the one I got. Her posture was relaxed, eyes sparkling with tears. "You'll continue to work the case though?"

"I will."

Smiling, she nodded quickly. "Thank you."

"Just doing my job."

"No, you're not." Evelyn nodded to the Police Department. "You're doing *their* jobs."

Couldn't disagree with her there.

"I heard what you said, by the way. That the money fluctuates." After digging in her purse, Evelyn held out a check. "I don't know what the total will be once you add up the hours, but at the bare minimum, once you find out what happened to my daughter, this is yours."

It read $10,000.00.

Whew.

Considering I charged less than $100 an hour, and I doubted this case would be a hundred and something hours' worth of work, I wasn't complaining.

"Are you sure?" I asked.

"You're the only one who seems to care about what happened to my baby." She tucked the paper back into her bag. "Expect more than your regular rate."

I couldn't object. "Thank you, Evelyn."

"Thank you for caring," she said. "So what's next? Are you going to stake out that apartment?"

"In a bit, yeah. But I did want to ask, do you have housekeepers?"

"I do. They haven't been in Quinn's room since everything happened. Why?"

"That dent in the wall," I said. "I wanna make sure it's new."

"Betty's thorough," Evelyn said. "If it's been there for a while, she'll remember it."

"Then I'd like to speak with her."

Chapter 12

STILL OUTSIDE THE POLICE DEPARTMENT, EVELYN CALLED THE maid, Betty, and asked if she had time to meet with me. After Evelyn hung up, she said Betty would be at a little restaurant off the highway in half an hour. Evelyn told me she could show me the way, but I wanted to speak to her alone.

When I was a kid, my mom cleaned houses under the table with a few friends to make ends meet, so I knew how the hierarchy worked. The people cleaning the houses wouldn't be their full selves around the wives writing their checks, much like how a server had a lot to say in the back room but smiled and chirped at the table they waited on.

I didn't dive into all that with Evelyn, but she agreed to leave. Apparently, she was going off to an appointment with a client.

And once I got cozy in the booth, no matter how guilty I felt about leaving Tempest in the car, I was glad it was just me and Betty. The moment she sat on the other end of the booth, I realized I was in like company.

She was somewhere around middle-aged, light blonde hair turned ashy gray at the roots. The round apples of her cheeks were bright pink from the wind outside. No makeup lined her blue eyes or naturally red lips, but her smile was friendly.

Our outfits were almost identical. Hoodie, sweatpants, and tennis shoes. The only difference was that she smelled of fresh laundry detergent, while I smelled of dog.

Finishing up the introductions, passing our menus to the server, Betty said, "So what do you need from me?"

"I just have a few questions. Mostly about this." Holding out my phone with the picture visible, I pointed to the dent in the wall. "Do you remember this being there the last time you cleaned Quinn's room?"

Betty slid her glasses on and eyed the photo for a moment. "Definitely not, and I've got the pictures to prove it."

"What do you mean?" I asked.

"I clean for a lot of people." Digging around in her purse, Betty gave me a look that said I should've seen what she was getting at. "Some of them aren't as nice as Mrs. Barnes."

I gave her a questioning look, encouraging her to keep going.

"When something goes missing, or if something breaks, they like to blame the help." She swiped open her phone and clicked around for a moment. "So after a lady deducted three hundred bucks from my pay over a vase, I started inventorying everything I do at a job." Angling the phone my way, she showed me a neat and organized checklist. "Go ahead. Take a look."

I did.

And I saw exactly what she meant.

Every single item in each house she cleaned, she checked it off the list and attached a photo of the job before she started, as she did it, and then once she'd put everything back into place. For the bathroom counters, for instance, there was a before shot with an array of personal hygiene items scattered around with some jewelry lying about. The second shot was once she'd removed everything from the counter and wiped it down. The third shot was with all the belongings that'd lain haphazardly over the surface now organized and squeaky clean.

"For insurance purposes, mostly," Betty said. "I didn't think it'd help an investigation, but I hope it does."

"It might. Could you show me the pictures you took in Quinn's room the last time you were there?"

"Sure." After taking the phone and flipping through for a few heartbeats, she handed it back to me. "Funny enough, that was the day I took her curtains down and washed them. I do that every six weeks."

And there it was.

Three days before Quinn's death, there was no dent in the wall below that window. There was no drywall powder on the floor below, either.

"Do you happen to have a before picture of the floors?"

"Yep." Betty took the phone, swiped around a bit, and handed it back. "Quinn's room stayed mostly clean since she went off to college."

Zooming in, I saw no blood splatters on the hardwood. I supposed they may not have been visible without a careful eye. It wouldn't hold in court. But it had merit to me. "Would you mind sending me all that? With the timestamps, please."

"That's no problem," Betty said. "Is there anything else I can help with? Because I loved that little girl. She used to follow me around the house while I cleaned. I even gave her a rag to help me dust sometimes."

"Maybe a few things. Did you ever see Quinn getting into a black luxury car?"

Betty shook her head. "No, always her little Prius."

Damn it. "What about a boy? Did you ever see Quinn with someone?"

She chuckled. "When she was in high school, there were a few, but no one notable. She told me about that Troy a few months ago. He's a cute kid."

"She never mentioned anyone else?"

"Not that I can think of. I'm sorry," Betty said. "You think this happened because of a boy?"

"I don't think much of anything aside from finding it highly unlikely that Quinn did this to herself," I said. "Did Quinn ever mention the book *The Strange Case of Dr. Jekyll and Mr. Hyde* to you?"

Betty paused, thinking for a moment. "Not the book, but she did play this song with a lyric about that a lot. On repeat, sometimes."

Interesting. Music was always a valuable insight into someone's thoughts. I should've considered that when I was sweeping Quinn's phone. "Do you know who sang it?"

"Hang on, let me look." Betty turned back to her cell, clicking away. "I always play music while I clean. Quinn was home over Christmas, and I asked if she wanted me to play anything in particular, and—Ah! Here it is."

"Could you text it to me?"

"You've got it," she said. My phone dinged a second later. "What does that have to do with anything, though?"

I explained that Quinn bordered on obsession with the book. Her friends weren't exactly scholars who debated high lit for fun. I'd just wondered if it was something she and Betty had in common.

"No. I'm not a big reader," Betty said. "Quinn always was, though. She was sweet and quiet. I think a lot of her existed in between those pages she always had her nose in. Like a part of her *was* the books she read, you know what I mean?"

Prior to meeting Grace, I wouldn't have known what Betty meant. But now that I saw that preteen girl constantly reading—and quoting— Shakespeare, I understood. Like with any culture, the media we surrounded ourselves with molded us into the people we were.

All those cop shows I watched as a kid certainly played a part in making me.

"Yeah, I know what you mean," I said. "Is there anything that stands out about Quinn that might help me?"

Betty's face scrunched up in thought for a few heartbeats. Then her brow arched. It fell just as quickly. "No, nothing off the top of my head."

"Nothing at all?" Certainly looked like something had struck through her. "Absolutely nothing?"

"I'd smelled some pot in her room over Christmas, if that means anything."

Not at this point. "I know she partied a little."

"But that's about it." Betty shrugged. "If you have any more questions, just let me know. You've got my number."

* * *

THE SERVER WAS JUST BRINGING MY PLATE OVER AS I STOOD FROM the table. I asked her to make it to-go and headed to the register to pay. The longer I stood in that spot, waiting, the deeper my knee ached.

It hadn't been too bad today but skipping that exercise routine this morning was a big mistake. Especially since I was gonna be staking out an apartment all night.

Which reminded me.

After I let Tempest out on her lead and fed her some kibble, I sat in the driver's seat with my lunch sprawled out on the passenger side. Gobbling down fries as I hopped on the highway, I called Bentley.

On the fourth ring, he answered with, "Hey, you."

"Hey, are you busy?" I asked.

"On my lunch. What about you?"

"Same, actually," I made out between chews, glancing in my rearview as I merged into the left lane. "Don't be mad at me."

"Why would I be mad at you?"

"Because I've gotta bail on our plans for tonight."

"It's your knee that's gonna be mad. Not me." There was a teasing edge to his voice. "What's going on?"

I explained my agenda, ending with, "Which I know my knee will also be mad at me for, but a job's a job, ya know?"

"Shit, for ten grand, your knee can complain when it starts paying the bills."

"My thoughts exactly."

"What are you even gonna do with a check that big?"

"Pay off the trailer. That'd bring my rent down three hundred bucks a month," I said. "Then put the rest away, I guess."

"That'd be the mature call," he said. "But hey, if you're getting that kinda money, maybe you *should* get me more than socks for my surprise."

I laughed. "Shoes instead?"

"That's more like it." His smile was almost audible. "But that's alright. Good luck tonight. If you get bored, give me a call. Let me know if you wanna get some sets in tomorrow."

Hopefully, I'd be home at sunrise, just in time for our morning schedule. "Will do."

"And if you lay down the seats in the back of your car, you might have enough room to do at least some of your exercises. Anything's better than nothing."

"Valid point. I'll try that."

"It's worth a shot. Be careful tonight. I don't know who you're stalking, but you better make it home in one piece."

I wasn't sure why my cheeks felt warm, but I was grateful there were only sound waves through a speaker connecting us. "I plan to. Thanks for worrying about me."

"Always. Have a good—" A beep cut him off.

A glance at the screen told me it was Ox. Meaning he'd likely gotten those background checks done. I told Bentley so, and he hung up just in time for me to catch Ox before it went to voicemail.

"Hey, did you find anything?"

"Depends on what you count as relevant," Ox said. "Possession of marijuana arrest from Troy Austin?"

"Nah, not valuable."

"Underaged drinking for Chelsie Johnson?"

"Any charges attached to that one?"

"No, looks like she got busted at a party right after she turned eighteen."

"That's about what I expected." Grabbing my sandwich from the to-go container, I held the wheel with one hand. "It was more precautionary than anything. Thanks for looking into it either way."

"Gave me something to do," he said. "Who are these people?"

With a sigh, I went into it, explaining all the ins and outs I'd gathered about the case, ending with where I was headed now.

"Hm," he said.

"What?"

"It's weird," he said. "I understand Alex's findings. I even understand overlooking the dent in the wall and the condensation on the window. Anyone could miss that, but after finding a message written on the glass, there's definitely a story there worth digging into."

"Right? Like the other stuff, fine, but pair that message on the window with Quinn's typical route of consumption, and something doesn't add up."

"I'd say so," he said. "You don't need any help, do you?"

Outside of the background checks, no. There wasn't much anyone could do at this point. It was just a matter of research and learning Quinn better. I had the feeling that finding the secret boyfriend was the missing piece, and hopefully I'd have that before the night was over.

"I think I've got it," I said.

"Are you sure?" he asked. "Couldn't even use an extra set of eyes for your all nighter?"

"I doubt I'll be able to sleep in the car either way."

"What about someone to talk to then?"

Ox's tone was flat more often than not. He was a blunt man with a straight-to-the-point attitude. That last bit, however, was tinged with a dash of desperation.

"Are you asking if *I* need help? Or are you asking if you can hang out with me?"

"I'm bored out of my damned mind, Maddie." Of course. The big tough guy couldn't simply admit that he wanted to come. He had to answer the question in a way that didn't *actually* answer the question. "I've been in this house for four days. I haven't even walked outside. There's only so much TV you can binge."

Thinking back to the recovery from my injury, I understood his pain. Being cooped up in the house all day, every day, had been draining. Even though I did close to nothing during that time, I was exhausted.

The irony of it wasn't lost on me. One of the fights we'd gotten into before we broke up was because I wanted to go for a run, and he said I was pushing myself too hard. A year or so later, he was the one on the road to recovery after taking a bullet, and desperate to get out of the house.

Anything to stimulate that boredom would've helped my mental recovery in an immense way. At some point tonight, I'd make a quip about the tables turning, however. "If you wanna come, you can come."

"Thank god," he said under his breath. "Wanna text me the address and meet me nearby?"

"Sounds like a plan. I'll see you soon."

Chapter 13

THIS WASN'T THE SORT OF PLACE I COULD SEE QUINN SPENDING her free time. It wasn't the sort of place I could see *anyone* spending their free time.

The building was standard red brick, stacked six stories high. One window on the fourth floor was shattered. Another was lined with foil. Cigarette butts littered the concrete outside the double door, only accessible with a key fob or numerical code.

That much I knew because after we'd arrived, my initial idea was to look at the mail slots on the other side of that double door. Through the foggy glass window, I saw someone checking theirs and hoped the names of the renters would be on the slots. Since there was no way past that door, and since I didn't have X-ray vision, that idea was a bust.

Still, from our hilltop perch in the parking lot across from the complex, I'd taken headshots of everyone who'd walked in and out since we'd arrived. A young mom with a stroller, a couple guys in hoodies, a drunken middle-aged man, and someone who'd likely just snorted a lot of something, judging by how much they were rubbing their nose.

A few minutes prior, Ox had shown me the names of all the renters in this building from public records. Not one of them looked familiar, nor seemed to have any connection to Quinn's family, college, or even her hometown.

"I agree there's more to this than the police reports say," Ox said, "but I'm not sure you're gonna find it here."

"I'm not sure that I won't, though." Laying my phone in my lap, I grabbed a candy from the center console. "Evelyn's paying me to be here, so I'm gonna stay right where I am."

As Ox was famous for, he answered with, "Hmmm."

Reaching to the floorboard beside his feet for Quinn's copy of *Dr. Jekyll and Mr. Hyde,* I said, "For a man who's been so bored, you sure make for some entertaining conversations."

"You haven't started one either."

"No, but I wasn't the one pleading for company."

He narrowed his eyes. "I didn't plead."

"Close to it." I held up the book. "Ever read this?"

"In high school, I think. Why?"

Swiping onto YouTube to play the song Betty had sent me, I explained its relevance to Quinn, ending with, "Do you think it'd have any connection to the case?"

"It could. The whole plot is about a man who leads a double life, one where he's an astute citizen and another where he's a monster. That sound like your victim?"

"Maybe in her eyes?" Spinning the dial to raise the volume, I swiveled to face him better. "But I wouldn't call what I've gathered so far a double life. She was typical. Look up 'smart college kid' in the dictionary, and there'd be a picture of her."

"Then maybe she equates someone else in her life to *Dr. Jekyll and Mr. Hyde.*" Ox tilted his ear closer to the speaker to hear the lyrics. After a moment, his brow arched. "This show up in her playlist?"

I'd confirmed after leaving the restaurant, and yes, *Jekyll and Hyde,* by the 2000's grunge band Plumb was the first song to pop up in each of Quinn's playlists. That meant she didn't only listen to it once or twice, but repeatedly.

Giving Ox a nod, I listened closer for the lyrics.

And my stomach churned.

From what I gathered, the song had far more to do with an abusive relationship than old English lit. It fixated on the singer's struggle to love the man she referenced as Jekyll and Hyde, wanting to escape a facade where they had to keep their love secret.

That was my interpretation of it, at least.

"Hmmm," Ox said when it stopped playing.

"Do you know how to use words?" I asked.

He shot me another look. "I was thinking."

"You can think without going 'hmmm.'"

"Do you want to hear my thoughts or not?"

"That'd be more helpful than 'hmmm.'"

A glare that time. I laughed, and the corner of his lip twitched into the faintest hint of a smirk.

"Jekyll and Hyde is a universal experience, isn't it?" Ox asked. "That's why that little hundred-and-fifty-year-old novella is still referenced so often today in pop culture."

I wasn't sure I saw what he was getting at yet. "Uh-huh."

"Everyone knows a Jekyll who has a Hyde inside them. Vanzant, for instance. We always saw Jekyll." Shifting in the passenger seat to face me better, he nodded to Tempest lying in the back. "She saw Hyde."

My mom had been the same way. Despite her obvious struggle with addiction, she was sweet as pie to my teachers at school or when the CPS workers brought me home. "Right."

"It's almost a take on narcissistic abuse," Ox said. "Or at least, that's the universal reality many people relate it to in this day and age."

"You saying that whoever Quinn thought about when she heard this song was a narcissist?"

"Maybe," Ox said. "Especially if you're right, and it is about a romantic partner. Whether the guy's married or not, forcing her to keep their relationship private is a textbook sign of abuse."

"Speaking of textbooks." Again, I held up the book. "Nothing else to do. Wanna read it?"

Ox's nose wrinkled. "Aloud?"

"I read a page, then you read a page," I said. "Someone who's just oh-so bored would prefer it to staring at a building."

After grumbling something impossible to decipher to himself, Ox said, "Well, start then."

* * *

So, WE READ THE BOOK, PAUSING ONLY TO CAPTURE PHOTOS OF THE people entering and exiting the apartment building.

Quinn had marked the entire novella with a variety of highlighter shades. There were notes in every margin. Some questioning and critiquing Stephenson's use of semicolons and em dashes, others pondering if the elixir Dr. Jekyll created was an allegory for alcohol turning him into a monster. That much seemed like basic critical reading.

All comments like that were highlighted and written in blue. In pink were comments that seemed more personal. In the first chapter, she'd highlighted a line that said, *But he had an approved tolerance for others; sometimes wondering, almost with envy, at the high pressure of spirits involved in their misdeeds.* Quinn had written, *Oof. Same, my man. Same,* in the margin.

In the same chapter, in pink, she'd highlighted, *the street shone out in contrast to its dingy neighbourhood, like a fire in the forest.* Quinn's comment on that bit was, *Beautiful storytelling. All the monsters I know live in the best of homes too. Isn't that a statement about humanity? Everyone puts on a face for the world in their own way, like saying 'I'm good, how are you?' for the sake of pleasantries. For most of us, that's as deep as it goes. We say we're good because we don't want to disrupt anyone else with the chaos of our lives. Others form fanciful facades, not to blend in, but to stand out. Monsters wearing masks of men paint their walls in gold so when you're looking at them from the street, you'll focus on their sheen instead of the beast that roams within them.*

"That makes me think whoever she'd visited here," Ox had said, "isn't her Mr. Hyde."

Watching a man in a hoodie pass something to a woman in a

minidress and six-inch heels on the street corner, I say, "Not exactly walls of gold."

"So, what are we even doing here?"

"Even if whoever lives here isn't Mr. Hyde," I reply, "they're a missing piece of the puzzle. The more I know, the more I'll find. Keep reading."

He did.

There were a handful of other deep, heartfelt notations like the one about the golden walls. Others were more casual. Like, *"Black-Mail House is what I call that place."* Quinn had written *LOL* beside it.

One I found interesting was from the quote, *Master Hyde, if he were studied... must have secrets of his own; black secrets... secrets compared to which poor Jekyll's worst would be like sunshine.*

Quinn had written beside it, *I love the irony of this foreshadowing, but damn, it hits hard. It makes me wonder if it isn't only everyone around Dr. Jekyll who sees him as flawless, but even Dr. Jekyll himself. Sure, he feels guilt later for what he created, and what he became, but Mr. Hyde feels nothing for anyone aside from himself. I'm not sure I believe real world Mr. Hydes can feel the guilt that Dr. Jekyll does. But then, does he? Does he have any remorse for the awful he does? If he did, wouldn't he stop? I know he tried for a while, but he opened himself back up to the same evil he claims to resent. Idk. I don't think Dr. Jekyll is as angelic as Stevenson wants us to think he is. He chooses to continue doing harm. It's not remorse if you consciously decide to continue hurting those around you.*

Truth was, I could relate to both Dr. Jekyll and Mr. Hyde. I didn't become a monster when I was using, but I knew it was causing me more harm than good and had continued to use.

All until Ox made that comment about me turning into my mom, who *had* been a monster. Out in the world, she wore the face of Dr. Jekyll as best she could, but anyone could see the cracks in her shiny exterior to Mr. Hyde underneath if they looked hard enough.

That was just it though, and where I agreed with Quinn. Whoever caused the pain was not remorseful if they consciously continued hurting those around them.

But who the hell was her Mr. Hyde? Who'd hurt her?

I didn't know, and I didn't find any clues within that novella. Ox dozed off somewhere around halfway through, so I read it again. And again. And one more time for good measure.

On the third read, I caught one bit that Quinn had highlighted in pink and circled in red pen. *O my poor old Harry Jekyll, if I ever read Satan's signature upon a face, it is on that of your new friend.*

Beside it, Quinn wrote, *Even when you look him in the eye, Mr. Utterson, you can't see him for who he is. Why does no one see him for who he is?*

"Why do you, Quinn?" I murmured to myself, reading that line over a dozen times. "Who do you see for who they are? Who is he?"

Chapter 14

Ox had always done this on stakeouts.

More often than not, they were *his* stakeouts. After all, he was the detective. I was just an officer. But I went along with him because it was the type of work I preferred. Writing out speeding tickets got monotonous. Sneaking around and watching drug dealers who were causing real harm to the world, who needed to be stopped, was more climactic than the typical day in the life of a cop.

Still, Ox was always passed out by the time the sun was coming up.

I hadn't minded then. I didn't mind it now either.

As much as it surprised me, I enjoyed it. The night together had been fun.

Sun pooling in through the windows, shining on his golden waves, highlighting the sharp angles of his dreaming face, reminded me of why I'd fallen in love with him. He'd always been broody and snappy, but when the sun shined on that blond hair and cast the right shadow on his strong jaw, he looked like an angel.

That wasn't to say that I wanted him back.

Nope. Angel-like jawline or not, big fat *nope*.

I loved Ox. I'd probably always love him, but I liked who I'd become since he'd stopped being the focal point of my life. When we'd met, I was barely out of my teens. I'd lived on my own for a few years out of high school, but I hadn't been a woman yet, not really. I wasn't one when we fell in love either.

The last year was the first time in my adult life that I *felt* like the woman I'd always dreamed of becoming.

Then again, I hadn't felt that way for all of the last year. Just the last few months. Since I'd gotten sober, paid my bills, and had a life outside of the man I'd shared a bed with.

Independence had always been a goal of mine. Sure, I was still struggling on the financial end of things, but in some regard, I was finally who I'd always wanted to be. Somewhere along the way, I'd found a dose of happiness.

The ball of fluff who sat up between the seats and licked my cheeks may've played a part in that.

Chuckling, I petted Tempest's scruff. "Need to go outside?"

She licked my face faster, whole ass wagging with her whip of a tail.

"Alright, I hear you."

Stepping out and guiding Tempest out the rear door to a patch of grass at the far end of the parking lot, I kept an eye on the building. No one had come in or out since three, but it was almost that time of the morning when people woke up for work. I expected movement soon.

Tempest did her business, and we walked around a bit, only in line of sight of the building. My knee needed the stretch. Tempest did too.

Once we made it back to the car, I held the door open for her and told her to get in.

She stared up at me from the cement. As if to say, *Seriously?*

Patting the seat, I commanded, "Come."

With her ears back, she hopped onto the bench.

Guilt bubbling through me, I gave her scruff a pet.

Today, I had to squeeze in some time to take her on a walk. A long one, whether my knee would tolerate that or not. German Shepherds needed constant stimulation. She hadn't gotten much of that yesterday and was a few hours from an outburst of some kind if she didn't get to expel some energy soon.

But I had to give her credit. She'd done excellent considering how much time she'd spent locked in the car.

"We'll go see Bentley and Grace later, alright? Then you'll get to run off some of that energy."

Tempest's tail wagged at the mention of their names.

Smiling at her, I scooped out her food from the Tupperware container on the floor and filled her bowl with water. Between her slurps, I hand fed her. The resource guarding had been less of an issue lately, but we hadn't been in one another's lives very long yet. No matter if it felt like I'd had Tempest for a decade. Daily, I put in the effort to make sure I had her trust.

Yawning and stretching his arms above his head, Ox craned to look at me in the back seat. "Shit, when'd I pass out?"

"Four-ish."

"Did I miss anything?"

"Just a deal at the corner." Petting Tempest one more time, I moved to the driver's side. "Nothing special."

"I'm surprised it was only the one." Yawning again, he focused ahead. "You're looking for a luxury vehicle, aren't you?"

Following his gaze, I watched a silver Mercedes slow to a stop at the meter just before the building. Not the vehicle the librarian had described, nor the one that'd been following me. It wasn't the kind I'd seen roll through these streets all night either.

Not even shutting the door, I grabbed my phone from the seat and swiped to the camera function. Hitting record, I zoomed in on the driver as he stepped from the vehicle. He wasn't anyone I'd seen around Quinn's college, but he would've fit in there.

Somewhere between five ten and six feet. Average build, covered by a sweater and vest. His khakis were ironed to perfection. The graying hair atop his crown was tousled with a bit of product, but nothing extravagant.

None of that was a direct tie to Quinn, but they belonged to the same social class.

Zooming in closer, I noted a cord tied around his wrist.

It was vibrant in color, decorated with a dozen or so beads.

Almost identical to the friendship bracelet Chelsie wore.

"Come." I tapped my hip for Tempest. She jumped from the car and joined me at my side.

"Was that for the dog or me?" Ox asked.

Shooting him a half smile, I shut the car door. "I don't need you. But you're welcome to join me."

My knee didn't thank me for the speed I took down the hill, but those double doors locked. I needed to talk to this guy before he vanished inside. He was still fiddling with his phone when we were halfway down. We were at the foot of it when he stepped out and headed to the meter.

"Excuse me, sir," I said, trekking faster across the street. The man looked up, then behind him as if to check if it was him I was talking to. "Do you have a minute?"

"I have somewhere to be—"

"It won't take long." Only a few strides apart now, I gestured to his wrist. "I just wanted to ask about that bracelet."

He glanced at it, then back up at me. "I'm sorry?"

"It doesn't match your aesthetic." I forced a smile. "Is there a story behind it?"

"Yeah." Studying me, then glancing at Tempest at my side and Ox beside me, he tucked his hand into his pocket. "I'm sorry, do I know you?"

"I don't think so, but I'd like to change that." Extending a hand, I dug in my hoodie pocket with the other. "My name's Maddie Castle."

Still confused, he took the hand I offered. "Can I ask what this is about?"

"Quinn Barnes." Smile falling, I squeezed his hand tighter. "Did she give you that bracelet?"

He'd already been confused at the mention of her name, but his blue eyes widened. Practically yanking his hand from my grasp, he stepped toward the apartment building. "I'm sorry, I need to be going."

Tempest walked between him and the door. Raising a lip, she growled low.

He stirred back a step.

"How do you know Quinn?" I asked.

"I don't know what you're talking ab—"

"She came here every Thursday." Voice harshening, I squared my shoulders. "A nineteen-year-old girl came to this apartment building every Thursday, told no one where she was going, and you show up here wearing a bracelet almost identical to one she'd made for her best friend. I think you know damn well what I'm talking about."

Breaths quickening, he glanced between me and Tempest. "I'd appreciate it if you moved your dog."

"And I'd appreciate it if you told me about your connection to Quinn Barnes."

"I don't know what you're talking about."

My blood was boiling now.

By my standards, Quinn was a child, involved in something far too big for her to understand. Although the affair may have been consensual, I saw those quotes from that book. I listened to that song she played over and over.

She felt isolated, trapped, and heart-broken every day since she'd fallen for the mystery man.

Legally, there was nothing wrong with what Quinn or this man had done. Morally? This man was dogshit on the bottom of my shoe.

With a glare that could shatter stone, I snapped, "A girl is dead, and you won't even admit that you know her? You made her hide from the beginning, and you're gonna continue making her hide from the grave?"

Color drained from the man's face. "Quinn's dead?"

At least he admitted he knew her. But I wasn't sure I believed he hadn't known she was dead. "Yes, she is. How did you know her?"

Blinking hard, he braced himself against the car.

"She asked you a question," Ox said, voice firm. "Now would be the time to answer it."

Confused, he met my gaze. "How do *you* know Quinn?"

"I'm a private investigator. Her mother hired me to look into her death.. Time to return the favor. What is your connection to Quinn Barnes?"

The man rubbed a hand down his face, saying nothing.

This guy was getting on my last damn nerve. "If you were having an affair with this girl, that'd make you or your wife the prime suspect—"

"Affair?" He shook his head. "No, no. Nothing like that. I—I don't understand. Quinn was murdered?"

"Her mom thinks so," I said. "So do I."

The man's face was paler than a cloud. Holding a hand over his stomach, his gaze grew distant with disbelief. That was the expression of an innocent man. The shock was genuine. He was hiding something, though.

"If it wasn't an affair, why was she here every Thursday?" I asked. "Because I've got most of her life sorted out, but you're a mystery."

"I can look into him," Ox said. "It's not my jurisdiction, but I can run records. There's something he doesn't want us to know about. Maybe I'll do enough digging and publish his name and information about this place online. That'd—"

"It wasn't an affair." The man's tone deepened. "She's my daughter's age. We made these bracelets together." He waved an arm in the air in gesture. "I could never see her that way."

"Then how did you see her?" I asked.

Tightening his lips to a line, color gradually returning to his face, he gestured toward the apartment. "I'll show you. But I ask that anything you're about to see remains discreet."

"If it connects to Quinn's death, and I have to turn it over to the police—"

"It doesn't. Please, just assure me that what you're about to see, as well as this address, will be kept off any public record, at least in connection to my name."

Depending on what *this* was, that might not be feasible. But I needed to know what was going on inside this place. "Sure. What is your name, by the way?"

"Steven Benedict." Careful to avoid Tempest, he walked to the keypad.

Either he was flustered or stupid, but he didn't cover his hand as he typed in the code.

4-9-0-2-5

Noted.

* * *

I WAS MORE GRATEFUL FOR OX'S PRESENCE THAN I THOUGHT I'D BE as we ascended the apartment building staircase. Ox was a big guy over six feet with even bigger shoulders and arms—the kind of guy people noticed, and avoided, in public settings. My gun was in my hoodie pocket, of course, and I would've had my finger on the trigger if I were doing this alone. With him behind me, I settled for my hand on it with the safety engaged.

The outdoor carpet underfoot was worn, torn in some places, making it difficult to tell if the color had originally been brown or an odd shade of green. Flickering fluorescents shined overhead, accentuating the smog stains atop the tall white walls. The scent of cigarette smoke and marijuana almost disguised the smell of animal urine.

Rounding the bend to the door for the third floor, Steven held the door open for us. Ox put a hand on my back, placing himself between me and Steven. Once the door clicked shut behind us, Steven walked ahead of us again. At apartment 303, he stopped and dug in his pocket for his keys.

Reaching inside to turn a light on, he said, "Have a look."

Ox kept that hand on my lower back as we walked inside.

Not sure what I'd expected, but it wasn't this.

Live plants hung from the ceiling and sat around in pots, adding a layer of warmth and comfort to the space. Tucked on the far right beside an apartment-sized fridge was a coffee bar, featuring what looked like a cappuccino machine, baskets of packaged snacks, and water bottles. There was a couch with a chaise between two windows, and a black lounge chair sat before it.

All four walls were a cozy shade of yellow. Photos of flowers, forests, and waterfalls decorated each one. A stenciled inspirational quote framed them overtop, each letter a different color of the rainbow.

It read, *Today, I'm alright.*

I recognized it from the inspirational quotes and photos Quinn had saved on her phone.

As the door clicked shut behind us, Steven said, "I was her therapist."

"There's no history of therapy in her medical records." Turning to meet his gaze, I gestured around. "And why would you have appointments here? You don't have an office?"

"I do have an office. It's where I met Quinn when she was fourteen." Walking to a desk beside the coffee bar, he said, "She reached out to me last fall and asked if there was a way I could counsel her without it showing up on her medical bills."

"And you set this entire place up for her?" Ox's voice made it very clear he didn't believe that.

"I already had this place, but for the same reason." Steven shuffled through some papers in a filing cabinet. After finding a manilla envelope, he flipped through it for a few seconds. He walked toward me with a sheet of paper. "I cater to a particular class of people. People who appreciate discretion."

Eyeing it, I caught Quinn's signature at the bottom. It was legitimate. Looked just like the signature on her schoolwork.

"There's a stigma around psychology and therapy in some circles," Steven said. "There are a thousand reasons people like to pay off the books for this sort of thing. In a custody battle, if it comes out that a mother has depression, a father might use it against her. Some careers won't allow you to work if you see a therapist. I offer therapy here, with no paper trail, so people have someone to talk to when they feel like there's no one else."

Damn it. Now I liked this guy.

"You're licensed?" I asked.

He nodded to a certificate on the wall. "This apartment isn't zoned for commercial use, but everything else I do is legal. I just don't accept insurances. I have detailed confidentiality agreements, stating that I will not store my patients' records on a computer, that I will repeat nothing about their treatment to another person, and the details of how to contact me confidentially."

"So you cater to rich people," Ox said.

"My patients usually come from wealth, yes," Steven said. "Hence why I practice here. They're unlikely to happen upon anyone they know on their way in and out of our sessions. Again, it all comes down to discretion. Even me telling you this is violating my contract with Quinn."

"Even in death?" I asked.

"Yes. Patient confidentiality doesn't change in the event of a person's death. If anything, it's more important to protect her privacy now than it was." Lowering himself to the lounge, he frowned. "I can't give you access to my records, but if you have any questions, I'll let you know if I can answer them."

Access to his records would cut out the middleman and make my life easier, but I'd do my best with what I had. "Quinn started seeing you in the fall, correct?"

"Yes."

"Was she seeing you in regard to a mental health condition?" Ox asked.

Steven's face said no, that wasn't the case, but his lips said, "I can't answer that. For what it's worth, though, I'm a therapist. Not a psychiatrist. I would refer a patient to psych if I believed they needed that type of care."

Quinn's records had no medications listed, which told me she wasn't in psychiatric care. She saw Steven for therapy. Likely to talk about issues with her second boyfriend.

"Is there anyone in Quinn's life she was afraid of?" I asked. "A partner who may've hurt her in the past?"

"Quinn never discussed intimate partner violence with me," he said. "She never mentioned being afraid of anyone in her life."

"Just because she wasn't afraid of a partner in the past doesn't mean he couldn't have harmed her later," Ox said. "Was she in an abusive relationship of any form? Even emotional?"

Steven inhaled and exhaled slowly. "I'm willing to confirm that she never mentioned being threatened by people in her life. But I can't tell you about her love life."

Because she *was* having an affair with someone. That knowledge coming out would tarnish her reputation, which the document I held swore Steven Benedict wouldn't do.

"You know the statistics as well as I do, I'm sure," Ox said. "Other forms of abuse can turn physical."

"They can."

"And you can't confirm or deny that she wasn't in an abusive relationship of some kind?"

"I can't confirm or deny any of her personal information."

"You just confirmed that she didn't feel threatened by anyone in her life," Ox snapped. "But you won't confirm that a partner may've been abusing her?"

"Quinn never told me about any abuse." Steven's voice had an edge to it now, but the look he gave me answered my question. He couldn't directly state his *opinion* on a patient, but he had one. "Again, confidentiality extends to death."

"Guess you can't tell me if she was seeing a married man then, huh?" I asked.

His expression said it all. The sharp look in his eyes, the stiffness through his shoulders. He looked a bit like Bentley when Darius sat too close to Grace.

Steven couldn't tell me who the guy was, but he was doing his best to tell me that, yes, Quinn was involved with a married man. No, he hadn't abused her, but something about the relationship made Steven defensive, protective.

If the man was married, I'd suspected he was older than Quinn. There weren't all that many married nineteen-year-olds, let alone married nineteen-year-olds who owned luxury vehicles. Whoever she was seeing worried Steven. Maybe not because he'd put his hands on her. Not because he was worried for her physical safety, but because he was worried about her overall wellbeing.

"I can't confirm or deny anything about Quinn's love life," Steven said.

"I understand," I said. "Can you tell me if the man she was seeing is one I would've happened upon in my investigation so far?"

Again, he shook his head. Which was what I hoped he'd do. "I'm sorry, I can't answer that."

So he wasn't someone closely associated with her. "What about her mental state? Did Quinn show any signs of suicidal ideation?"

"If she had, I would've had her institutionalized," he said. "It's my goal to help people. I would've made sure she got the care she needed."

Also what I'd expected. Quinn wasn't suicidal. She was only seeing a therapist to cope with the reality of being the other woman.

"You can't think of anyone, anyone at all, who may have wanted to hurt Quinn?"

"No, I cannot." Steven's expression was sincere. "I would tell you if I did."

Chapter 15

"You think he was telling the truth?" Ox asked, hand on my lower back again while we rounded our way down the stairs.

"I don't have any reason to think he was lying." Holding the rail for stability, I looked at the image of Steven Benedict on the website for his private therapy practice in Bedford County. I showed my phone screen to Ox. "His story checks out. Anything you found suspicious?"

"No. Just a pain in the ass that he wouldn't say yes or no to the partner abuse."

"Because Quinn didn't see their relationship as abusive," I said. "In Quinn's mind, it was a forbidden love story. But Steven knew the guy was taking advantage of her. That's an opinion though. He couldn't have told me that even with a court order."

"Which the police could've gotten if they were investigating."

"If they gave a damn." Making it to the landing of the staircase, I bent to adjust Tempest's harness. When I stood, Ox's hand was on my lower back again. "But I've got enough confirmation now. Quinn had another boyfriend. I just gotta find out who he is."

"Already looked through all her social media?"

"Wouldn't be doing my job otherwise," I said. Ox held the door for me and Tempest. "Maybe I can have Evelyn print out her phone records. I can compare her text and call logs to everything on there now."

"Might be able to find an inconsistency." His hand was still on my lower back as we stepped outside. "If you get a number, I can trace it to the owner."

As much as I appreciated his touch when we were walking upstairs, and even coming back down, he was standing a little too close. He was one step from tucking that arm around my waist and pulling me into him.

To not make it a big thing, I bent again to adjust Tempest's harness.

Ox dropped his hand to his side by the time I was vertical. That saved us from a conversation I really wasn't in the mood to have.

"Where are you heading now?"

"I guess to take you back to your car," I said. "I'll call Evelyn about those records. Then I'm gonna sleep for a few and go through them."

Ox never smiled, not really. Just the slightest upturn of the corners of his lips. "Sorry. I was supposed to let you do that."

"It's alright. Been a while since I did one of these. It was kinda nice," I said.

"It was." As shocking as I found it, that hint of a smile grew. "We should do it again sometime. Maybe not when you're stalking a therapist."

Was that a joke? It was close to one. The attempt was more than I expected from Ox.

But the undertone of that suggestion wasn't lost on me. "Yeah, maybe me, you, and Alex could get together. Summer's coming. You know how nice her yard is when she opens the pool."

"Or me and you could just go see a movie? Or dinner?"

I hated that there were butterflies and a knot in my stomach at the same time.

Last night, I'd felt normal with him. There was no hand holding or kissing, but there was never much of that back in the day, either. Ox's love language wasn't touch.

Actually, I had no idea what Ox's love language was.

Quality time, maybe?

Which I didn't mind giving him. But the mention of Alex was intended to send the message that I wasn't interested in any other dynamic. Not now, probably not ever.

Was it possible? Maybe, but I didn't even know where to begin.

This relationship hadn't just broken. It had gone up in flames. How could we rebuild when we only had ashes and an unstable foundation?

"I don't know." My voice came out softer than I knew it could. "I don't think I want us to go *out*, if that's what you're asking."

A glint of pain shined in his eyes, but that barely there smile stayed. "No, I know. I just meant as friends. It's been nice to have you visit me. Recovery would've been even more boring without you. But getting out of the house and spending time with you, it's been really good. I enjoyed it. You enjoyed it. There's nothing romantic about a couple friends going to dinner or a movie, is there?"

Was there? No, of course not. So why was my stomach still twisting and dancing? I couldn't tell if I was nervous, excited, or uncomfortable.

"Going out as friends sounds nice," I said. "As long as we're clear on the friends part."

"I don't think you're gonna stop reminding me any time soon." That time, the smile was more than a hint. It was the real thing. "I get it Maddie. I just miss you."

Damn it. My stomach didn't know what to do with itself.

I didn't know how to respond to that. I missed him, too. But even though he said he understood that I meant so in a platonic manner, I wasn't sure if *I* did.

I didn't want him back. We couldn't work as a couple again. I'd never be able to trust him. He worked a few doors down from Harper. Every moment he was at the office, I'd wonder if they were in a closet together somewhere.

Whatever my stomach was doing needed to stop it. Flattery would get him nowhere. We were friends. *Just* friends, damn it.

"I'm sorry," Ox said. "Did that cross a line? I didn't mean anything by it. We were together for a long time. Barely seeing each other has been weird. I'd just like to be more involved in each other's lives."

107

Over his shoulder, a black luxury vehicle turned onto the street. I couldn't be sure if it was the one I'd seen yesterday and the day before, but it had the blacked-out windows.

Mercedes, maybe? I couldn't tell from the distance. It was half a block away.

"Maddie, are you—"

The driver's side window rolled down just far enough for an arm to extend through the opening. The barrel of a gun slid through the crack, aiming right at me.

"Get down!"

Boom!

There was no coverage on the sidewalk. No garbage cans, no bins. Aside from Steven's car, which the bullet had just flown over, there was nowhere close to hide.

Tempest bolted to my left.

Ox grabbed my arm and shoved me toward the edge of the building.

Thumps and bangs sounded behind me.

I didn't turn to see the damage.

I ran.

Dropping into the alley, I ducked behind a dumpster. Tempest cowered at my side. Ox fell over me, knocking me flat onto my ass.

"Down," he told Tempest.

With a whine, she laid her head behind mine.

Caging me in place, shielding my body with his, Ox's eyes stayed open and focused on me.

A few bangs of gunfire sounded overhead, pounding off the dumpster.

Then the squeal of tires peeling out on cement.

Silence.

Ox said, "You okay?"

I nodded, heart pounding so hard, I felt it in my eyes. My knee wouldn't be happy later, but the adrenaline drowned it out for now. "You?"

"I'm good." He reached past me for Tempest, stroking a hand over her. "Looks like she is too."

"Then let's go."

But by the time we were on two feet, jogging toward the street, the black car was out of sight, only the faint purr of its engine in the distance. Even if it was still within our vision, my SUV was in the parking lot on the hill. Running at full speed, he still had a head start that we couldn't catch up to.

"Bullshit," Ox said under his breath, eyeing the street up and down.

That it was.

Tempy whimpered at my side, back legs trembling. This poor girl had watched her last handler die in a setting not much different than this. Out in the open. On a chase.

Bending to comfort her, I looked up and down the street, making sure no innocent bystander got hit in the crossfire. No one else was in sight, considering it was barely after sunrise.

Stroking Tempest, checking her paws to make sure there were no shards of glass stuck in them, I told Ox, "I'm gonna call 911. Can you go check on Steven?"

"As long as you get your ass in that doorway." He nodded to the apartment building. "You're a clear target out in the open like this."

The guy wasn't coming back. Not when I'd been so close to catching his plate, and not when he didn't have the advantage of shock on his side. But I agreed it was best to go somewhere with cover.

Scooping my arms beneath Tempy's torso, I hoisted her to my chest. "Good idea."

"What the hell are you doing?"

"We have shoes." Trembling at Tempy's weight, I walked toward the front of the building. "She doesn't. I'm not gonna make her walk on broken glass."

"Get her some shoes, then. Doubt this is the last time you'll be in this situation."

Valid point.

* * *

ONCE TEMPEST AND I WERE TUCKED INTO THE APARTMENT entryway, far enough to not be seen from the street, I called 911. After explaining that I was a private investigator and someone had shot at me, they said they'd send someone out right away. I could've gone to get coffee in the time it took them to show.

Steven was shaken as he waited at the foot of the stairs with us. He said he'd heard the gunshot, locked the door, and ducked below the windows for cover. Apparently, it wasn't the first time. Not a surprise given the look of this place.

Steven said it was the first time the gunshots had been so close, however. As he stood there, pale and quivering, I said, "Still not gonna tell me who might've wanted to hurt Quinn?"

He frowned. "I would if I could. But you don't have a warrant, and I have no proof."

Fair point. By law, he wasn't permitted to share that information with me. Since there was no pending case, we were screwed in the warrant department, too.

"Well, the bastard knows about your private *private* practice now," I said. "Be mindful of that."

Judging by the greenish cast that came to his face, that wasn't comforting either. He tucked his messenger bag closer to his body. Otherwise telling me without saying the words that there were files in there he had to protect.

So breaking in here later was out of the equation.

The local police for this tiny town arrived a few minutes after that conversation. It was a small department, no more than five guys. One squad car. I'd begun my statement with, "I'm Maddie Castle," only to be cut off with, "I know."

I'd thought he was referencing my involvement with the Country Killer. Which would've been uncomfortable. Instead, he hit me with, "I arrested your mom for possession a few years ago. She said you were a big cop in the city and you'd bail her out."

As much as I hated being known as the cop who'd put a bullet in the Country Killer, I preferred that to *the daughter of Natalie Castle.*

"Yeah, well, I didn't," I said. "Anyway, about what happened here today—"

"Did you catch the guy's plate?" His expression was stoic. "Make or model?"

"We didn't get the chance," I said. "But there are a fair number of bullets laying around. Ballistics might tell you something."

Officer F. Kennedy, his badge read, rolled his eyes. "Look, we get shootings like this all the time. Probably had nothing to do with you."

"That car's been following me since I started my investigation." My tone sharpened. "I have every reason to believe that this is the same man responsible for the murder I'm investigating."

Jotting in a notepad, he made a face that told me how little he believed that. "Investigating, huh?"

"Yes, investigating," I snapped. "I'm a private investigator. I have the certification to prove it."

Kennedy choked on a laugh as he scribbled some more notes. "I believe you."

"Then what's the attitude about?" I crossed my arms against my chest. "Because my mom was an addict? Because you don't think private investigation is a real job? 'Cause I'm looking around your city, sir, and it doesn't look like you're all that skilled at serving and protecting either. Especially if you guys 'get shootings like this all the time.'"

Glaring up from his notebook, he snapped it shut. "I got your names and numbers. We'll let you know if anything comes up."

"You've gotta be shitting me," I said. "That's all you have to say."

"Well, like you said." Kennedy clicked his pen and clipped it to his shirt pocket. "I've got a lot of work to do, protecting and serving my city."

Once he stomped back to his car, Ox turned to me, face scrunched up in disbelief. "What the hell is wrong with the cops out here?"

The truth of the matter, Ox wouldn't accept.

These little country towns had been idyllic once, like the one Quinn came from. Then, whether from inflation or economic crashes, poverty had fallen upon its occupants. With poverty came a bad image. Shit home values because the people living here couldn't afford the upkeep. Drugs moved in to comfort the victims of economic crisis. With drugs came addiction. Addiction meant more drugs, more drug dealers, which exacerbated violence, theft, and vandalism.

I came from a shit mom who'd given that cop a hell of a time once. She was the living personification of the issues that'd taken his town in a chokehold and strangled it to death. In his mind, I was no more worthy of his help than the rest of this city.

"It doesn't matter," I said. "Let's go talk to a different one."

Chapter 16

"Brought a friend this time." Fitz extended a hand. "Detective Jerry Fitz."

"Detective Lennox Taylor." Ox's jaw was taut. "Do you have a minute?"

"'Boutta head out, actually." Crossing his arms against his chest, he leaned against the reception desk behind him. "What can I do for you, Castle? Got any more holes in the walls you wanna show me?"

Gritting my teeth, I held up one of the bullets that'd smashed into the dumpster in that alley. "Maybe you'll find this a bit more substantial."

Eyeing it through the bifocals of his glasses, his face screwed up in confusion. "You found this in Quinn's room?"

"No, it almost went through my head in an alleyway," I snapped.

"What the hell are you talking about?"

"Every Thursday, Quinn went to an apartment building in Somerset County," I said. "Couldn't figure out why, so we staked it out last night. It was her therapist."

Now he looked even more confused. It lessened a second later. "Well, that increases the odds of a suicide, doesn't it?"

"Not according to him," Ox said.

"And that's not the point," I said. "When we were leaving, a black car fired at least a dozen rounds at us. A car that's been following me since I started this investigation."

Still, he looked puzzled. "Where at in Somerset?"

Swiping open my phone, I showed him the exact spot on a map.

He snorted a laugh. "I don't see what this has to do with Quinn."

"Are you that stupid?" My voice was acid, and I didn't care if it was unprofessional. "Some son of a bitch is following me. I saw the same car at Quinn's college. It was watching me when I was interviewing someone in Pittsburgh. Then I get close to figuring out what happened to her, and they shoot at me. And you don't see how this has anything to do with Quinn?"

"Did you get the plate?" he asked.

"No, but—"

"The make and model?"

"I didn't have much time when I was running for my life."

"Then what makes you think that shooting was even about you?" He nodded to my phone. "That's not a good area. Shootings happen there a few times a week. You were probably just in the wrong place at the wrong time."

"You've gotta be shitting me," I said. "This car has been following me ever since I started looking into Quinn's death, and—"

"And how do you know it was even the same car?"

In fairness, I didn't have proof. Every glance I'd gotten was so quick, I couldn't make out any identifiable markings. "Window tint that dark is illegal. I couldn't see a damn thing through it. Most cars don't have that."

"You want me to keep an eye out for a car with dark tint?" he asked. "I'll let the boys around here know. We'll make sure to pull 'em over for you, get their names, and check the car for a gun. If we find one, we'll bring the son of a bitch in for questioning. Is that enough for you?"

No, it wasn't. It was a step in the right direction, but it felt intentionally evasive. Like he was more concerned with appeasing me than catching a killer.

"It's a start," I said. "A search for the guy would be nice."

"I'll tell my guys to keep an eye out, but what kinda APB am I supposed to put out when you don't have a face, a name, a plate, or a make and model?"

That much was fair. It was his attitude on the subject that pissed me off.

"Acknowledging that this is tied to Quinn's death would be nice." Ox's tone was deeper than mine. "Acknowledging that the girl was killed would be better."

Fitz made a noise in the back of his throat. "I already told your little girlfriend here. There's no evidence of foul play. No marks on the body. No signs of a struggle—"

"Blood on the floor, a dent in the wall, and a message on the window are all evidence of foul play." Ox's eyes were narrowed to slits. "You can't look me in the eye and say that this was a textbook overdose, Detective. Not unless you truly are incompetent, in which case, you shouldn't be doing this job."

"Weren't you the lead on the Country Killer case? I think I remember that pretty boy face of yours on the TV." Glaring at Ox, Fitz squared his shoulders. "Tell me again about incompetence, Taylor. How many women died before you called in for reinforcements?"

"How many of those women were from *your* county? What'd you do to find the bastard?"

"I damn sure didn't send my girlfriend in to stop him."

Clenching his hand into a fist, Ox stepped in. "Watch your mouth."

Fitz huffed a laugh, coming in closer. "When you take a step back, I will."

Ox stood steady. "Why are you against reopening this case?"

"Because there is no case."

"Do you really think it's all coincidence?"

"I think kids do drugs and make dumb decisions. That's what Quinn did."

"All the evidence points to the contrary."

"They're straws, not evidence, and Barbie's"—he waved a hand at me —"grasping at anything she can get her hands on to make as much money as she can off a grieving mother."

I said, "To hell I am."

"We both know that's not true." If a look could kill, Fitz would be a rotting corpse from the one Ox gave him. "Why are you scared to find the truth?"

"I ain't *scared* of a damned thing, boy." Fitz was practically screaming in Ox's face now. "I'm under-manned, I'm out of leads on the girl, and it looks like you are, too. You don't have a damn place to go, and there isn't enough evidence to say this was anything other than an accidental OD."

"There's plenty of evidence." I began.

"There are some odd pieces that don't fit neat and tidy in the picture." Fitz turned his glower on me. "None of it is evidence of murder, Castle."

Now he was back to Castle. Only *Barbie* and *your little girlfriend* when he addressed a man. That said a hell of a lot about how he viewed women. Then again, so did his one hundred percent male police force.

"You're full of shit, and we both know it," Ox said.

"What do you want me to do? Huh?" Another vague wave toward me. "She's investigating You think she can do a better job than me, anyway. She can keep doing what she's doing, and if she finds proof of murder, I'll happily arrest the guy."

"If you were investigating, you could subpoena the therapist's records," Ox said. "Open the investigation just for that. Prove there's no one in those files who had the motive and means to kill Quinn Barnes, and we'll get off your ass."

Fitz had grown furious as this conversation progressed.

But when Ox said that, he took a step back. The vein on his neck pulsed faster. Even his breathing picked up.

Why was he nervous?

Did he know what was in those files?

"Tell ya what," Fitz said, calmer now, eyes averted. "This crosses into your jurisdiction, and you open the case, pretty boy."

Ox must've thought the same thing I did because he drew a hair closer. Fitz and he were roughly the same height, but Ox looked bigger when he stood with the right posture. Although I'd never been afraid of

Ox, I understood how he intimidated those he interrogated. If I was on the receiving end of that cold stare, almost chest to chest with a man of his stature, I would've pissed myself.

"What's gonna come out as Maddie digs into this case?" Ox asked.

"The hell are you talking about?"

"You tell me."

"Are you accusing me of something?" Fitz broadened his stance. "'Cause you're getting very close to a line you shouldn't cross."

"An innocent man would acknowledge the holes in this case and find a way to fill them in." Ox didn't flinch as he stared hard into Fitz's eyes. "So, you tell me. *Should* I be accusing you of something, Detective?"

Through bared teeth and flaring nostrils, Fitz said, "I'm not hiding a damn thing. The case is what it is. So. Back. Off. Don't come back unless you got something that'll lead me to an arrest."

Ox still didn't move. He studied Fitz for so long, I wondered how his eyes weren't dry.

When Fitz reached for his hip, I grabbed Ox's arm. "It's not worth it. Let's go."

Ox glared at the other man until he turned to the exit. He was out the door before me.

Just as I stepped through the threshold, still holding the handle, Fitz said, "Castle."

I looked at him over my shoulder. "You mean Barbie?" His harsh expression softened. "What, Fitz?"

"If I thought that girl was killed, I'd be out there hunting down the jackass who did it," he said. "I ain't crooked. I just don't see what you see here. There are only a handful of guys in this office. I don't have the resources to search for something that ain't there."

"I understand scarcity," I said. "I understand what it's like to be understaffed and underfunded. But it's there. *Something* is there. I don't know what yet, but Quinn didn't die by her own hand, and I'm not gonna stop until I find out who held her down and shoved those pills down her throat."

He tried to disguise it, but he shuddered at that mention. "You really think someone did that."

"I really do. And I think they were counting on your inexperience to cover their ass."

The anger returned. "I'm not a rookie, Castle."

"Maybe you know a thing or two about the opioid crisis, but you clearly don't know much about other drugs." I didn't say that in a condescending manner for a reason. "It'd serve you and your community if you educated yourself more thoroughly on the subject."

Fitz only licked his teeth in response.

* * *

"You think he's crooked?" I glanced from the highway to Ox. "That's the vibe you got?"

"I don't know." It came out closer to a sigh than a sentence. "I think he's stupid."

Chuckling, I took a glance at Tempy napping in my rearview. "He really doesn't have a grasp on narcotics."

"Guess most people out this way don't," he said under his breath. "Drugs don't operate like they did when he started working. I don't think ecstasy had any prevalence in the mainstream when he was young."

I wasn't sure of MDMA's history either but, considering it had only just gained popularity when I was in my college years, I had to agree. "It's still taught regularly. I'm sure he still has those pamphlets from D.A.R.E."

"Those pamphlets don't tell you shit. Hell, most of what I know about drugs is from you and my informants. Real life experience goes farther than words on a piece of cardstock."

Couldn't disagree with that. "Hopefully, he'll do some of his own research."

"Either he's an idiot, or he's hiding something. Could be a combination of both, I guess."

"You thought he was hiding something too, right?" I asked. "That reaction when you mentioned Steven's files, that was weird, wasn't it?"

"Definitely struck me as odd," he said. "Did he already know about Steven? Or was he surprised that you did?"

"Or maybe he didn't know about him at all."

"Or maybe he knows exactly what's in those files, and he's protecting someone."

Although that was possible, I wasn't sure. There was sincerity in his voice when he said he'd be out there looking if he thought Quinn was killed. Even so, he'd agreed to look out for a black car with heavy window tint.

It stood to reason that whoever had killed Quinn was the same person driving the car. If that were so, and it was someone Fitz knew, wouldn't he have recognized the description of the car? Wouldn't that have been the part he got so defensive over?

"I don't know," I murmured. "Maybe it isn't a person he's trying to protect, but the news of a murder in town? Maybe he doesn't want people to worry that the Country Killer's back? He brought him up both times we've met."

Ox growled his annoyance.

That piece of shit was a sensitive subject for both of us. We'd barely talked about him since it had all happened, almost two years ago now.

The case that had destroyed Ox. The case that had shattered my knee. The case that had killed Bear. The catalyst that had launched mine and Ox's life together into utter shit.

The Country Killer, named so by some journalists excited for their big break, had killed six women. Because he'd killed in the countryside, the state police had asked for Pittsburgh's assistance with the investigation.

By the second woman murdered, we'd known it was a serial killer. Ox hadn't called the FBI for help until after the third. I doubted he'd ever forgive himself for that, but it wouldn't have made a difference either way.

Chance had been the only reason I'd been able to confront the guy.

I'd been visiting my mom—the last time I'd visited her before her death—and he'd been right down the road.

I'd almost gotten him. But you know what they say about, *almost.* Something about horseshoes and hand grenades.

The prick got away. I'd gotten a knee replacement. We'd buried Bear. The trauma had created a void between me and Ox, and he'd filled it with my best friend. The Country Killer was still out there, six women were dead, and mine and Ox's lives imploded.

Suffice it to say, there were still few people we hated more than the Country Killer.

"Maybe," Ox said after a moment. "The Country Killer could be back, I guess. Assuming he's dirty might be my own bias. Ever since Vanzant, I'm a lot more careful about who I put my faith in."

When I glanced at him, his hand was on his chest, as if rubbing a phantom pain from the bullet that'd left him bed-ridden for weeks. That bullet came from the gun of a man Ox had seen as a friend—a man we'd both seen as a friend.

Although Ox's experience was far worse, I guessed we both knew what it felt like to be Julius Caesar.

"I meant to ask," I said. "You doing okay with that?"

He arched a brow at me. "I don't know what you mean."

"After the shooting earlier," I said. "You looked a little pale."

"And you didn't?" His confusion morphed to annoyance. "What—it isn't normal to feel off after you get shot at?"

Of course it was. But I'd seen Ox get shot at dozens of times, and I'd never seen him look the way he had this afternoon.

And his reaction answered my question. He wasn't okay after that. And he wasn't going to admit to it. Ox was a big, tough guy. Saying he was scared or that he'd had a flashback, or that a shootout shook him up more than it used to, would tarnish that persona.

If he were anyone else, I'd soften my voice and say it didn't make him weak to struggle. He'd gone through a horrific event caused by someone he'd considered a friend, and it was going to take time to heal from that.

Healing was not pitiful. He didn't need to be strong every moment of every day.

But if I said that, it'd either turn into an argument, or he'd go quiet and slam my car door when he got out. I understood. I also hadn't wanted to hear that it was okay to not be at the top of my game after I'd gotten injured. Nothing had pissed me off more at that time than Ox babying me.

So I just said, "You're right. I'm sorry. I just wanted to make sure you hadn't torn a stitch or anything."

Realizing I was referencing the physical damage opposed to the mental damage, his tight jaw softened. "No, the stitches are gone."

"Good." I gave him a smile. "Do you wanna put some music on? It's a long drive."

Thickness in the air subsiding, he said something under his breath before landing on a song he knew I loved by *Halsey*. He'd always mocked my "girly" music before. The fact that he played it now without any judgment was his method of nonverbal communication.

As if to say, *Thanks for not making me talk about how much of a mess my head is.*

Chapter 17

It was noon by the time I made it home. On the way, I'd called Evelyn. I told her I'd give her a better description later, but I was tired and needed to get my head on straight before passing on any definitive thoughts. Taking that as answer enough, she said she'd email over all of Quinn's phone logs since starting school. The attachments arrived while I was outside with Tempest.

The pain from that fall was hitting me hard by then. I coped with another hot bath, which only helped until the water cooled. I filled it up again, but by then, the tank was empty. Cussing with each step, I limped my way to the kitchen, grabbed an ice pack, and used a rolling computer chair to get back to the bedroom.

No doubt I took too much ibuprofen when I got into bed, but it was better than an oxie. Even though I would've killed for one right about then.

Lying in bed, staring at the ceiling and waiting for the meds to kick in, I reminded myself that I'd had days like this even when I was on the harder drugs. The more I took, the higher my tolerance got, and the less effective they were. They helped the mental pain far more than the physical in the grand scheme.

And I didn't have that.

It wasn't like my life was perfect. There were moments of sadness. Regularly, I swiped to a picture of Bear on my phone just to let myself wallow in the grief. Every time I walked past his dog tags, any time I glanced at his folded flag, pain ripped through my chest.

Then Tempest would lick my hand, or paw at the door to go outside, or attempt to guard my hoodie, and that pain would lessen.

What'd happened with Ox didn't hurt like it used to either. In a way, I was almost grateful for our breakup.

If we hadn't broken up, I wouldn't have ended up in this trailer. I'd hated it for so long, but it'd become my haven. Soon, if all went well with this case, I'd be able to pay it off. Maybe I'd steal Bentley's idea and start saving for a piece of land to move it to.

That was another thing I was grateful for. Bentley. He and I wouldn't have rekindled our friendship if I were still with Ox. Not only would we have been living in different cities, but Ox had always been the jealous type. Guys who worked with me knew better than to so much as look at me for too long when Ox was around. Then, I'd found it endearing, but now that I had Bentley back in my life, I wanted no part of a relationship where my partner felt insecure over my male friends. Let alone the implication that he couldn't trust me.

As though I was the disloyal one.

Most of all, what I loved most about where I was now was how I made it from one check to the next. Sure, some of my jobs were as simple as spying on cheating partners. Others were proving abuse so that a jackass who hurt their kids couldn't get custody in court.

Then there were cases like Quinn.

Evelyn had every reason to believe her daughter was murdered, and no one else would help her. But I could. I *would*. I didn't know when or how, but I was damned determined to find justice for that girl's death.

Pain finally subsiding as I focused on those notes of positivity in my life, I drifted to sleep.

* * *

POUNDING ON THE DOOR TORE ME FROM MY DREAMLESS REST. Grumbling a curse, I checked my phone. 4:45.

Ugh. Four hours would have to do if I wanted to get back on a normal schedule tonight.

The pain had lessened while I slept, so I forgot about it until I stood. Almost faceplanting when my knee gave out beneath me, I held the bedpost to bring myself upright.

Limping my way down the hall, I grumbled some choice words all the way to the door. Holding the wall for stability, I peeked through at Bentley on the porch.

He was smiling when I pulled it open, but he frowned when he saw how much pressure I was putting on my left side. "Didn't have time for your exercises, huh?"

"Coulda squeezed them in. I'm just stupid," I said. "What's up?"

"Dinner, if you're hungry. Wanna do some sets when we're done?"

As long as I wasn't too stiff to get back into our routine. "Aren't I always hungry?"

"Haven't turned down food yet, so I guess so."

"Hey, it's your fault." Grasping the other wall for support, I hopped in that direction. Bending to unlatch Tempest's crate, I gave him a smile. "If you weren't such a good cook, I wouldn't eat you out of house and home."

"Nah, you'd just starve." That was accurate. "Grace is making cookies for dessert, by the way. She wants you to try them. I guess she learned the recipe from home ec—"

My attempt to straighten from Tempy's cage ended with me stumbling forward. Before I could bang my face off the wall, Bentley caught my arms and steadied me. The pain still ripped up my thigh, but better one limb than two.

"Shit, you okay?" he asked, making sure I was steady before he let me go.

"Yeah, I'm alright." I blew out a deep breath to ease the ache. "Too much time in the car. It's my fault."

"It's your job." His eyes were concerned, but his tone was soft. "Gotta do what you gotta do. And it'll be worth it when you get that check."

Despite the pain, I couldn't help but smile. That support mattered so much more than he realized. "That's what I figure too."

"But you're not running back out there to catch bad guys until we get you walking steady." The concern was still there, but there was a playful edge to that mahogany gaze. "Deal?"

"Deal."

"Do you need a hand getting over to my house?"

"Nah, I've got it." Another smile. "I'll call for you if I fall and can't get up."

With a chuckle, he started back through the entrance. "I'll tell Grace to turn the music down."

* * *

"What'd you call this again, hon?" Bentley asked Grace between chews. "Sink cookies?"

"Kitchen sink cookies, yup." Grace was polite enough to cover her mouth as she chomped away. Bentley had no such manners. "Aren't they good?"

Better than sex, I almost said. Then I remembered she was a literal child and decided against it. "They're amazing."

"I wonder why they're called that." Bentley reached across the table for another one. "Weirdest name I've ever heard."

"Because it's 'everything but the kitchen sink,'" Grace said. "Get it? Because there are so many ingredients?"

Ingredients I never would've thought to combine. Chocolate chips were basic, and the hint of peanut butter was nothing special either, but the way they paired with the crunch of the potato chips and pretzels was divine. Not to mention the other crunchy bits I couldn't quite put my finger on. Maybe nuts? There was a hint of something fruity in there, too. A handful of dried cranberries?

"It has every food group, and it's genius." Holding up a hand, I said, "Good job, kid."

Finishing the high five, Grace beamed. "Thanks. I'm really proud of them."

"You should be. I'm gonna pay you to make me a batch of these twice a week."

"I could show you how." Excitement poured out of her. "They're not hard."

"Boiling water is hard for Maddie." Bentley shot me a smirk.

I tossed a hunk of pretzel from my cookie at him.

Chuckling, he stood and started to the fridge. "You guys want some more milk?"

"Yes please," I said.

"You really can't cook?" Grace asked. "Like, at all?"

"I can microwave stuff," I said. "And I make some kick ass ramen. I can do scrambled eggs too. And frozen pizza. I add my own cheese and everything."

"That doesn't count." Grace laughed. "You've never cooked, like, a real meal?"

"I have a couple times. Something usually comes out burned," I said. "Tacos. I can make tacos."

"How do you go through life without knowing how to cook?" Grace asked. "That's, like, the bare minimum for survival, isn't it?"

"You'd be amazed at how little you need to survive. Microwavable food might not be good for your arteries, but sustenance is sustenance."

"Every day though?" Grace asked.

"She gets takeout sometimes too," Bentley said, filling my cup. "Now stop bullying."

"I'm not bullying," Grace said. "I just don't get it."

I hadn't taken it as bullying. She was a kid, and she was curious. Tack on the social norm of women being expert chefs, and this conversation was no big shock. But I had the feeling she wasn't gonna stop until I gave her a real answer.

"My mom never taught me how." I raised a shoulder. "I could probably learn and get better at it, but it comes naturally to some people more than others. Especially when they're taught how to do it when their brains are still developing."

Grace's head tilted to the side. "Your mom didn't teach you at all?"

"She taught me how to use the microwave."

"Did your dad cook then?" she asked. "Couldn't he have taught you?"

"Grace." Bentley shot her a look, one that Grace didn't seem to understand.

"What?"

"Don't pry."

"She's not," I said, giving him an expression that said it was okay. It wasn't some big secret.

If he didn't want me to go on and told me so, I'd end the conversation. Sheltering Grace from the upbringings we had wasn't a bad thing, but I didn't want to lie or make her feel guilty for asking questions.

Bentley raised his hands at his sides. "Alright. But don't feel obligated to answer every question she's got. You can tell her to back off."

Which I also appreciated. He knew I didn't like talking about my trauma. Not with most people at least, but it was different with kids. Kids were curious. I knew her life story, so she wanted to know mine.

"I don't know my dad," I said.

"Oh." Grace's voice softened. "Did he...?"

"Die? Maybe." Another shrug. "I don't know. I can barely remember him."

Blinking a few times, as though trying to understand what I meant, Grace's mouth slowly fell open. "He just left?"

"Yep."

"What an ass."

I laughed.

"Grace." Bentley furrowed his brows.

"What else would you call someone who leaves their kid?" She asked.

Covering my mouth, I tried to disguise my laugh with a cough.

"I'd call them an ass. But you're thirteen, so you can call them a jerk."

"Fine. What a jerk," Grace said. "You never heard from him again?"

"Nope."

"How old were you?"

"Seven, I think."

"Was he, like, always an as—"

"One more time, and I'm taking your phone," Bentley said.

Rolling her eyes, Grace said, "Was he always a jerk? Or was it just leaving you that was jerk-ish?"

I had to laugh at the phrasing. But truth be told, no. None of the vague memories I had of my dad classified him as a jerk.

Once when Mom had been screaming, belligerently drunk, he came into my room, locked the door despite her beating on it from the other side, and asked me if I wanted to make a pillow fort. We did, singing along to classic rock that played from my Barbie Boombox to drown out the sounds of her yells. Although stinking of booze as he sang me to sleep that night, I was in his arms, and I was the happiest I could've been.

I wasn't sure how old I'd been, but I'd tried to make myself some cereal one morning. Of course, I'd tried to wake Mom and Dad first, but they were both too messed up from the night prior to so much as stir. After climbing onto the counter to get myself a bowl, full of pride, I held the shelf of the cabinet for stability on the way down. And everything that'd been on the shelf fell to the ground with me.

Crying, bloodied from the glass I'd fallen on, Mom came out of the bedroom in a rage. She didn't ask what'd happened. She didn't check if I was okay. She just started beating my ass for shattering her dinnerware.

Dad came out a moment or two later and got her off me. They argued until she was hitting him instead of me.

Mom had been petite, and Dad somewhere around Bentley's size, barely smaller than Ox. He could've hurt her. As I watched it go down, as I watched her hit him, I'd wished he would hit her back.

But he didn't. Not once.

Grabbing her arms, he screamed, "Not in front of the damn kid, Natalie!"

She'd snapped something about how I mattered more to him than she did, that I was the source of all their fights, that she never should've had me. For a split second, watching fury burn in his eyes, I'd thought he was gonna hit her for that.

But he hadn't.

Instead, he released her arms, walked to me, and scooped me up. Didn't say another word to her. Didn't say anything to me either, not until we were in the car. Still in our pajamas, feet bare, he smiled at me in the rearview as he reversed from the drive. "How about we go spend the whole day at the park, Mad dog?"

I'd nodded in answer, and we listened to rock music the whole drive there. Then we played all day, bare feet or not. Somewhere in the cavern of my mind was a brief memory of him taking me into the bathroom of the playground. He'd locked the door on the way in, then told me to wait by the sink while he went into the stall. A few moments later, he came out with powder on his nose. I hadn't known what that meant then. He'd looked sick when we were on the playground, and he looked better when he came out of that stall. Supposed in my young mind, he'd just taken some medicine.

Later, he'd scraped some change from his car together to get me a Happy Meal for lunch, only nibbling off my plate. He'd said he wasn't hungry, but I knew it was because he didn't have enough money for both of us, so I'd said I wasn't hungry and gave him half of my burger. Somewhere at the tail end of it, I'd asked if that was true. If I was the reason they fought. If he wished he'd never had me too.

Blue eyes so gentle, so sad, he took my chin in his thumb and forefinger. "You're the best thing that's ever happened to me, Mad dog. Don't think for one *second* that I don't want you."

One night, not long after that, they'd fought again. After Mom stopped screaming, he opened my door. I pretended to be asleep when he sat beside me. I didn't say anything when he stroked a hand through my hair, nor when he muffled a sob, Even when he whispered that he'd loved me, and that he was sorry, I stayed quiet.

Then he'd left.

He'd walked out the door, and the engine of his car turning over sounded a moment later. I ran to the window and watched as he pulled out, whispering a quiet plea that he would come back for me. That he wouldn't leave me with my mom. I loved her, but she was mean, and he wasn't.

Even when he'd been high out of his mind, even when he'd been drunk, he'd been kind. His smile was warm, and his eyes—no matter how tiny the pupils—were always full of light. He loved me. He protected me. He couldn't leave me.

But he had.

He left.

Once he was gone, when I'd been the only target Mom had to let her rage out on, and I wasn't big enough to hold her back like Dad had been, the abuse escalated. The next five years were spent in and out of foster care. They'd tried to get ahold of my dad, but they could never find him. Or maybe they did, and he'd said he didn't want me. I didn't know.

By the time I was twelve, I'd learned that most of the foster homes were just as bad as Mom. At least if I was with her, I knew how to avoid her outbursts. So I'd hidden the bruises at school. I'd kept my head down until I was old enough to leave her, too.

"Just leaving me," I told Grace. "He wasn't too bad outside of that."

"Did you ever try to find him?" she asked. "Like, online or anything? Just to tell him off?"

Chuckling, I gave a nod. "No social medias. Every year or so, I search death records, but with the life he led, he might be buried as a John Doe somewhere. And I don't worry about it too much either. I'm the kid, ya know? He's the parent. If he wanted a relationship with me, he could've made an effort."

"Would *you* want a relationship with him?"

"No." Especially now that I, too, was an addict. Recovering or not, being around people like that could ruin my sobriety. "Like I said, I don't worry about it."

"Good for you." Grace chomped into her cookie and wagged it at me. "You don't need that negativity in your life."

Smiling, I held up my milk. "I'll drink to that."

Chapter 18

"ARE YOU DONE DRILLING HER NOW?" BENTLEY ASKED GRACE.

"I wasn't drilling her," Grace said. "I was just wondering."

"Uh-huh," Bentley said. "When you're done with that cookie, you need to go to your room and work on that English paper."

Grace's jaw dropped. "But it's Friday."

"And you want to go to a sleepover tomorrow night. You're gonna be up late with your friends, and you'll be exhausted on Sunday. So do it now, or you're staying home."

Pouting, Grace glared. "Are you gonna do the dishes, then?"

"That's the rule," Bentley said. "But English paper needs done before I take you over there."

Another eye roll as she stood. "Fine. But don't eat all my cookies."

"*Fine.*" Enunciating the word just as she had, he walked to the sink. "Bring it out here when you're done."

Her face told me how ridiculous she found it that *he* needed to look over her prose. "Night, Maddie."

"Night, kiddo," I said, watching her drag her feet to her bedroom. Once she was out of sight, I turned to face Bentley better. "'That's the rule?' What do you mean?"

"I cook, she does the dishes. Tonight, she cooked, so I do the dishes."

Flicking on the water, he looked at me over his shoulder. "Bella started it when we moved in together. She was real strict about it when Grace entered the picture. Said it was bullshit for us to not split the work. She didn't want Grace growing up thinking housework was just one person's responsibility."

"In that case"—I struggled upright and wobbled to the sink—"you wash, and I'll dry."

"Guests don't count."

"I practically live here." Reaching to the drawer beside the sink and retrieving a towel, I wiggled my fingers. "It'll go twice as fast. Give it."

With a sigh, smiling, he handed me the bowl Grace had used for the batter. "If you need to sit, you can sit."

"Sitting so much is why I'm having such a hard time walking." I dried the bowl and set it to the far corner of the counter. "You taught me that."

"True, but standing in one spot isn't good either," he said. "You need to get your joints moving."

"Wanna go for a walk when we're done, then?" I nodded to Tempest in her crate. "She's been stuck in that thing for too long."

"I'm down. And hey, sorry about Grace."

"Don't worry about it. She sees me as a friend. Friends know things about each other's lives. She seemed surprised when I mentioned my dad leaving, though. Doesn't she know about yours?"

"Not in detail, no." Passing me a plate he'd just scrubbed, he nibbled his lip. "She asked about him when she was little. Hasn't really come up again. I'm grateful for that."

Like me, Bentley came from an abusive household. His mom had been his safe haven, and she'd never left, but his dad had been in and out all his life. They'd break up when he hit her or one of the kids, and then she'd take him back when he showed with flowers and a check to help her get through the next month.

That cycle continued until our teens, when Bentley's dad had died of a heart attack.

"It's just easier to say he's dead. If she gets involved with the wrong crowd and I need to tell her to stay away from guys like that, I will. But for now, it's not worth it." He shot me a smile. "I don't worry about it too much."

"I'm not someone worth quoting." I smiled back. "But for what it's worth, having a dad like you's gonna make her expectations for men very high."

"God, I hope." Finishing the last dish, he flicked off the water and walked past me to put away the ones I'd dried. "Ready for that walk?"

Tempest shot up in her crate and wagged her tail.

"Someone is," I said.

*　*　*

GRACE STAYED HOME WHILE BENTLEY AND I WENT WITH TEMPEST. I wobbled for most of the walk, relying on Bentley's forearm to keep me upright. Tempy kept looking up at me and wagging her tail. Like she was saying, *I'm so excited for this, but you're moving slow, and I wanna run, Mom.*

Bentley picked up on that and asked if he could help her burn off that energy. I obliged, planting myself on a tree stump. For ten minutes or so, I watched the two of them jog up and down the street. Tempest wasn't ready to quit when Bentley bent over, holding his knees.

The walk back to Bentley's was easier. Pain was odd in that way. More of a spectrum than a scale. Doing nothing hurt worse than doing the work and hurting good. Rather than a searing ache, it was more of a dull throb as we settled onto the floor to do our exercises. Throughout them, it wasn't pain so much as a tightness from the muscles stretching. The kind of hurt that almost felt good.

Attempting to get up, however, brought back that stabbing pain.

Grumbling a curse, I gripped the couch to hoist myself onto it.

"No better, huh?" Bentley asked, sitting beside me.

"Sorta." I explained that fluctuating spectrum, ending with, "As long as I stick to our schedule, the pain stays tolerable. I shouldn't have let it get this bad."

"Life happens. You can't blame yourself for that. Massage might help, though."

When I still had insurance, my physical therapist had helped in that department. Problem was, paying out of pocket at a parlor or the PT wasn't an option when I had to check my account before even buying ramen. "Bold of you to assume I can afford that."

"I'm not certified, but I know a thing or two in that department. Want me to try?"

I might as well have punched myself in the face if I turned down that offer. Massage was a godsend. But even though Bentley's offer had been as casual as the offer to take Tempy on that run, my stomach did something weird. The same weird thing it'd done when Ox asked to go out this morning. The only difference was this sensation had no discomfort attached to it. Just a fluttering that stretched through my chest.

"I haven't shaved my legs in a while," was, for whatever reason, my blurt of an answer.

"Huh. Neither have I." He smirked. "Humans grow hair, Maddie. I don't care."

Why did I? What did it matter if my best friend saw my hairy legs?

Scooting back a bit, Bentley tapped his lap. "It'll help. And I'm not letting you leave until I'm sure you can make it around without falling."

"You're not *letting* me?"

"Nope. You're not gonna get yourself killed fighting criminals because you can't walk. Not on my watch." Another smile. "Either that or take the rest of the night off and rest. You've gotta have balance. Even when you're working a serious case."

Damn him for being right, and in a way that didn't come off condescending.

"Only because I have more work to get done tonight." After rolling up my pants and lifting my legs to his lap, I relaxed against the arm of the sofa behind me. "But I'm gonna be mad at you if it hurts more when you're done."

"I'll be gentle." The smirk he gave me and the feel of his warm, rough fingertips on my bare knee brought back that fluttering feeling in my belly. "Only deep tissue hurts."

All those fluttering feelings went away when he pressed his thumb into my skin, pain shooting deep into my leg. "You're a damn liar."

"It won't hurt when I'm done."

Despite my annoyance, after a few seconds, the pain subsided, relief taking its place. It was like that stiff stretch of the exercises. The kind of pain that felt good.

"Better?" Bentley asked.

"A lot. Did they teach you this in paramedic school?"

"They did not. And it's two years of college followed by a rigorous training course. Not *paramedic school*."

I smiled. "Where'd you learn it then?"

"Massage training." Each deepening rotation of his thumb through the muscle was somehow bliss and misery at once. "It was years ago, but I don't think the procedure's changed much."

"You're a masseuse? Why didn't I know this?"

"I'm not really," he said. "Bella and I met my freshman year of college. By Christmas, she was pregnant."

My eyes widened. "Damn."

Bentley laughed, nodding. "I had one semester of credits toward my goal. But she was heartbroken because she didn't want to drop out and lose momentum. She wanted to be a teacher by the time she was twenty-three."

"So you dropped out and became a masseuse?"

"I took a break, yeah. Saw an ad for a massage school. It said I could get certified in six months, and I could get a job shortly after. I had a baby on the way, ya know? We needed money. If I could make a decent wage by the time Grace was born, I could take a few years off from college, work, pay for daycare, and go back once Bella got her degree."

There came those spins and flutters again.

Since I'd met Bentley as an adult, I knew he was a good dad, but I hadn't realized how much he'd sacrificed for Grace. College had been his dream since we were kids. Yet, he put that on the back burner to do right by his little girl, and to make sure the woman he loved got what she wanted out of life.

"It worked out. Bella had her degree by the time Grace was three. She had a solid income going when I went back to school, but I did some massage work on the side so we could get a house. At twenty-five, I was a certified paramedic." Pausing, his eyes grew dismal. "At twenty-six, Bella died. Her life insurance was enough to pay off student loans, and that sorta supplemented what she made. Still have some of it left for that piece of land I wanna buy."

My heart ached for him. "You're amazing, you know that?"

A quiet laugh. "I'm alright. Thanks though."

His humility was endearing, but *alright* didn't do it justice. Not only did he go into a field designed to help others, to be the first on the scene of disaster and comfort people through some of the worst moments of their lives, but he was an excellent parent and partner.

So why was I picking apart that fuzzy feeling in my stomach? What was the use of analyzing it?

Of course, I had butterflies. Who wouldn't? Bentley was everything any woman wanted.

The perfect combination of modest and confident, an exquisite balance of compassionate and smart. He cared about his health, but he wasn't a gym rat who spent every waking moment lifting weights and obsessing over his muscles. That boyish smile was beautiful on its own, but there was no denying the sex appeal when he smirked. Tack on that well-maintained beard and his soft brown ringlets, and he was far from hard to look at.

But those butterflies didn't have to mean anything. *Couldn't* mean anything. Not because there was anything wrong with them, not because he was a red flag I needed to stay far away from, but because he was the brightest green flag in my life.

Bentley was my best friend. Aside from Alex, my *only* friend.

Even if I wanted to see if Bentley and I could be more than that, I couldn't risk saying so and losing him. If it didn't work out, if I went back to having one friend who lived an hour away, who worked sixty or more hours a week, I'd be alone again.

I didn't mind being by myself, but that wasn't the same as being alone.

This was enough. It had to be enough.

"That's funny coming from you." Bentley shot me another smirk, tracing his thumb along my knee, softer than the rest of the massage had been. "The one with the badass battle scar."

Those butterflies turned to spins.

I didn't hate the scar. Hearing him call me a badass for it was almost empowering. But thinking about that when I'd been admiring him brought back a reality I didn't wanna acknowledge.

I wrote off my discomfort with sarcasm. "Ah, yes. The badass who lost her knee."

"Every hero has scars."

"I think *anti*hero is more fitting," I said.

"Nah, you're just a hero."

Easy for him to say. He didn't know I'd let a mafia lord take a man captive. "I'm really not a hero."

"That's not what people say around town."

"What do they say around town?"

"That you saved a whole bunch of cops." He raised a shoulder. "According to Phoebe, anyway, but she didn't know the whole story."

"The cops would've been fine." I shook my head slightly. "I probably kept a teenage girl from being killed, though."

"Grace's teacher would've corrected your grammar there."

"That wasn't grammatically incorrect."

"No, but you weakened your language. You didn't keep her from being killed. You saved her."

"Tomato, tom*a*to. Still means the same thing."

Holding my gaze for a few seconds, smiling softly, he shook his head. "Sounds like it means two different things to you."

Because it did.

Getting that girl out of her house the night the Country Killer broke in was instinct. It was my job. Doing it wasn't heroic.

Shortly after the attack, when they'd tried to interview her, I was the only one she'd speak to. I'd gone straight from the hospital to the police department to do so. Not because I was a hero, but because I'd seen what he did to her. He hadn't killed her yet, but the scars he'd given her that night would never go away.

No one called her a hero for living to tell the tale. Sure, I hurt my knee, and that pissed me off every second I breathed, but I was no more a hero than she was.

"Sorry," Bentley said. "You don't have to talk about it if you don't want to."

"Just a sensitive topic," I said.

"I get it," he said. "It's the same for me when I talk about Bella. Saying she died isn't so hard. Talking about how I was first on the scene hits a lot harder."

"Oh my god," was all I could manage.

"It was bad." Pulling in a deep breath, he pressed a bit deeper on my knee. A minute prior, I would've told him it hurt, but I couldn't bring myself to now. "Talking about the scar on its own doesn't hurt too bad. The details of how you *got* the scar feels like you're giving it to yourself all over again. Like reliving it brings you back there, and then you replay every second of that day from start to finish. But it does no good to tear the scar open again."

Like reliving it takes you back there, and then you replay every second of that day from start to finish.

I thought of Quinn.

"What's that face for?" Bentley asked.

"Hmmm?"

"You've got your thinking face on."

"I'm sorry. I was listening. Go on."

"It's alright. Sorta walked myself into a wall with that anyway. What is it?"

"Quinn." Chewing my lower lip, I scratched my head. "I don't know what she did the day she died."

"I thought you said she was at her boyfriend's."

"She spent the night there, but she left early that morning to go back to her parents'. Her body wasn't found until Monday morning, but Alex reported her time of death sometime late on Saturday night. What did she do all day?"

"You're the investigator. Why're you asking me?"

"Good point." I started to pull my leg away to stand, but Bentley caught my thigh.

Which should not have made me feel the way that it did.

"Let me finish this before you run off," he said. "Stopping mid-massage will definitely make you sore."

I made a noise in my throat that expressed my annoyance. "Fine, but I need to make a call."

"Go for it."

Chapter 19

While Bentley massaged my knee, I called Evelyn and asked if I could come take another look at Quinn's car. Just like with my other requests, she had no objections—even said she'd give me a partial payment. Apparently, she felt guilty that I was doing so much work with nothing upfront.

Considering the fuel light had come on when I was on my way home today, and that I had only six bucks in my account, I wasn't gonna tell her no.

Bentley insisted I give him five more minutes on my knee, which gave me time to compare the phone logs to Quinn's call history. Getting roped into that, Bentley continued massaging my knee for another ten. Which I also wasn't gonna complain about.

After finding no inconsistencies and grunting my frustration about it to Bentley, he asked if I checked her app download history. That she may've used an untraceable texting app to communicate with the boyfriend. Bentley had caught Grace doing that with a boy from school last year.

And sure enough, Quinn had done just that.

But since she'd deleted the app, even once I'd reinstalled it and signed in with her auto-filled account info, everything was wiped. As though she'd deleted him from existence.

It was another dead end, but I had two more roads to take.

So, I headed down the nearest with Tempest in the back seat. It was almost eight by the time I arrived at Evelyn's home. She met me at Quinn's car, driving information already pulled up on the dash. After showing me how to click around to the daily breakdown, I selected the day of Quinn's death.

As I jotted each address down, Evelyn said, "So something happened today? Or are you back to square one?"

"Something happened," I said under my breath. "But I'm not sure what to do with what I found yet."

Frowning, I explained Quinn's confidential therapy with Steven Benedict. I couldn't describe Evelyn's reaction as shocked. It was closer to hurt.

"Quinn wasn't depressed." She repeated it as a statement, but I assumed it was a question.

"According to Steven, no," I said.

"I don't understand." Facing me, expression hard to decipher under the dim glow of the car lights, she shook her head. "Why wouldn't she have told me she was going to therapy?"

"Because you would've asked why. Then she would've had to tell you she was the other woman," I said. "That's my best guess, anyway."

"Did Steven confirm that? That Quinn was seeing a married man?"

"Not in words. Patient confidentiality and all that. But it seemed like he was trying to say so without saying so."

"Does that extend to me? I'm her mother. She had me as the emergency contact on all of her information."

"Quinn saw him at this office under this specific contract and paid in cash to protect all her personal information."

"But in an investigation, we can..." Trailing off, annoyance tightened her jaw. "There is no investigation. Not within the courts. So we can't subpoena those documents."

I nodded. "Knowing where she went the day she died might lead me to who she was with, though."

For a few heartbeats, Evelyn only held my gaze. Then she reached into the pocket of her sweater, pulled out a checkbook, and began scribbling in it. She held it out. "Early payment, as promised."

"Thanks." I glanced at it, doing my best not to smile when I read $5,000. "I appreciate it."

"I appreciate everything you're doing," she said. "I'd appreciate you even more if you could find a way to get those records."

Silly me for thinking it was mere appreciation. "Are you asking me to break into Steven's office, Evelyn?"

"Of course not." Her tone said otherwise. "I'd never encourage anyone to break the law. I am an excellent attorney if you ever need one, but that's irrelevant."

It obviously was not irrelevant.

Would I break into Steven's office? Practically, I could make it work. The apartment wasn't in a heavily policed area, I knew the key code to the building, he had no security systems or cameras to protect his patients' privacy, and picking a lock wasn't difficult.

On a moral level, I wasn't above breaking and entering. As long as I was unarmed, if I got caught somehow, the worst that'd happen was a slap on the wrist and some fines.

I was, however, above being *paid* to break the law.

Alongside that, I had the feeling Steven was the kind of man who kept confidential documents somewhere safer than the filing cabinet of his apartment in a shady area. Especially after telling him we'd been shot at just outside his building.

"Before I do anything morally questionable, let me explore these other avenues." I held the check out for her. "I don't need this."

"I saw your car," she said. "And your shoes. You need it."

Ouch. "I mean that I don't take bribes."

"Your entire job is accepting bribes in exchange for information."

"Legally."

"There's nothing illegal about me paying you for hard work."

"You know what I'm saying."

"I do. And I know that you misunderstand what *I'm* saying." Shoulders squaring, her expression became what I imagined it looked like in a courtroom. "I already told you I'm paying you more than your regular rate. Write up the invoice however you like so it doesn't look suspicious. I've seen P.I.s charge as much as two hundred an hour. Between travel, the interviews you held at the college, the time you spent here, and all your research, I have no doubt you've spent twenty-five hours on my daughter's case, which only makes us even. But either way, you're the only person who gives a shit about what happened to Quinn. So yes, Madison, I'm going to pay you your worth. I will pay you extra *should* you go above and beyond."

Doubted she used some of those choice words in the courtroom, but with a tone and stare like that, I understood why she could afford the life she led.

"Damn, two hundred an hour?" I asked. "I need to up my rates."

* * *

FOLLOWING EACH STOP OF QUINN'S DAY MEANT RETURNING TO THE college. Sure, I could've just glanced over each location on Google Maps, but I wanted to see the day exactly as she had. It wasn't just the locations that mattered, but things along the way.

From Troy's fraternity, I followed a maze of backroads to a shopping center. Starbuck's was Quinn's first stop of the day, and Target was next. She spent close to two hours there. The reason why women—myself included—could spend so much time in that store and walk out emotionally rejuvenated was a scientific phenomenon that needed exploration.

Nonetheless, the time stamp said she got back on the road just after noon. For the next hour, her drive was a peaceful one, looping around her hometown on the mountain roads. Despite gas prices and the rough bumps and dips in the cement, even some dirt paths, I saw the allure. It was one thing I'd missed when living in the city. Quinn's trip had been during the day, while mine was just after sunset. Coasting through the vegetation, admiring the early spring blooms, with the windows down and the music playing, was just as soothing as a hot bath with candles and a glass of wine.

Everyone from the countryside or a mountain town had done this from time to time. When the weather was nice, there was nothing more tranquil than alone time in the car, accompanied only by the vibration of the speakers and the critters who scurried along the roads.

Which only verified all the thoughts I'd had already.

Quinn was finding contentment in her life. After cutting off mystery guy, starting strong with Troy, full of hope to rekindle her relationship with her best friend, she used her Saturday morning as a makeshift therapy session.

So, what happened?

The next stop on her drive, I hoped, would answer that question.

It was a gas station about ten minutes from her parents' house.

Giving Tempest a scratch on the head, I cracked the windows, pumped some gas for myself, and headed inside. The man on the other side of the register was in his mid-thirties, wearing a stained shirt embroidered with the company logo. Fiddling around on some handheld gaming system, he muttered a curse to himself as I approached the register.

With a grunt, he set it on the counter. "Sorry about that. Can I do something for you?"

"Maybe." Holding out a photo of Quinn on my phone, I said, "Do you know this girl by chance?"

"Yeah, that's Quinn. Why?"

First name basis? Interesting. "I'm investigating her death."

His mouth fell open. "Seriously?"

"Unfortunately. You guys knew each other?"

"Sorta. She's been coming in since she got her license. David always told her to get her gas at the same place every time. That's good for your car. Stopped in once a week or so." Sitting on a bar stool behind the counter, he blinked a few times in disbelief. "Someone killed her?"

"The cops don't think so, but I do. So does Evelyn," I said. "You know her family?"

"My brother worked for David at his shop for a while. We weren't friends or anything, but small town, ya know?" he asked. "It wasn't the Country—"

"No, nothing like that." Maybe that was why Fitz was trying to keep Quinn's death below the radar after all. "The day she died, she stopped here for gas. Do you remember that? Two weeks ago tomorrow?"

"Yeah, I think. I can pull up the cameras if you wanna have a look."

"That'd be great. Is there anything you remember from that day?"

Clicking onto the computer behind the desk, he nibbled his bottom lip in thought. "Not really. Quinn was sweet. She always was, I guess, but she got her gas, grabbed a tea, and talked to me for a minute. Said school was going good, asked about my wife and daughter, and that was about it."

"Didn't seem upset at all?"

With a shake of his head, he turned the monitor to face me. On the screen, Quinn stood at the register, chatting casually with the man before me. He'd shown her pictures on his phone, I assumed of his kid, and she laughed, saying something I couldn't distinguish.

Although she looked happy, she didn't seem overly excited, like she was high. Her demeanor, her dusting of barely there makeup, all pointed to what I knew. She'd used that Saturday as a self-care reset.

"She seemed like she always did," he said. Then his brows furrowed. "I don't know if this'll help you, but about a month ago, she stopped by on a Friday night, and someone pulled in while she was pumping her gas. She argued with them."

"Did you see who?"

"Not really. They parked in that corner." He pointed to the edge of the lot, framed by the woods. "I couldn't catch what they were saying either, but Quinn was pissed. I got a glimpse of him, though. Thought it was kinda weird, actually. He was in a suit, and he looked older. I saw his hand come out the window."

"For what?"

The cashier scratched his head. "Well, almost like he was trying to..."

"Hit her?"

He made a gesture toward his jaw that I still didn't understand. "Maybe like he was trying to kiss her? She slapped him away and stormed off."

So mystery guy was not only an older man, but familiar with this area. Likely meaning, he knew where Quinn lived.

"Do you have footage of that?" I asked.

"Sorry, I wish I did. The storage only goes back a month. The car was nice, though."

"Did you catch the make and model?"

"Like I said, it was dark. But high end. Maybe a Bentley? Audi? I don't know, but it purred."

At least I finally had confirmation. Not an ID, but I had a witness now who wasn't bound by a contract of confidentiality. "If I'm able to track down that guy and his car, would you recognize them?"

"I can't say for sure about the guy, but the car, yeah. No doubt about it."

Number one objective then: track down that car. The only way I could think to do that was with Steven's files. If I could get Quinn's mystery guy's name, I could find out if his vehicle matched the one that shot at me and Ox, and there'd be a solid case against the guy.

Evelyn's proposition sounded more enticing than ever, but the chances of his files still being in that apartment were slim to none. Beyond a doubt, he'd secured them after that shooting this afternoon, if not after my interrogation of him.

Steven was a decent guy. Maybe if I talked sweet enough, I could get him to leave Quinn's file on his desk while he ran to the bathroom. It wouldn't be the first time someone wanted to help with an investigation, but their hands were tied legally.

"Is there anything else you can think of that might help me?" I asked the cashier.

"Not off the top of my head," he said. "Sorry."

"That's alright." I passed him a business card. "If anything else comes to you, give me a call. Day or night."

"Sure thing. I'll ask around a bit too," he said as I started to the door. "I hope you find out what happened to her. Quinn was a good kid."

"I'm not gonna stop until I do." I wasn't sure if he caught that part because I was already outside, swiping through my phone.

Dialing Ox's number as I climbed into my car, grimacing at the pain in my knee, I clicked my seatbelt into place. He answered on the third ring. "Hey, you alright?"

"Hangin' in there. Could you find an address for me?"

"Steven Benedict?" he asked. "Found it when I came home, in case you needed it."

"You're the best." Pushing my key into the ignition and turning it over, I put the phone on speaker just as the text came in. "I'll let you know if I come up with anything."

"Sure. Before you jump off though, I talked to some of the state boys," he said. "They're keeping an eye out for the car that shot at us today. It isn't much to go on, but if they find the guy, they have your number. They'll hold him so you can interview him. Hopefully, get a confession."

"Fingers crossed. Searching for a black car with dark tint across three counties is searching for a needle in a haystack." Following the GPS, I turned onto the road toward Somerset. "Thanks for putting in a word for me."

"As soon as they heard your name, they were willing to help. The sergeant I spoke with is Derek Ames. If you need anything, ask for him," he said. "Do you need backup?"

Derek Ames and I went way back. He was the first to arrive when I called 911 at eight years old, while Mom was in a drunken stupor. He'd gotten me a candy bar and a pop while we waited for social services to collect me.

When I was back in Mom's care after she "got her life on track," he'd come to check on me with a candy bar and bottle of pop in hand. Those foster parents had been worse than Mom. I didn't tell him so, but he read between the lines.

Over the years, he checked in from time to time. Also arrested me for possession of marijuana when I was fifteen. He hadn't filed the charges, but he got me a candy bar, a pop, and told me I could make something of my life, despite where I'd come from.

In part, I had Derek Ames to thank for the woman I was now.

"Backup to talk to Steven? No, I think I have a better chance with him if you're not there," I said. "But I'll be careful. I haven't seen that car again since this morning."

"Shooting at us was a distraction to keep us from catching his plates," he said. "He's probably laying low to keep you from seeing him again."

Or maybe he'd shot to kill the person he thought would discover all his dirty secrets.

"Either way," I said. "I'll be careful."

Chapter 20

STEVEN'S CLIENTS MAY'VE BEEN WEALTHY, BUT JUDGING BY HIS home, he was upper middle class. He lived in a suburb—the kind where the houses all looked the same but were far enough apart that it didn't *feel* like a suburb.

The car was in the drive, and the lights inside the house were off. Seemed a little early to head to bed, but he was at work by six in the morning.

After knocking for a moment and getting no answer, I called, "I'm sorry to bother you at home, Mr. Benedict, but I really need to talk to you."

Silence.

Groaning, I pounded harder. If someone was banging on my door like this, Tempest would've been going berserk. Guessed he didn't have a dog.

Which was worth noting in case he refused to give me Quinn's files, and I needed to come back for another look around. Peeping through the windows, knocking again, I searched for a security system. Those were usually close to the door, glowing on the wall, but I didn't see one. There weren't any at the corners of the porch roof either.

"Steven, I could really use—"

"He isn't home," a voice called from my left. A woman stood on a neighboring porch in a robe. "Who are you?"

Telling her the truth made this less weird. It'd also give her a name to give the cops if I *did* end up breaking in.

"A private investigator." I stepped off his landing to the walkway. "Are you sure he isn't here? The car's right there."

"Yeah, and he left in an ambulance."

My heart dropped. "He *what?*"

She nodded to the end of the street. "He was on a jog this afternoon, and someone ran him down. Then they drove off."

Stomach bubbling, my mouth fell open. So much for shooting at us to keep us from catching his plates. "When was this?"

"Right after dinner." She propped either hand on her hips. "You're a P.I.? What're you investigating Steve for?"

"I'm not," I murmured, unease stretching through me. "I'm investigating another case, and he knew the victim. Do you know if he's okay?"

"Haven't heard yet, sorry," she said. "You don't think it was connected to whatever you're working on, do you?"

I didn't see how it *couldn't* be connected. Which meant I'd put the target on his head.

I needed something stronger than tea before bed tonight.

"Did you see the accident?" I asked. "Happened on this street, you said?"

"Yeah, at the corner down there." Another wave down the road. "Colleen saw it, though. She already talked to the cops, but she might be able to help."

It was worth a shot.

* * *

NORMALLY, I WOULD'VE WALKED DOWN THE ROAD. MY KNEE WASN'T cooperating though, so I drove and parked at the corner, as the neighbor had said. Four knocks on the door later, Colleen answered in her pajamas.

When I told her I was investigating Steven Benedict, she said she'd already spoken with the police. Showing her my business card, I explained that I believe this may've been connected to the death of a young girl, and the woman's eyes filled with tears. She was stressed enough already, and I was sure that didn't help, but it got her onto the porch.

Sitting beside me, she said, "I didn't see much, really. I just heard the bang, and then a scream, and I ran to the window. Then I saw Steven, and there was a car racing down the road there." She pointed off into the distance. "But it was so fast, I didn't catch the plate."

"Was it a black luxury vehicle?"

"I think, but I was more concerned with Steven." Eyes filling with tears, she shook her head. "We were in the PTA together. He's a good man. Seeing him like that was just—" A sharp breath cut her off. "I just got off the phone with his daughter. He's in the ICU."

Hell, this guy was taking no chances. I should've assumed as much this afternoon, but Ox and I both agreed those had been warning shots.

"Would you be willing to give his daughter a call for me?" I asked. "I think this could've been about some files Steven had on a patient. If she can get me access to them, I might be able to find who did this."

"Sure. She has it off right now, but she said she'd call me with an update. You have a number you want me to pass along?"

"Yeah, it's on my business card. Let her know she can call any time. No pressure to wait 'til morning." Especially since I'd been plotting how to get into the man's house once the neighbors were asleep. "I'm so sorry you had to see your friend that way."

Giving a short nod, she swallowed hard. "Just let me know if you find the asshole."

"I will." Standing, gritting my teeth at the pain in my knee, I gestured ahead. "It was right there, you said?"

"Right at the stop sign. The police said it was okay to clean up the blood."

"You don't mind if I look around, do you?"

Colleen shook her head in answer.

With that, I limped off the porch to the stop sign at the corner. It was a few hundred feet from the porch, and there was no sidewalk. Not uncommon in areas like these. It'd help the bastard in court, though. He could say he didn't see Steven, panicked, and drove off. No matter what, he'd get charges for the hit and run, but unless I or the cops could prove he was connected to Steven through his files, he wouldn't get attempted murder.

Or flat-out murder, if Steven didn't make it.

Shaking that thought off, I eyed the tire tracks in the edge of the grass just before the corner. It looked like the tires had spun, which made deciphering the make and model difficult, but the prints couldn't have come from a truck or SUV. They were too small to have come from anything but a sedan.

One thing worth noting, however, was the stop sign itself.

It bowed slightly up hill. Examining it, right above hip height, was a strip of black. As though when he'd plowed Steven to the ground, he scraped either his mirror or the side of his vehicle. That was worth noting. The guy would have some type of damage to his front left fender, judging by Colleen's account of the direction he drove off.

Still, I was back at the same dead end.

All this information or not, I had jack shit pointing me to the car's owner. Every bit of evidence told me this was Quinn's mystery guy, but I had no way to track the bastard down.

Only that file.

Chapter 21

ALREADY WATCHING OUT FOR THE LUXURY VEHICLE, I DID A DOUBLE take at each black car I saw on the way home. None of which had damage that matched that stop sign.

Steven lived closer to me than Evelyn, so the drive home wasn't long, pulling in just after eleven. Normally, I'd climb into a bath and crawl under the covers by now. But Steven's daughter would hopefully call soon with permission to search his belongings, so sleep was off the table for tonight.

Bentley's light was still on. There was a better chance of staying awake if I wasn't staring at a wall all alone, so I texted to ask if he was still up. Responding in a handful of seconds, he said to come over.

As we settled in on the sofa, he asked if dissecting the last day of Quinn's life had brought me anything conclusive. I explained it hadn't and told him about Steven.

At which point, Bentley's jaw dropped. "He tried to kill the guy over some paperwork?"

"And the kicker is, that's what solidifies his guilt." Tucking myself into the corner of the sofa, I chomped into one of Grace's cookies. "If he hadn't been following me, if he hadn't shot at me, I wouldn't have anything conclusive against him."

"Do you think the daughter'll give you the files?"

"No reason not to. Giving me permission to go in the house and look around isn't putting her dad's job at risk, and it might help me find who did this."

"True." Chewing a cookie, Bentley cocked his head to the side. "If she doesn't, you're gonna do it though, aren't you?"

"Break in?" I smirked. "Never."

He laughed. Concern drifted through his expression a moment later. "You don't think he's gonna try to kill you next, do you?"

"It's a possibility." I shrugged. "But a hit and run against my tank wouldn't work. I have cameras at my house, so if he followed me home, he'd see so and run before doing anything incriminating. Plus, trying to kill someone here isn't smart. Every other trailer, someone's sitting on their porch. Kids are constantly playing on the streets. Way too many witnesses."

Credit where it was due in that regard. In the suburbs, there was a false sense of community. People in the trailer park and other lower income environments had stronger ties to their neighbors.

Suburbanites worked stricter nine-to-five type schedules, while people in areas like mine were more likely to have odd jobs with inconsistent schedules. We also had a surplus of unemployed folks, whether due to age, health, or otherwise, who got most of their human interaction by hollering from one porch to the next. Because we were poor, most kids weren't involved in after school activities like sports. Similarly, while every kid in a suburb had a phone or an iPad, only a handful in my area did. They spent more time with the other neighborhood kids as a result, and there was always an adult somewhere on the street who kept an eye on the dozen or so of them.

"Valid point, but you should be careful," Bentley said. "Seems like this guy's gonna stop at nothing to cover his ass."

"I'm always careful. Grace at her friend's already?"

"Yup. I dropped her off after you left." Stretching his arms overhead with a yawn, he cracked his neck from one side to the other. "Remind me that this is a good thing. Kids do this. They go to sleepovers with their friends."

"Are you that worried about her?"

"I just don't like when she's outta my sight."

"This isn't her first sleepover, is it?"

"No, she's been to a few. Just the first one here. She's fine. I'm sure she's fine."

"There's no reason she wouldn't be. You have her location, don't you?"

"Always."

"Then it's not much different from her being right there." I nodded down the hall toward her bedroom. "That why you're still up? Panicking over her not being here?"

"I'm not *panicking*." Bentley's eyes narrowed, but he smiled slightly. "And that's only part of the reason I'm still up, thank you."

"What's the other part?"

Taking a gulp from his water, his smile grew.

Glancing at the third bedroom, I noted the light on under the door. "Ooh, it's about my surprise."

"It might be."

"When are you gonna give me this surprise?"

"It's not really something I can *give* you." He paused. "Well, I guess I could, but it'd be redundant."

"I don't understand."

"You will when you get it."

"But you just said I won't get it."

"You'll get it, but you're not gonna, like, walk away with it."

"That makes no sense."

"It will."

"Can't you just show it to me?"

"Then it won't be a surprise."

"Considering I have literally no idea what it could be, there's no way it *couldn't* be a surprise."

"It's not finished yet."

"I'm cool with a work in progress."

Looking me over for a moment, he sighed. The smile was still there as he stood. "C'mon."

Grinning, I struggled to my feet and trailed behind him. "Is it a pony?"

"Damn it, what gave it away?" I reached past Bentley for the handle. He beat me there and raised a finger. "Cover your eyes."

"Really?"

"Or no surprise."

With a dramatic exhale, I put both hands over my face. "Happy?"

"Yup." The squeal of the hinges sounded, and the thump of his footsteps was next. "Alright, open them."

I did, and it was...

A treadmill.

A pink treadmill, to be exact. It took up almost as much space as a twin-sized bed, far from compact. Judging by the screen between the handlebars, it was a few years old at least. The flower decals on it were cute, I had to admit.

"Don't look at it like that." Bentley laughed, walking toward it. "I know it's not fancy, but it is your style."

"It is." Smiling, I shook my head. "But I don't get it."

"I knew you wouldn't, which was why I wasn't going to tell you about it until I was done with it." He leaned against the handrail. "Last week, I was bullshitting with a coworker. Your knee came up. His mom had a knee replacement last year. He said that her physical therapist recommended getting a treadmill and walking on it backward for an hour or so a day. I googled it, sure enough, it's a thing. Walking backwards on a treadmill is proven to help knee pain. Then I was driving home from work, and I saw someone taking this out to the trash. And I thought of you. So I grabbed it, brought it home, and started working on it. Actually, I just got it working before you texted that you were home."

Damn it. My stomach was doing that thing again.

"You want me to walk on that backward?" I asked.

"You've tried a thousand other things. If it'll help the pain, why not?"

"If I don't break my neck first." I walked that direction, looking it over. "It is cute though."

When he clicked it on, a beep and high-pitched squeal sounded. Barking, Tempest barreled toward us, nearly pummeling me toward the ground. She jumped onto the treadmill and quickly gained traction, walking in sync with its pace. Then hopped off. She cocked her head from one side to the other, then jumped on it again. She walked for a few paces, then skipped off, tilting her head from side to side.

"See, even Tempest can do it." Smirking, Bentley offered a hand. "I won't let you fall and break your neck."

Why—*why*—did such a simple sentence make my chest feel so warm and my hands so sweaty? Maybe it had nothing to do with the sentence and everything to do with the meaning behind it. Not only had he thought of my health, encouraging me to do whatever it took to minimize my daily battle with my body, but he even thought of my style. It was a simple thing, really, but Ox had always mocked my love of pink. For the life of me, I couldn't picture that macho man loading a pink treadmill into his car and driving it home.

But Bentley did. Casually thoughtless and thoughtful at once. Incorporating me and my needs into his life while considering that I'd love it simply for its aesthetic.

"Just try it." Bentley wiggled his fingers. "If you hate it, Grace'll use it. If you love it, it's yours anytime you want it."

"Alright. I'll try it." Accepting his hand, I used the handrail to climb onto the footrests on the sides, telling Tempest to go lie down. She plopped down on the exercise mats in the corner, resting her head between her paws, as if waiting for her turn on the new toy. "Face you, you said?"

"Yeah, there ya go." One hand, he clasped with mine, and the other, he held out beside my waist. "It's on low, so you won't go flying off or anything."

Holding the rail and squeezing his hand tight, I stepped onto the moving belt. As expected, I stumbled.

Bentley's hand found my waist before I had time to fall.

"Told you I won't let you fall." Bentley smiled. "You got this."

"I don't feel like I got this." Looking at the treadmill belt below, watching my feet travel backward, I grabbed the rest harder. "You're sure this is safe?"

"It's recommended by physical therapists everywhere. Just give yourself a minute. Your body's not used to it yet."

"Easy for you to say," I muttered, watching my feet.

"Don't look at them. You'll think about it too much. Just look at me." When my eyes found his, he was still smiling. "See? You're doing it without thinking about it."

"What I'm thinking about is how much it's gonna hurt when I fall."

"I won't let you fall." That hand on my waist tightened, and that was exactly how it felt. That spinning sensation in my stomach—that's what it was.

It felt like I was falling.

"How's your knee feel?"

My knee.

Right, my knee.

"Huh," I muttered.

"Does it feel better?"

"Sorta? It's like there's less pressure, or something? I'm not sure how to explain it."

"It doesn't hurt though?"

I shook my head.

"Did it hurt when you got on?"

"A little stiff." Paying closer attention to it, I searched for the words. "Now it feels like stretching. But it's stretching in a place that doesn't get stretched when I walk forward."

"I think it's using the muscles on the back of your legs, so it's taking pressure off the muscles that usually do the hard work." His thumb brushed along the back of mine, and that falling sensation deepened. "It's probably gonna take some time to get used to it, but hey if it helps, why not?"

I probably looked ridiculous, but all I did was smile in response.

Bentley laughed. "Are you mocking me? Because I'll show you the articles. I didn't make this up. It's supposed to help."

"I'm not mocking you."

"What's that smile for, then?"

"Thank you." My voice came out soft. "For everything you've done for me lately, but for this, too. It's really sweet."

"Meh. It was free. The part was only twenty bucks. It's no big deal."

It was.

Whether he saw it as a simple gesture, or was being modest, everything he did for me was a big deal. Making dinner each night, letting me come over at midnight, letting Tempest out if I was away from home for too long, and every other tiny thing he did that made my life easier, that made me happier, was a big deal.

To a man who'd dropped out of college for several years so his wife could get her degree first while he worked, maybe this was small. To a man who' devoted his entire existence to helping everyone else, finding a treadmill in the garbage and popping a new part in wasn't a large task.

But for someone like me, who'd never had much of a support system, it was everything. Bentley had always been that for me, even when we were kids. Until he came back into my life, I hadn't realized how much of an impact he'd made on me.

"And I promise, it's not like the bike," Bentley said.

I laughed. "I forgot about the bike."

"Phoebe has not, and she reminds me of it regularly."

When I was thirteen, Bentley's had gotten a flat, so he'd borrowed mine. He left it in his driveway and his dad ran it over, breaking the wheel. For the following three days, he avoided me, going so far as to have his mom drive him to school so he didn't have to see me on the bus.

Then he'd shown up at my house one night with a bike that was a hell of a lot better than the one I'd let him borrow. With a thousand apologies, he showed me all the cool features about the new one, carefully avoiding mentioning where he'd gotten it. He ended his anxious speech by asking if this one was okay instead.

I'd told him it was fine, and we went to the field in the center of the park like we did most days. Only for his sister to find us there and punch him in the face for taking money from her piggy bank to buy me said new bike. He'd insisted he was going to pay her back, but she took the bike as collateral until he did.

"You know I wasn't mad, right?" I asked. "I didn't care about the bike."

"Well, you shoulda been mad. My dad shoulda replaced it."

He should've, but that wasn't the point. "I was mad that you blew me off for a week."

"I thought you were gonna kick my ass." Bentley's smile hadn't gone anywhere throughout this conversation, and it was only wider now. "I'm sorry."

"Just don't let it happen again." I smiled back. "No more long breaks apart, alright? I don't want another decade to go by without you in my life."

"Neither do I." His hand on my waist tightened, thumb brushing over my ribs. "I don't know why we didn't keep in touch when I left."

"Think it was my fault," I said. "I didn't have a phone when I left."

"Where did you go after graduation?" he asked, glancing past me when something beeped on the treadmill. "I don't think you told me."

"Got an apartment outside Pittsburgh. waitressed at night, and trained at the academy during the day."

"And you stayed there until when?"

Until I met Ox. We moved in after dating for three months because he said I wasn't safe on that side of town. I'd disagreed. No one had bothered me in that apartment. Except the roaches. My other neighbors had been too stoned to interfere with my life. Those damn roaches, however, had woken me several times crawling on my face.

But I didn't want to talk about Ox. Or the roaches. Especially not with Bentley's hand around my waist.

"Until I was twenty-two. Then I got my first K-9 and got certified in dog training. Sorta took up all my time from then on. But I shoulda called Phoebe and found out where you were."

"I should've found you on social media."

"Ah, but you wouldn't have."

He furrowed his brows. "What do you mean?"

"I don't have any. Just a bunch of burner accounts I use for research," I said. "When I became a cop, there was this girl who got acid thrown on her by some guy she turned down. He knew exactly where she was because she'd posted an update with her location. After that, I shut down all my socials."

"Shit." He paused. "Do you think I should let Grace be on those?"

"Eh. Social media's awful for kids, but she's been on them for so long, it might make her think you're punishing her," I said. "So much of the modern world is run online. There's no way to keep her away from it. Maybe checking her settings and making sure she never attaches her location to any posts would be a—"

The treadmill belt skipped.

My foot jutted out.

And slammed Bentley in the shin.

Down we went.

I lost my balance.

There wasn't time to brace for impact, but I didn't need to, because Bentley's hand was still around my waist. The hand that'd been holding mine caught my knee before it slammed into the ground.

My legs were around his hips, and my chest was against his.

I expected pain to rip through me, or for Bentley to groan in agony, but he laughed instead. "Okay, I lied. You fell. Are you okay?"

"Are *you* okay?" I looked him over, noticing his head only inches from his bench press. "You didn't hit your head, did you?"

"No, just my ass. And my shin."

"I'm sorry." I laughed too. "I told you this thing was a bad idea."

"And I told you it wasn't ready yet." Still laughing, he smiled so widely that the corners of his eyes wrinkled. "But you didn't break your neck, so still better than expected."

"You almost did." Touching his jaw, I tilted his head from one side to the other to check for blood, still laughing. "Are you sure you're okay?"

"I'm fine. Are you okay?"

This angle wasn't great, but most of my weight was on Bentley's lap.

I'm sitting on Bentley's lap.

His hand was still on my waist, the other resting on the outside of my knee.

Each of my palms were on the carpet beside his head, propping me upright, my chest was only a few inches from his. We were so close, I could feel the heat of his breath on my cheeks.

"Maddie," Bentley said, "are you okay?"

"Yeah. Yeah, I'm fine."

"You sure?" That hand on my knee came to my face, touching my chin. "Your face is red."

I believed the phrase for that was blushing. "Just what a lady likes to hear."

Chuckling, his fingers slid to my cheek, thumb on my chin just below my lips. "I'm sorry. You're beautiful."

Now his cheeks were red too.

God, it was like we were thirteen again. Every surface of my skin was on fire, and my chest was warm, and it felt like I was falling.

When we were thirteen though, we were in the field in the center of the trailer park, lying on a blanket, watching the stars. Mom had busted my lip because I'd gotten an attitude with her, because there was no food in the fridge, and Bentley's dad had just left for the thousandth time. We'd been talking about how badly we wanted to get out of this place, and I'd told him, "You're the only thing I'll miss."

Then he'd kissed me.

And for that moment, everything was right with the world. It didn't matter how sore my neck was from when Mom pushed me into the wall, or how scared I was that she'd be awake when I got home, because Bentley's arm was around me, just as it was now, and I was safe. I was with my best friend, the boy I loved, and nothing else mattered.

Until I remembered that simple fact.

He was my friend.

Boyfriends and girlfriends broke up all the time. Bentley's presence was the only place in the world that felt safe, and if I hadn't ended that kiss, we could've become that, and I could've lost him for good.

Did I still think that now?

Staring into his eyes, feeling his fingers on my cheek, the thump of his heart pounding against my own, both ready to explode out of our chests, did I truly believe I'd lose him for good if I leaned down and touched my lips to his? I'd lost him before. For years, he'd been gone, and that wasn't because of a kiss.

What if I did kiss him, and we fell in love, and we went up in flames just like Ox and I had? What if he hurt me like Ox had, and I grew to hate Bentley just like I'd grown to hate Ox?

But what if we didn't go up in flames?

What if it all worked out?

Was *that* what I was afraid of?

"I'm sorry. Was that outta line?" Bentley asked, hand on my cheek, dropping to his side. "It was. I'm sorry. I—"

"It wasn't," I said. "It was sweet."

His smile returned. As he opened his mouth to speak, the ring of my phone cut in first.

I wasn't sure if I was relieved or annoyed.

Finding it in my hoodie pocket, I slid the green bar for the unknown number that flashed across the screen. Answering with, "Maddie Castle," I tried to figure out where to go from here.

Sit up? Crawl off Bentley's lap? Roll to the side and pray my hair didn't get caught in the treadmill?

As embarrassing as it was, I settled for a mixture between the last two.

"Uh, hi, this is Alice Benedict. Colleen gave me your number?"

"Yes. Yeah, I'm Maddie Castle." Like I hadn't already said that. "I'm a private investigator. I think the case I'm investigating might be tied to your father's accident. Is there any way you and I could meet?"

"I'm at the hospital with my dad right now. I don't think I can really leave," she said. "Is there something I can do for you? Colleen mentioned something about a file?"

"Yes." Struggling upright, holding Bentley's bench press for stability, I said, "Yes, I believe that a college girl was murdered. Your dad was her therapist. I think whoever killed her knows his name is in your dad's file, and he hit Steven with his car to keep that information from coming out. I believe he took that file home with him today. Is there any way I could take a look around his house for it?"

"Wait, I don't understand. You think someone tried to *kill* him? It wasn't just an accident?"

Of course she didn't understand. All that information tumbled out of me in an incoherent ramble. "The car that hit him seems to be the same one that's been following me since I started the investigation. I don't have proof yet, but there are too many coincidences for it to not be connected."

"Oh my god," she murmured, silence following for a few heartbeats. "Is it illegal for me to let you have his files?"

Technically, no. "It's illegal for him to turn over confidential information. It's not illegal for his daughter to let me in his home."

"Are you sure?"

"A lot of gray area, legally," I said. "But I really think this could help me find who did this to your dad."

A long moment of silence passed. "Okay. Alright. I'll text you the garage code."

Relief washed through me. "Thank you. How's your dad doing?"

"I don't know." Her voice cracked. "He's in a surgery right now."

Poor kid. And poor Steven. "I'm sure he's gonna be fine."

"I hope," she said. "Please let me know if you find anything."

I told her, of course, and hurried off the line.

Just as Bentley stood. Scratching his head, face still bright red, he said, "That the therapist's kid?"

"Yeah, I'm gonna head back to his place now."

"Right. That makes sense." His smile that'd been so playful all night now, was uneasy. Much like I must've looked as I shoved my hands in my pockets. "Well, I'm not gonna be able to sleep 'til I know you made it home, so shoot me a text when you get back."

I blurted a "will do," practically ran to Tempest's crate, and bolted to my car.

Chapter 22

I drove with the windows down. The heat in my cheeks and the fluttering in my stomach were a distraction. The stakes of this case had climbed higher in the last day, and I needed my head in the game.

When I pulled up to Steven's house, the stakes climbed even higher.

Light shined behind the curtains.

No one had been here earlier. Alice was at the hospital with her dad. There was no reason a light should've been on.

There was no black sedan parked on the street, so if the mystery guy was in there, he'd walked from somewhere nearby. I parked on the street to not alert him of my presence. Gun in hand, I left the key in the ignition and shut the door, making sure it didn't click so I could hop in and chase him by car if I had to.

Usually, I'd bring Tempest in with me, but this son of a bitch was trigger-happy enough to attempt murder today. Great partner or not, I wasn't risking her life like I had Bear's.

Tiptoeing to the porch, I noted the broken window framing the front door.

Definitely not a family friend or a cop.

I slid open the front door, already unlocked and ajar.

Luminance shone from the rear of the house. Shuffling sounded. I wasn't sure if it was footsteps or someone fiddling with something in a cabinet, but the light was moving. It was a soft shade of fluorescent blue, like the glow of a flashlight.

It was my only guidance. Using my own flashlight would alert him to my presence.

Thank God the floor was carpeted, because my damp sneakers would've squeaked on anything else.

Keeping my steps quiet, adrenaline easing those sore muscles in my knee, I stalked closer down the hall. Passing a powder room, I glanced at the kitchen on my right. The light came from the left, about a dozen strides ahead.

A figure rushed through the opening.

Nothing more than a blur as he scurried into the hall.

Then he stopped.

The light turned on me.

It blocked out the details of his appearance, but I wouldn't have been able to identify him ,anyway. Wearing gloves, a black hoodie, and a ski mask, only the slightest glimmer of his eyes was discernable. What I could make out was a manilla folder tucked against his chest with one hand as the other held the flashlight. Meaning he had no way to grab his gun.

I steadied mine in the center of his torso. "Hey, thanks. I was looking for that."

He tucked it under his arm.

"If you reach, I shoot," I said. "Put your hands above your head."

He stood still.

"There's a gun aimed at your heart," I snapped. "Put your damn hands above your head."

The flashlight clunked to the ground.

He darted toward the kitchen.

Damn it.

I took off after him.

He only had a few feet on me, but I wasn't as fast as I once was, adrenaline-fueled or otherwise. The son of a bitch was out the kitchen door just as I entered it. When I made it to the opening, he was at the bottom of the porch steps.

My gun was still on him. I had a clear shot.

But I wasn't a cop. He wasn't armed—not from what I could see. This wasn't my home, so I couldn't use the *Stand Your Ground* law as a defense if I killed him. Killing someone, even shooting someone, carried a hefty penalty. Even for cops, but especially for civilians.

If I got him on the ground, though? Well, no one would bat an eye.

Jogging behind him, relying solely on the light of the moon overhead for guidance, we ran into the woods framing the property. I knew this area. This patch of foliage was only a few acres wide. On the other side of it was a shopping center.

If I chased him into civilization, there was a better shot of cornering him.

Thorns and twigs snatched at my ankles as I trailed him into the early spring blooms. He was only a dozen strides ahead of me. The deciduous trees provided excellent camouflage, but while I saw the bushes and branches continue to rattle with his movement, I wasn't stopping.

Until the flash of gunfire lit up the forest.

Ducking sideways, I relied on a thick pine for cover.

Another jolt of orange blared, accompanied by a *boom*.

That one was farther away, almost a dozen yards to my right, uphill.

Running uphill wasn't gonna be easy for either of us, but could slow him down enough for me to catch my breath.

When a few heartbeats had passed without another shot, I took off in the direction the last shot had come from. He was louder than me, panting hard, rustling branches and bushes. Trailing him wasn't difficult. His aim was shit, too.

As long as I stayed quiet, as long as he couldn't see me, trailing him out of this patch of trees would lead us to that shopping center. Now that the state police were on board, that could be our saving grace. If he'd parked in that lot, one of the cameras had to have gotten his plates, or at least a concise make and model.

About fifty feet ahead of me on the right, I vaguely made out his figure. Grasping at branches, trekking slowly uphill, he glanced behind every few feet.

I walked slow, not taking my eyes off him for a heartbeat.

Cresting the hilltop into the clearing, only a few dozen feet behind him, I tried to line up a shot. But he had the higher ground. I was better camouflaged than him, but he'd already shot at me. The bastard had tried to kill a man today. He clearly had no assault rifle, but I didn't know how many bullets he had in that clip. If he unloaded it in my direction from where he stood now, where the trees were further apart and thinner than they were at the bottom of the hill, I'd be the next victim to his spree.

I tiptoed close behind, making it to the top of the hill as he traveled toward the right.

Not toward the shopping center, but toward a small highway.

Damn it.

Running again, now that he was on level ground atop the hill, I remained a few dozen strides behind, staying as quiet as possible.

Until a crack of a heavy branch sounded underfoot.

He spun toward me.

I dropped sideways behind a tree.

Boom!

Searing pain ripped through my bicep.

I rolled backward, catching myself in a bush of thorns and jaggers.

Vision distorted, blackening around the edges, the thumps of footsteps sounded. Hot blood rolled down my arm. My breaths becoming unstable, legs weakening. I tried to calm my breaths, patting my chest to my shoulder. Reaching my outer arm, the pain soared all the way to my hand. Squeezing my gun tighter, the agony burned all the way into my chest.

Shoulder wounds hurt like a bitch, but I wasn't letting this bastard get away.

That's what I told myself as I took off in his direction, but his figure was gone now. I heard his footsteps somewhere in the distance. Vision getting blurry, my heart slammed against my ribs.

I ran still. I ran after him because if I didn't get the bastard now, when would I? How could I?

I ran that direction until I was at the highway.

The glare of headlights blinded me. My stomach churned and my head pounded. Legs becoming gelatin beneath me as I looked in either direction, searching for the man who'd shot me, I grabbed a tree branch for stability and lowered myself to the ground.

Fainting mid chase wasn't gonna help me catch him.

Dropping my head between my knees, searching for the phone in my pocket, I used voice command to call the nearest state police department. Once I had the operator on the line, I said, "I need you to connect me with Derek Ames."

* * *

"You should really let me take you to the hospital, kid," Derek said, glancing from the road to me.

"So they can charge me five grand and order physical therapy?" Pulling the towel off the wound, I studied the slash the bullet had left. Past superficial, but more than a graze, roughly an inch wide and about half as thick. Seeing my tissue exposed wasn't comforting, but it was hardly an emergency. "I have a friend who's a paramedic. He can stitch it up."

Derek made a noise in his throat. "Just as stubborn as you were at ten years old."

"Yep." Grimacing at a bump in the road as he turned onto Steven's street, I held the wad of cloth tighter to the wound. "You got something I can tie around this 'til I get home?"

"Got a jacket on the floor there." He pointed to the floorboards. "I shouldn't even let you get in your car. How the hell you gonna hold the wheel, Maddie?"

"I have two arms." Raising the injured one, I did my best to maintain a poker face. "And I can move it fine."

Another noise in his throat, followed by a shake of his head. "Whatever you say, kid. But ya know, you should really have a partner. If you'd have passed out, you coulda lost a lot of blood before anyone got to you."

"But I didn't," I said. "I do alright on my own. Don't worry about me."

Not dignifying that with a response, he only nodded to the troopers parked in Steven's driveway. "My guys are looking through the house now. I'll let you know if we find any files that mention the girl."

"Thanks."

As he shifted the car into park behind my SUV, Tempest jumped to the front seat, ears perched high. Even from the distance, I saw her tail wagging.

"She trained?"

"Yeah, her handler died. I took over from there." I struggled with the jacket, trying to tie it around my bicep one handed. Derek helped, giving me a look that said *You need to go to a hospital, kid,* when I winced at the tightness. Before he could say so, I kept the conversation going. "She's a good partner."

"And you left her in the car."

"Better he shot me than her."

"If you die, she's got no one."

"I have a few friends who'd take her," I said. "You want me to come to the station tomorrow to give a written report?"

"If you've got the time. I have my guys on the streets looking. He couldn't have gotten far since you placed that call. That whole area's getting canvassed. We're pulling over every black car we see."

"Thanks. And I've got all my notes explaining how this connects to Quinn Barnes," I said. "You think it'll be enough for an arrest warrant?"

"The accident is what'll get us the arrest warrant," he said. "From there, once we have his name, we'll connect it to everything you've got. It's up to the D.A., but with everything you've told me, once we identify the guy, charging him with the girl's murder shouldn't be hard."

Chewing my lip, I nodded. "Be mindful of Bedford County. I think that's where he lives. He's probably headed that way."

"I know." He took a moment to study me. There was a frown across his lips, covered in a thick gray beard. His warm ebony skin had aged well. If not for that gray hair, I wouldn't have known he was approaching sixty. "You sure you're alright, kid?"

"I am. The blood loss wasn't too bad. I just need some juice and a nap."

"That wasn't what I was asking." His warm brown eyes said everything his mouth didn't. "I saw you limping. I know you got hurt last year. I'm wondering how you deal with that pain."

"Ibuprofen. Daily exercise. Massage, recently." Giving him a smile, I shook my head. "I'm not my mom, Derek."

"I know you're not."

"And you know I'm living in the trailer park. But that's because I'm poor, not because I'm high," I said. "This might not have been what you pictured for me when you said I could make something better for myself, but I'm happy with where I'm at. Things could be better, but I'm okay. Really."

He studied me a moment longer. "You like the whole private investigation thing?"

"I love it. And I'll love it more once I find the bastard who killed that girl and shot me."

Another sigh. The worry in his eyes was still there, but it wasn't so accusatory. More like the way a father would look at his daughter when she said she was going to school for social work. He may've found it admirable, but he knew it was a hard job with little room for growth.

"Alright, kid. Go on then. Get your friend to stitch up your arm." In response, I thanked him for the ride and started from the car. Just as the door shut, his window rolled down. "And if you need backup, you call me. Any time. Day or night. Alright?"

I gave him another smile. "Yes, sir."

Chapter 23

Every time he heard the rumble of a car, he ran to the window.

Which was lunacy.

That's how Bentley felt—like he was losing his mind. His heart hadn't stopped racing since that fall off the treadmill. His stomach kept twisting and turning. Even his hands were sweaty.

It was almost two o'clock. He should've gone to sleep. That's what Maddie would do when she got home. But when he lay in bed, he'd heard the rumble of an engine and ran to the window.

To see if it was her. To ask if she wanted to come over. To talk about what she'd found at that therapist's house, and to talk about what'd happened earlier.

Should he have kissed her? The last time he'd done that, it hadn't ended well. But he swore that he could feel the same longing come from her. When she had kneeled over him, when she was smiling down at him, when she was laughing against his chest, he'd thought it was what she'd wanted.

If Maddie were any other woman, he would've. But he couldn't risk it. Had he kissed her, had he been wrong about what her expression meant, Maddie would think that's all he wanted. She'd think he was only being kind to her because he wanted a relationship.

That wasn't the case. Their friendship was why he was kind to her, not because he expected anything in return. Having her in his life at all was plenty. Yes, Bentley had begun to realize he wanted more than friendship. Every day that went by, he wanted it more.

If Maddie made the move, he'd leap. But he could read between the lines. She hadn't kissed him. She didn't want him in that way, and it was okay.

They were close, but they were still getting to know the people they'd become since they were teenagers. Maybe she wasn't ready to dive into anything with someone she was still learning about. Maybe she didn't want to risk their friendship. Or maybe she was incapable of seeing her childhood best friend in a romantic light.

That was okay. It'd have to be. Bentley didn't want to lose her friendship. He wasn't in any rush to enter a relationship either.

So why did he keep running to the window like a stalker?

Shaking his head, he pulled in a deep breath and watched the TV in the corner. He was overthinking. Her exit was awkward, but nothing had happened. Maddie went to work. That was all. She said she'd text him when she got home. She hadn't packed up and run because of an almost kiss.

Everything was fine. It was—

A knock thumped at his door.

He hadn't even heard a car rumble.

Butterflies filling his stomach, he walked to the door. When he pulled it open, all those butterflies were gone, a sinking sensation replacing it.

Maddie's arm lay limp at her side, wrapped in a blood-soaked cloth. Her skin was pale, dark circles lining her eyes. She smiled, though, as she often did at the strangest of times. Struggling with Tempest's leash in her free hand, she gestured to her bicep. "You don't know how to take care of a bullet wound, do you?"

"What the hell happened?"

"Can I tell you about it while you stitch me up?" It was a grin she gave Bentley then. "I'm getting a little lightheaded."

"I'm not a doctor." Bentley reached for his jacket. "Come on. Let's get you to the hospital—"

"I can't afford a hospital, and I don't need one," she said. "The blood looks bad, but the damage isn't."

"You're full of—"

"I'm not going to the hospital, Bentley." Her tone harshened. "I can stitch it up myself if you won't."

He growled his annoyance, took Tempest's leash from her hand, and guided her inside with a hand on her back, prepared to catch her if she fell. "If it's bad, you're going to the hospital, damn it. Even if I gotta drag you kicking and screaming."

She waved him off.

* * *

THE WOUND WAS HARDLY SUPERFICIAL, BUT BENTLEY WAS MORE worried about infection than the damage itself. He told Maddie so, to which she replied that seeing a doctor for an infection would be far cheaper than seeing a doctor for a gunshot wound.

With no anesthetic, Bentley stitched the wound, listening as Maddie explained what'd happened. Just as he tied it shut, moving on to cleaning the drying blood off her arm, she said, "And if they can't find those files, I'm back to another dead end. Those files were the only chance I had of finding this guy."

"I'm sure you'll think of something," Bentley said. "But you need to get some rest, Mads. If you can't even think straight, you're not gonna find anything valuable."

She rolled her eyes, then jumped when he grazed the wound. "Ow."

"Hey, this would be numb if you'd gone to the hospital."

Glaring, she gave a half smile. "Don't patronize me."

"'Don't patronize me,'" Bentley said in a mocking falsetto.

She shoved his shoulder. "Listen, if I could afford the hospital, that's where I would've gone."

"Maybe with that big check, you should buy yourself some health insurance." Carefully, he wiped at a piece of dried blood. "Might cover some more physical therapy."

"Who needs physical therapy? My best friend's a masseuse."

Bentley laughed, and Maddie smiled back at him. It was the same expression she'd given him a thousand times, easing the worry that'd settled through him while she was gone. What happened tonight may've been awkward, but it didn't change anything.

He still was worried, however.

Only now, he was worried about how light her skin looked and how dark the undersides of her eyes were. She would've fainted by now if she needed a transfusion, but she needed to take the rest of the night off. Making tomorrow a sick day wouldn't be a bad idea, either.

"Well, as your makeshift doctor, I'm ordering rest," Bentley said. "You're gonna eat, you're gonna drink some water, and you're gonna sleep."

Her smile faltered, just a bit. "Please don't do that."

"Don't do what?"

"Treat me like I'm fragile." Maddie's eyes were soft, voice somewhere between sad and hurt. "I'm not dying. I'm not broken. I didn't get hit because I was stupid. If I were still a cop, I would've gotten him before he got me. But I'm not, so I would've gone to jail. It would've ruined my career. And that's what this is. It's my job to find this guy. And yeah, it would be a lot easier to do if I had a badge, and if I wasn't so slow because of my damn knee, but I find a way to make it work. I'm not fragile, Bentley."

Fragile? Bentley would never put Maddie Castle and fragile in the same sentence. Reckless, sure. Adrenaline junkie, yes. But never *fragile*.

Brows furrowing, Bentley's head tilted. "You're the strongest person I know. Of course you're not fragile." Maddie's expression softened. She opened her mouth to speak, but Bentley beat her to it. "But you are human. I'm telling you to take a break tonight, maybe even tomorrow, because you can barely lift your phone, let alone a gun. You're injured. You're exhausted. You lost a good bit of blood, and you need to rest. Not because you're *broken*. Because you're not a machine. I'm sorry if I'm going into dad-mode, but it's not because I think you're incapable, Maddie. It's because I care about you. I understand your job is dangerous, and I respect you for doing it, but you're not gonna be able to if you pass out from exhaustion."

Maddie only held his gaze for a moment, reddened blue eyes dewy. Not with tears, but comfort. Like that little speech meant the world to her.

"I'm sorry. I didn't mean to snap at you," Maddie said. "It was a frequent issue for me and my ex after I got hurt. He was always telling me to take it easy. That I didn't need to work so hard. He treated me like I was crippled, and now it's sort of a sore spot when anyone tells me to slow down."

Frowning, Bentley began dressing the wound. "I hate that word. Crippled."

"Me too." Maddie winced when the gauze touched the sensitive skin. "I'm not. No one is. Cripple means deprived of strength or efficiency. Having to do something differently doesn't mean I'm not efficient."

"Or that you're weak," Bentley said. "Makes you a hell of a lot stronger. You do everything everyone else does *while* you're in pain. Really ups the bar for 'strength,' don't you think?"

She smiled at him. Then he grazed that sensitive spot again, and she muttered a curse.

"Sorry. I just want to make sure this is covered, so nothing gets in here and makes you go septic," he said. "Did you mean Ox? Is he the ex?"

Maddie's expression said the mention of that hurt more than the bullet had. "Yep."

"Take it you don't wanna talk about it?"

"Not really, no."

"Then I'll shut up," Bentley said, standing. "And I'm gonna get you something to eat. Just leave your jacket off so you don't tear those stitches."

"You got it, doc."

Chuckling, Bentley walked to the kitchen. Out of the corner of his eye, he saw Maddie lie back on the sofa and reach to the floor below with her good arm to pet Tempest.

Fragile. That word ran circles through Bentley's mind as he spooned some leftovers onto a plate and put it in the microwave.

Maddie Castle could never be fragile. Injured knee or not, Bentley meant what he said. Maddie was the toughest person he'd ever met.

That girl had broken up a dogfight between a boxer and pit bull at ten years old, then hid the wound she'd gotten in the chaos to make sure the dogs wouldn't get put down for it. When Bentley twisted his ankle at eight, Maddie had carried him piggyback style all the way to the other side of the trailer park, barely breaking a sweat. After every beating Maddie's mom had given her, Maddie shrugged it off with a quick, "I'll live."

Last year, a serial killer had shot her, and she'd lived to hate him for it. Tonight, she ran headfirst after a murderer to avenge the death of someone she'd never met. Since Bentley had come back, Maddie kicked addiction in the face daily. At almost thirty, she had started life over and created a profitable business, all on her own.

And Ox told her she didn't need to work so hard.

Had he never known her at all?

Her entire life, Maddie had worked harder than everyone around her, simply to survive. To succeed, to thrive, nothing could stop her. Expecting Maddie to "take it easy" because her knee didn't work like it used to was no different than telling her to lie down and die. Maddie would never. Until she took her last breath, Maddie would give anything she set her mind to a hundred and ten percent.

That was what Bentley loved about her. Maddie always gushed about Bentley's kindness, his understanding nature, but Bentley loved the opposite about her. Maddie was sweet in her own right, which Bentley adored, but it was her fury and determination that he admired so much.

If Ox had tried to diminish those parts of Maddie, he'd never deserved her.

When the microwave dinged, Bentley grabbed the plate, a fork, and a bottle of juice. Walking to the living room, he said, "It's better fresh, but anything's better than nothing."

Only to realize Maddie's eyes were shut.

Groggy, she lifted a finger over her lips, assuring Bentley she hadn't fainted, but the exhaustion was taking its toll. With a chuckle, he laid the plate on the coffee table, sat in the recliner, and turned the TV down a few notches.

Chapter 24

RING-RING-RING!

The phone dinged in my hoodie pocket, pulling me from my sleep. As my eyes opened, I jolted. Pain ripped through my arm as a result.

Instead of my pink bedroom walls, or the floral prints covering my living room, these were sage green. Rather than my lumpy mattress, cushy memory foam cradled my spine. The smell was the first identifier of where I was. Earthy, like cedar with a hint of sandalwood.

Bentley's cologne.

The next telltale was the photo of him and Grace on the dresser.

I was in Bentley's bed. That, I'd have to unpack after I answered the phone.

Sitting up, I slid the green bar and lifted it to my ear. "Maddie Castle, what can I do for you?"

"Hey, kid, it's Derek," he said. "Got a minute?"

Heart skipping a beat, I hurried from the bed. As soon as the burn of pressure on those pulling stitches stretched to my wrist, I regretted that decision. Slowing, I used the bedframe to bring myself upright. Trying not to let the pain show through my voice, I asked, "Did you find him?"

"We didn't, no. None of Steven's records were at the house either," he said.

Was I disappointed or annoyed? I couldn't tell.

Struggling to pinch the phone between my shoulder and my ear, I tugged Bentley's blankets to the top of the bed. "What about Steven? Have you heard from him?"

A sigh echoed through the speaker. "He's not doing good. Still unconscious. He had a brain bleed, they said. Fifty-fifty chance he'll wake up."

I rolled my head back, growling my frustration. "So we've got nothing."

"Well, if he wakes up and his mind isn't impaired, we got something," he said. "I got a judge to sign a warrant for his records. I know he doesn't have those at his house or in his office, but if he wakes up, he won't be bound by HIPPA laws to keep the information about that girl concealed."

True. But if Steven's condition was so poor, a fifty-fifty chance wasn't something to bank on. "You checked the records at his main office, right? Just in case he stored one there?"

"We did, yeah. All we've found so far is a consent form from when she was fifteen. That's not what you were looking for, right?"

"No. But just a consent form? You don't have his notes from back then?"

"They're password protected, so it's taking us a minute to get into it," Derek said. "Why do you ask?"

Because anything was better than nothing. "It's worth looking over. I don't have anything else to go on."

"Hmmm." A moment of quiet passed. "Well, it is an ongoing investigation, Maddie."

The kind way of telling me he couldn't let me have a peek at them. "Quinn was a minor then, so her mother has the rights to those documents, doesn't she?"

Another, "Hmmm," followed by a pause. "I'm not sure, actually. Psych laws are stricter than the rest of medical information."

"Evelyn's a hell of a lawyer," I said. "Let me give her a call and see what she says. Is it alright if I pass your number to her if she knows the specifics?"

"Sure. As long as she'll sign off on you looking them over, I'll forward them to you once we get into his system."

"Thanks. Keep me posted."

I tugged the phone from my ear to end the call, but Derek said, "Hang on, kid."

"Yeah?"

"Your arm alright?"

"Honestly? It hurt less than my knee. More of a scratching pain of torn flesh compared to the dull ache that wouldn't quit. Bentley said it didn't go deep."

"You're lucky it hit your arm instead of your shoulder," he said. "Rotator cuff pain hurts like a mother."

"I'll take your word for it. But I should get going—"

"Bentley Roycroft?" Derek asked.

"That's the one."

"Yeah, I've seen him around. He's a good worker." It made sense that their professional paths would cross from time to time. "I'm glad y'all are spending time together again."

"Uh-huh." Just like Derek was glad I spent so much time with Bentley when we were kids. "I really gotta go, sir."

"Yeah, yeah," he said. "Let's keep each other in the loop."

Once I'd thanked him again, I did my best to make Bentley's bed look decent with my limited mobility while I called Evelyn. It went to voicemail, so I left a message asking her to call me back.

The bed looked good enough by the time I was done, so I headed to the door. As soon as I was through its threshold, the smell of bacon and pancakes greeted me. Tempest was next, of course, rushing my way as soon as she heard the squeal of the hinges. I petted her, telling her good morning, and continued to the kitchen.

At the stove, Bentley stood in a faded T-shirt and gray sweatpants, spatula in hand. There was nothing provocative about that and yet, my stomach did that spinning thing again.

"Do I have memory loss?" I asked. "I thought that was a brain injury thing, not a bullet wound thing."

Looking at me over his shoulder, face screwed up in confusion. "What don't you remember?"

"How I ended up in your bed."

Cheeks burning red, his mouth opened and closed a few times, as if just seeing the implication of that sentence. "I took the couch."

The fact that he was out here, and the blankets were only disturbed on my side, told me that much. That reaction also told me he'd carried me into his room. Which wasn't a shock.

But it didn't lessen that falling feeling in my stomach.

However, it did remind me that last night's interaction had been awkward, and now was the chance to get back to our casual friendship.

Smiling, I leaned against the wall behind me. "You didn't have to do that. I was fine with the couch."

"Well, there wasn't enough room to elevate your arm." Tension loosening through his posture, he spun around and laid a plate on the table. "It just made sense."

"Next time, don't worry about it." I walked his way, grabbed a mug for some coffee, and filled it up. "You do enough for me already. You don't need to give up your bed."

He topped off my cup with some creamer. "Let's hope there isn't a next time."

Waving him off with a dismissive hand, I sat at the kitchen table and had a sip of my coffee, thanking Bentley for breakfast.

As always, he said it was no big deal while he finished preparing his plate. But it was a big deal. Not only because of that fluttering feeling in my belly, but because he'd done more for me in the time since he'd moved back than almost anyone else. Emotional tension aside, he was my best friend, and the list of things he'd helped me with was a mile long.

Outside of picking Grace up from the bus stop a couple times, I couldn't think of any ways I'd returned the favor. Intentionally or not, it was almost like I was taking advantage of him. I needed to correct that somehow.

Sitting across from me at the other end of the table, he lowered his mug to it. Hot liquid tipping from its brim, he cussed as it burned his fingers.

"Are you alright?"

"Yeah, I'm fine." He slurped the top of his coffee to keep it from spilling again. "Who were you talking to? Got any leads?"

"Just dead ends."

Cutting through my pancakes, I studied the liquid in his cup. It was at an angle, which was why he'd spilled it on himself. A handful of times, he'd complained about how in the move, one leg got damaged, so the table was uneven now. The top wasn't in excellent shape either—old and dingy with a blond, nicked up finish.

As much as Bentley cooked, and as much time as he'd spent at this table, he deserved a decent one. With the check Evelyn had given me, and the next one I hoped would come soon, I could get him a new one. That'd level the field for that treadmill.

"Maddie." Bentley snapped a few times, only inches from my face. "Anybody in there?"

"Huh?"

"You zoned out for a minute." His eyes flicked between mine, and he leaned in closer. "Maybe we should check your vitals. Let me grab—"

"I'm fine. I was thinking." Bentley's face told me he didn't believe that, but I laughed it off. I was less focused than usual, though. "I'm sorry, what'd you say?"

"Did you talk to the local cops about what happened last night?"

"Yeah, that's who I was on the phone with. Derek Ames." Forking pancakes to my lips, I took a bite before continuing. "They got a warrant for Steven's files since there's enough evidence to say Steven's accident was attempted murder, but it's gonna take them some time to get into his operating system. Those files will only contain Quinn's notes from when she was a kid. I don't see what good that's gonna do me, though. Her weird behavior started when she went to college."

"Eh." Sipping his coffee, he leaned back in his seat. "You're the one who says every bit of information you get on someone helps the investigation."

"It's not gonna help me find the married man she was seeing." I paused. "God, I hope not, anyway."

Bentley's nose wrinkled. "If she was fifteen when she started seeing this guy, next time you run into him, don't hold back."

Arching a brow, I leaned back in my seat. "Are you telling me to kill him?"

"I wouldn't *tell* you to kill anyone." A casual sip of his coffee. "But ya know. I've got a good shovel."

Laughing, I shook my head. "Either way, fourteen isn't much different than eighteen. Just because it's legal doesn't make it any better. I can rationalize why an eighteen-year-old would be interested in a married man, especially one who'd lost their dad."

"But there's no rationalizing a married man going after an eighteen-year-old," Bentley finished my thought. "What would a man at that age even see in someone so young?"

"Control." The image of that bondage equipment in Quinn's closet flashed through my mind. "She was easy to manipulate."

"Ugh." Wrinkling his nose, Bentley shuddered. "No one's grown at eighteen. I had a kid at eighteen, and I wasn't grown. It's like I grew up with her, ya know?"

I was about to respond when my phone rang. Sliding it out, Evelyn's name blinked across the screen. I answered with, "Hey, how are you?"

"Hanging in there," she said. "Sorry I missed your call. I guess I left my phone in the car. What's going on?"

"A lot. You aren't busy, are you?"

Evelyn said she wasn't, and I described the chain of events from last night. Everything from Steven's accident, to the burglary, to my gunshot wound. I wrapped it up with, "I'm not sure what the laws are about those records, but if it's possible, I would like to take a look at them."

"I'm certain I have legal rights to those," she said. "I just have to double check since there's now an open investigation. Let me make some calls and get back to you."

"Sure, I'll be here."

"Before I let you go though, can I ask why you want these? Those files are from years ago. I don't see how they'd be relevant."

As much as I hated it, transparency was a part of my brand. I'd told Evelyn I wouldn't keep information from her. The sad truth was, although those files didn't seem valuable, it was the only thing I had left.

"Neither do I, Evelyn." Rubbing my tired eyes between my thumb and forefinger, I searched for the words. "But I've looked at everything. I've torn apart Quinn's phone. I followed the path she took the day of her death. All her friends' stories check out. All the evidence points to her death having been a homicide, but this guy's good at covering his tracks. He tried to kill a man and put a bullet through me to keep those records from coming out. I don't know if I'm gonna find anything worth exploring in those files, but I do know it's one stone I haven't turned over."

Evelyn was quiet for a few heartbeats. "That makes sense. I understand."

The melancholy edge to her voice made my heart hurt. "I'm sorry I don't have more for you. I'm doing everything I can."

"You have nothing to apologize for." Her tone was still gentle. "Are you okay? Your arm, I mean?"

I glanced down at it, noting the bit of blood that'd seeped through the gauze. As long as I kept it relaxed, the pain was just a pinch. "I'm a little less mobile than I'd like to be, but I'm alright."

"Let me know what the hospital bill comes to. I'll take care of it."

Well, I wished I would've known that sooner. "I've got it covered. Thank you, though."

"If you change your mind, give me a call. What's the name of this officer you want me to give confirmation to?"

"Derek Ames. Let me grab his number for you."

Putting the phone on speaker, I sifted through my recents and read it aloud to her. Once she repeated it back to me, I brought the phone back to my ear and confirmed she'd gotten it right.

"Perfect, I'll call right away. But there's one thing I don't understand."

"What's that?"

"The state police in your county are opening the investigation. Why didn't the police in mine?"

A valid question, and a valid point.

One more stone I hadn't seen the bottom of yet.

"Steven's accident happened here, so it's their jurisdiction. Considering Steven had taken his files home, and that after the hit and run, someone broke into his home and stole the files, that's probable cause for a warrant. Whatever's in those files is what got Steven run over."

"Huh." Evelyn was quiet for a moment. "Have you relayed this to Fitz?"

"I haven't." And I didn't want to. Now that I was up against a wall, I wanted to do a deep dive into that man. "For the time being, could you keep all this quiet, too?"

"I already have," Evelyn said. "Ashley and I have talked briefly about what you've found, but I haven't shared information outside of that."

Ashley Harper was not a concern. If she played any part in what happened to Quinn, she wouldn't have given Evelyn my number.

"Thanks," I said. "Just let me know when you get confirmation on those files, alright?"

"Of course. Thanks again, Maddie. Take it easy today."

Judging by the look Bentley was giving me from the other side of the table, I didn't have a choice. "Will do," I said, exchanging a few more pleasantries before ending the call.

* * *

"She gonna get you those records?" Bentley asked.

"She is," I said. "So I guess I'm gonna sit around twiddling my thumbs 'til then."

"Your body'll thank you for the break." He smiled. "When we're done eating, I'm gonna run over to my mom's. She needs help with a few things around the house. She mentioned you last week. Said it'd be nice to see you if you wanna come."

Julia Roycroft had been one of the shining lights in my life as a kid.

She may've been married to a scummy man, but she was a wonderful person. Always had dinner on the table, always made sure her kids had decent clothes—even bought me things from time to time and made sure to let me look through Phoebe's hand-me-downs before donating them.

Bentley's mom was the best role model I'd had back then. Spending some time with her would be lovely. But I was a wreck. There was a bullet wound in my arm, I stunk of mud from the forest I'd trudged through last night, and my hair desperately needed washing.

"Maybe another time." I asked. "I think you're right about the machine thing."

He made a face at that.

"That's what you said last night. I'm not a machine." Smiling, I shrugged. "And you're wrong, because I *am* a machine. But even machines go out of service for maintenance. I'm gonna go home and rest a bit."

"That makes more sense," Bentley said. "That's wise of you."

"I thought so."

But I didn't plan on *only* resting.

There was information on Jerry Fitz somewhere. I had to find it.

Chapter 25

Bentley wouldn't let me leave until he checked my wound. No signs of infection. Insisted I should still see a doctor, but I waved him off.

Tempest needed a walk, so I took her out when Bentley left. I stayed in my neighbor's driveway, keeping my eyes peeled for any suspicious vehicles. Not to my surprise, I saw none. Like I'd thought before, the trailer park was too busy for mystery guy to follow me here.

When we made it home, Tempest pranced to her crate and plopped down on her belly. Panting and exhausted, she smiled up at me.

I was quite proud of her.

Tempest's entrance to my life had been a rough one. She had her own host of trauma and survival behaviors when she'd arrived, but she'd come a long way. It was about time she got what was missing from that crate.

Rolling onto my tiptoes, struggling at the linen closet, I grabbed the pile of linen I'd tucked up there last week. Holding it in my good arm, I walked back to the living room. "Look what I got."

Tempest's head perked up, cocking to the side.

Sitting on the couch, I laid the massive pile of plush at my feet. "Come."

Tempest did, sniffing as she approached.

I patted the purple, memory foam dog bed. "Come."

Tail wagging, Tempest hopped onto it and spun in a few circles. Sniffing, roughing it up with her paws, her tail wagged faster and faster.

"Yeah, it's yours," I said. "But you try guarding it, and it's going right back where it came from."

Tempy paid me no mind. With excitement, she whirled around a couple of times. Then plopped onto her back and rolled from side to side.

I laughed. "Do you like it?"

"A-woo-woo," she howled, still lying on her back, tongue flopping from the side of her mouth.

"I mean it, little girl." Reaching down to scratch her head, I kept my voice firm. "You better be good."

She resumed rolling from side to side.

That dog bed had been sitting in the closet for a while now. I would've loved to give it to her sooner, but when I'd gotten her, Tempy had a serious problem with resource guarding. If I hadn't been cautious, she may've taken off my hand for a jacket I'd left lying on the couch a few times in the beginning.

Rules had been established early on. Tempest wasn't allowed on the couch. She didn't have unlimited access to her toys. As soon as she was done playing with them, they got put up in a basket on a high shelf. Not once had I given her any type of treat that'd take her a substantial amount of time to eat, like a bone, because she would've guarded it. There'd been an incident with her food bowl once early on as well, so I'd hand fed her for a while. When I transitioned to letting her eat from a bowl on her own again, I moved the bowl as soon as she was done, so she understood it wasn't hers.

To date, Tempy hadn't guarded her crate. But she did sleep in it. She spent a lot of time in it when we were at home, in fact, and I always felt bad when I saw her lying on that cold plastic tray.

It wasn't what I wanted, but Tempest was dangerous. A big dog with the ability and training to attack. If I hadn't gotten those behaviors under control, and she broke off her leash, or if she mauled a guest, her life was at risk. It was better she was uncomfortable on that plastic tray than buried in the backyard.

I'd done it though. I'd gotten Tempest under control. This dog was the light of my life lately. Her personality was big and bold, and I loved every second I had with her.

So long as she didn't attempt to guard this bed, it'd be an added amenity to her crate.

Leaning back on the couch, I smiled down at Tempy as she pawed at the bed, rolling from side to side. I grabbed my icepack from the side table and tightened the elastic band around my bicep to fix it in place. With my good hand, I set my laptop on my thighs, adjusting my arm on a throw pillow.

Just as I opened my browser, my phone rang.

Struggling to reach it on the coffee table, Ox's name lit up the screen. This would be a fun conversation.

"Hey, what's up?" I answered.

"Just checking in," he said. "How's that case coming along?"

After a huff of annoyance, I explained everything I'd gathered since we last spoke. It wasn't a surprise when he said, "You got *shot?*"

"It's a graze. Bentley took care of it. I'm fine."

"He should've taken you to the damn hospital."

"In his defense, he tried."

Ox growled his frustration. "Where are you?"

"On my couch. Safe. Healthy. Fine. I'm just doing research today. Don't worry."

"I will worry." A sweet sentence, but somehow it came out sharper than a blade. "You need to go to the hospital."

"Not happening."

"I'll call an ambulance myself if you don't—"

"And I'll deny care, as is my legal right." Putting the phone on speaker, I laid it down and typed Jerry Fitz into my browser. "I can't afford it, Ox. If it gets bad, if it gets infected, I'll get it looked at. But there's nothing they can do for me that Bentley didn't."

Another sound that I could only describe as a growl.

"Seriously, I'm fine."

In Bedford County, I saw no results for Jerry Fitz. Jerald Fitz, maybe?

Ox sighed on the other end. "Are you alone right now?"

"Tempest is chilling on her new bed." At the mention of her name, Tempy shot up, tilting her head from side to side again. I gave her ear a scratch. "Why?"

"Because Tempest can't call 911 if you go into shock."

"You don't go into shock a day after the trauma, Ox."

"If you start losing blood again, you can," he said. "And with a wound like that, gangrene can set in within forty-eight hours."

I rolled my eyes. "I'm not developing gangrene."

"You could be."

"You're insane."

"And you're reckless." Like always, that tone was as rough as the jagged edge of shattered glass. "I'm coming over."

"No, you're not."

"Yes, I am." A car horn sounded in the background. "I'm halfway there, anyway. I was at that farmer's market in Westmoreland. You can't be alone right now."

There was literally nothing wrong with being alone in my current state. My vitals were fine. The wound was manageable, and it hurt far less than my knee. Being first aid certified meant I knew the warning signs to watch out for.

More than that, I didn't want to sit beside Ox on this couch. As nice as it'd been to stake out Steven's apartment with him, I didn't want to feel the way I had when he asked about going out.

Not after all those flutters and spins in my stomach last night with Bentley.

There was no potential with Ox. He wanted something I couldn't give him. Yes, there were unresolved feelings, but they meant nothing. I couldn't *let* them mean anything. It wasn't happening. Forgiving and forgetting was out of the question.

I didn't know what I wanted to do about the feelings I was developing for Bentley, but I knew it wasn't fair to let Ox think there was a chance.

Spending time together, on my couch, completely private, wasn't a good idea.

"Ox, I'm fine. Really," I insisted. "You don't need to—"

"Well, I am. I'm grabbing food too. I'll see you soon."

He hung up.

Gritting my teeth, I dropped my phone to the couch.

* * *

Ox arrived about half an hour later with takeout in hand from a Chinese restaurant I loved. Telling him to leave was useless. He was as stubborn as me. In his mind, I was in danger, and there was no convincing him otherwise.

Which was fair. No matter how rocky our relationship had been, I wouldn't let him be alone after getting shot, either. And as much as I hated admitting it, the hand he lent when I was struggling to get on and off the couch made life easier.

With the TV playing in the background, we relaxed on the sofa, talking circles around each other about the case. Flipping through Quinn's annotated copy of *The Strange Case of Dr. Jekyll and Mr. Hyde*, we dissected every note she'd left, just like we had the other night. My fingers were crossed, praying we'd catch something we'd missed, but nothing stuck out to either of us.

This was what we'd done back in the day. When Ox had gotten stuck, when whatever case he was working on had no obvious culprit, we'd talk through it. Although, talking *at* one another was a better way of phrasing it. I'd toss out an idea, and he'd explain why it didn't work. He'd blurt a missing piece, and I'd point to the spot in the paperwork that showed we'd already explored every avenue that it led to.

It was a loop. An entertaining one, but a frustrating one in a case like this.

"Ya know what I keep coming back to?" Ox said, squinting at all the notes laid out on the coffee table.

"What's that?"

He flicked through the papers, then scooched closer, clicking open my laptop. Once he was in my photos, he zoomed in on the one of Quinn's bedroom window. Or rather, the note left on it. "This doesn't compute in my brain."

"Me neither, but it can't be a coincidence."

"I don't think it is, either. Especially considering"—he flipped to the photos Betty sent me from her last cleaning—"this. The photo was taken three days before Quinn was killed. But why? How?"

Huh. A valid point. "Quinn wrote it there, but if she could write a message on the window, why couldn't she get to the door?"

"Hell, why couldn't she shove a finger down her throat to induce vomiting? If someone had just shoved a bunch of pills down my throat, that's what I would've done."

"Unless she was tied up," I said. "She would've had to have been."

"So, how did she write it?"

He nibbled his lip in thought, clicking around on my keyboard until he was back at the image of the Quinn's bedroom just after Betty had cleaned it.

"The chair's directly beside the window." I pointed to it. "So if she was tied up there, she might've tried getting out."

"Hence the dent in the wall."

"Maybe she used her nose?"

Ox's face told me he didn't understand.

"Think about it. She's tied up, can't get out of the chair, realizes she's dying, and leans in to blow on the glass and fog it up," I said. "Then she uses the tip of her nose to spell out a message."

Understanding, Ox nodded, still studying the image. "But why say *this*? Why say 'I love you, Mom?' Why not spell out her killer's name?"

"True, but if she was high and short on time before he came back in, maybe that was what was on her mind. In her final moments, she wanted to make sure her mom knew she loved her."

Dropping his chin to his hand, Ox studied the image a moment longer. He shook his head. "Maybe. But my gut says this means something."

My gut said it all meant something. Everything laid out on the table before me carried a meaning I couldn't decipher. Like I was missing a chunk of the story.

"Okay, we need to recenter." Ox flipped the laptop shut, collected all my notes into a pile, and flipped them face down. "Ten-minute break, then we go back with fresh eyes."

"Yeah, good idea." I reached for my cup on the edge of the coffee table and gritted my teeth when the pull of the stitches stung across my bicep. "Can you pass me that fortune cookie?"

He did, even tore the packaging open for me. "You alright?"

"I'm good." Breaking the cookie in half, I let the scrap of paper fall to my lap. "It doesn't hurt unless I move the wrong way and put tension on the stitches."

"A sling might help."

"A sling will also make me immobile. I'm fine. Really. The wound's not that bad."

Shaking his head, he smiled.

I wasn't used to that. Mostly the part where Ox smiled, but also his presence feeling so casual. It used to.

Sitting on the sofa, or at the kitchen island, had felt like the most natural thing in the world. For the last year, just his face had made my jaw tighten and my heart lodge in my throat. The smile he wore now wasn't quite as comforting as it once had been, but it still brought me a wave of familiarity that I hated to admit I'd missed.

"What're you smiling about?" I asked.

"You," he said.

"What about me?"

"How far you've come. Everything you've accomplished. This. This job you turned into a business, into a career." The smile stayed. "You've worked really hard to get here, and you're kicking ass."

I laughed. "A bullet went through me last night, I've got no leads, and I'm still kicking ass?"

"You are." From Ox, I would've expected a backhanded compliment, or a smartass remark, but there was no condescension in his voice. "You almost got within arm's reach of the guy. We both know that means you're close."

"God, I hope so."

"You're gonna get him. I know you will. Everything you've been doing, everything you've accomplished since you moved here, there's no way you're gonna let this bastard get away. I believe in you. And I'm proud of you." Damn it. Damn him and damn those butterflies. "Thanks for letting me help, by the way. I've missed going back and forth with you like this."

"It's always what we were best at."

"I wouldn't say that." A smirk. "We were great at what we did during our ten-minute breaks, too."

As much as I hated the heat that rose to my cheeks, he wasn't wrong. We used to pause our research or brainstorming session, get something to eat, then a casual kiss would turn into a bit of physical stress release. The kind that only couples could give one another.

It usually did the trick. Our heads were clear after the endorphin rush. We'd get back to work with level minds, and we were far more productive.

I laughed. "Usually turned into more than a ten-minute break."

"You never complained."

"Neither did you."

Smiling, Ox looked me over. "Those were the days."

"That they were." I smiled back, and it felt effortless. It didn't hurt either. This conversation should've hurt, but it didn't. Not really. "For what it's worth, we're a good team either way."

Ox's blue eyes twinkled as he looked me over. Like that sentence melted him.

And then he leaned in.

Chapter 26

I DON'T KNOW WHY I DIDN'T PULL AWAY.

Maybe because it felt casual. Effortless. Just like the rest of today had. Maybe because that was the first time Lennox Taylor said he was proud of me. Despite the way things had turned out between us, it brought me a pathetic amount of joy to hear that everything I'd worked so hard for made him respect me.

When his lips touched mine, when his hand found my cheek, all those feelings I'd buried tore their way out of me. Holding his jaw, breathing in that signature sage cologne of his, a wave of familiarity, of comfort, washed over me.

For a second, I was back where I'd been a year ago. We weren't in a trailer. We were in his condo. It wasn't Tempest at my feet, but Bear. I was at peace, certain about what came next for me. There was a wedding in my future, and a house in the suburbs with a wraparound porch, and an acre of land for Bear to run through. My job, my income, was stable. All my limbs worked like they were made to. Everything made sense.

Everything was *right*.

Then Ox came in closer, edging me backward onto the sofa, and pain shot from my knee up my thigh.

And it all came back.

That bullet tearing through my leg. Burying Bear. Those texts on Ox's phone. Packing my bags. Overdosing. Moving into this trailer.

All the pain, the drama, the chaos that had led to this moment.

Just as Ox reached for the bottom of my shirt, I caught his hand. Eyes still shut, I tugged away and shook my head.

He was still over me, breaths uneven. Releasing my shirt, I heard the remorse in his voice when he whispered, "I'm sorry."

The air was thick as he straightened on the other side of the couch. Sitting up, grimacing at the pain in my knee from the angle, I cleared my throat. "That shouldn't have happened."

"I know. I got lost in the moment." He didn't meet my gaze. "I'm sorry."

"It's okay." Adjusting my clothes, I cleared my throat again. "I shouldn't have kissed you back."

Nibbling his lip, he still avoided my gaze. "Because of him?"

"What?"

Finally turning to look at me, he made a vague half nod toward Bentley's trailer. "Are you two together?"

"No. Nothing like that."

"You're a shit liar."

"I'm a great liar, thanks, but I'm not lying."

At least, not completely.

Bentley was part of the reason I stopped that kiss before it could become anything more. Ox felt familiar, but Bentley felt familiar in a different way. A safer way.

Bentley had never hurt me.

Ox had.

Ox's jaw tightened, and he got quiet again.

"It'd be easier if you were right," I said. "It'd be so much easier if my childhood best friend swooped me onto his white horse. It'd be easier for you too, wouldn't it? Because then you could blame him." My tone got more defensive with every word I spoke. "Because then it'd be simple. He'd be the bad guy who stole your chance. But that's not it, Ox. It's because of you, damn it. I don't want to let you in again because of what *you* did. Because I can't trust you. I love you, but I can't trust you. I'm not gonna put myself through that."

"I wouldn't do it again, Maddie." While my tone was aggressive, his was a plea. "If you'd just give me a chance, I wouldn't mess it up again. I wouldn't."

"But you *did!*" Tempest jolted at the volume my voice raised to, and I forced my tone to ease. "You already messed up, Ox. I told you the other day, I don't want what you want. I want you in my life, but I don't want to be with you. I'm sorry if that hurts, but these are the consequences of your actions, and it isn't fair to make me feel guilty for that."

Once more, he grew quiet, only holding my gaze. I couldn't be sure, but it almost looked like tears were forming. Finally, he said, "You're right. I'm sorry."

This time, I didn't say it was okay.

I nodded to the door. "I think you should go."

Pressing his lips together, he craned down to pet Tempest, stood, and walked to the door. When he grabbed the handle, he looked at me over his shoulder. "If I could go back in time and stop it from happening, I would."

I said nothing.

Once he walked outside and the door clicked shut, I wished I would've said what I felt. That if we did have a time machine, I wouldn't change a damn thing.

Except for Bear. I'd save Bear if I had the chance.

Cheating may've been one of Ox's biggest regrets, but it had led me to where I was. And I was proud of the Maddie Castle I'd become. I was proud of my career, and my trailer, and how hard I'd worked on my body after the injury.

The facts were simple.

Ox and I weren't meant to be. The most fun the two of us ever had was picking apart a case together. All we ever had in common was our career.

Bentley and I had fun every time we were in each other's presence. We had the deep, heart to heart conversations Ox's shield of steel wouldn't allow. Ox wanted to mute the colors on our wedding cake, and he wouldn't let me put pink anywhere in the decor of his condo aside from that tiny powder room. But Bentley liked my floral wallpaper. He got me a pink treadmill.

When Ox told me not to work so hard, Bentley acknowledged that I had to work harder than everyone else, and he cheered me on as I did.

I didn't know if Bentley wanted what I wanted. I didn't know if risking our friendship was worth it. But if I was gonna fall for any man in my life, it would be him.

Shaking that off, I lifted my laptop to my thighs.

Ox and I had scoured Fitz's social media page. A mutual friend of Ox's and Fitz's lent Ox his password so we could see all Fitz's private posts. We hadn't found anything.

But there had to be something.

Once I got his full name, Jerald Edward Fitz, and came back with nothing suspicious, I plugged his name into a background checker. The website cost a hundred and fifty bucks a month for the yearly membership, but I considered it a good investment. At least it was a write off.

That was when I found his address.

And his previous address.

The last one was a small house in the suburbs. When I searched the address itself, I found it on a realty website. The listing was inactive now, but the landing page description was clear.

HANDYMAN'S DREAM!

This two bed, one and a half bath is move in ready. Minor updates may be necessary, but it's got great bones! Cash only.

Foreclosure

Huh. Foreclosure. So he'd defaulted on his mortgage. Why? Where was he living now?

Typing his new address into Google Maps for a street view, my eyes widened.

This place wasn't a house. It was a damn mansion, not much different than Evelyn's home. From the street view, I could hardly make it out through the thick foliage, but what I could see made it very clear that this place was not the sort a cop could afford.

Not without help, at least.

After scanning a few dozen websites, trying to figure out how to hunt down lien and deed information, I found it on the county tax assessor website.

When the second owner's name appeared on the screen, something clicked.

Carlyle Moore.

Somewhere, I'd seen that name. I couldn't remember where, and I knew I hadn't interviewed him.

I typed into my search engine, *Carlyle Moore Bedford County*. A dozen articles came up, all of which praised him.

Local Author Carlyle Moore Gets Six-Figure Publishing Deal
Best-Selling Author Carlyle Moore
Professor Carlyle Moore Wins $50,000 in Writing Competition
Professor.

Carlyle Moore was Quinn's English Literature professor.

According to the first article I found, Carlyle Moore married his high school sweetheart fresh out of college. Carlyle Moore was in his mid-fifties, roughly six feet tall judging by the photos, fit for his age, and as much as I hated to admit it, a good-looking man. Judging by the way he held his hand around the journalist's waist in the photo, the kind of attractive, rich man who loved having a young, pretty girl on his arm.

My blood was boiling by the time I clicked back to Fitz's social media page. Sure enough, when I searched for Carlyle Moore, there he was on Fitz's friends' list. Fitz stood beside him with pride at their thirty-year high school reunion, a wife on either of their arms. After a moment of flipping through Carlyle's photos, I found one of him and his wife Cheryl, parked before a beautiful lake.

They posed against a shiny black sedan with window tint so dark, there was no way to see inside.

Teeth pressed so tightly together, I wasn't sure how they didn't shatter, I grabbed Quinn's phone and began flipping through her schedule.

Sure enough, she'd been in his class every Wednesday.

I noticed, however, that when I typed *Moore* in the search bar, all the way back in December, Quinn had Saturday evenings blocked out. *Tutoring with Prof. Moore.*

Fingers crossed he was holding a session tonight.

"Ya wanna go for a ride, Tempy?"

Chapter 27

QUINN HAD A MAP SAVED ON HER PHONE LISTING EACH PROFESSOR'S name and location, so I knew where I was headed when I made it to the college. Carlyle's light was the only one still shining as I walked down the hall. Voices echoed off the high ceilings, bouncing from the linoleum underfoot to the wainscoting-covered walls.

When I got to his door, gun clasped in my hoodie pocket, I gritted my teeth at the small gathering of students packing their bags. Eleven, if I counted correctly. One of them was a guy. The other ten were girls.

Quinn was an honor's student. Why the hell did she need tutoring? Unless this wasn't tutoring. Extra credit, maybe? An opportunity for Carlyle to spend more time with his favorite pupils?

If nothing else, there was no denying that each of them fit his type. As they stood, collecting their belongings, I noted the similarities that every single one of them had to Quinn. Not a single blonde. All around Quinn's height. Each of them sharing the same body type, even. Thin. Little curves through their waists. Small busts and small butts.

They all looked young. Just as Quinn had. If I didn't know better, I'd say that every one of them were minors.

I couldn't release my tight jaw as they brushed past me.

As Carlyle packed up his briefcase while the last of the students left,

I tapped on the doorframe. He looked up. And I saw what Quinn had seen.

A friendly, almost fatherly smile. Kind hazel eyes. A strong jaw and confidence through his broad shoulders. The aesthetic was attractive too. Nice slacks, a fancy button-down, covered in an expensive black jacket.

"Can I help you?" Carlyle asked.

"I believe you can." Walking toward his desk, I held out my business card. "I'm investigating the death of one of your students."

Not even a flinch.

"Maybe it was last semester." I held out a photo of Quinn on my phone. "Quinn Barnes?"

"That's right." He frowned, and it didn't look even the slightest bit genuine. "Yes, it was last semester. Such a shame. She was bright."

"That's what everyone keeps telling me." My hand tightened on my gun. "Would you be able to tell me a bit about the type of student Quinn was? Anything about her that you remember?"

"She did very well in my class," he said. "She was quiet, though. We didn't talk much."

"Huh." I tilted my head to the side. "Why did she come to tutoring sessions if she did very well already?"

"Oh." He laughed half-heartedly. "Well, she'd gotten a poor grade when class first started. This was extra credit."

I bet it was.

"I see." Glancing him over, I watched the vein in his neck throb just a little bit faster. Behind his head, centered on a bookstand, rested a copy of *The Strange Case of Dr. Jekyll and Mr. Hyde.* I nodded to it. "That a part of your curriculum?"

Turning to look at it, he shook his head. "No, just a favorite of mine."

"Hey, it was Quinn's favorite, too." My chuckle was as phony as his. "Guess you guys had that in common."

The lighthearted look in his eyes fading, he pushed up his glasses. "Interesting. But is that all? My wife's waiting for me."

"I'm sure she's used to that."

"Excuse me?" He furrowed his brows. "What are you implying?"

"You know what I'm implying. And so does the State Police Chief. I called him on my way here."

That wasn't true, although I wished I had.

Carlyle snorted. "I have no idea what you're talking about, but I don't have time for this."

When he started past me, I sidestepped into his path. "Quinn's therapist is lying in a hospital bed after getting hit by a car that looks a hell of a lot like yours. So, you gonna keep lying, Professor? Or are you going to explain it to the police chief? The one who isn't willing to cover up your affair."

Mouth falling open, head shaking. "I didn't kill anyone. I certainly didn't hit anyone with my car. You can have a look at it on your way out. It's just outside this door. My name's on the parking spot."

I wasn't sure I believed that, but his shock seemed genuine. "But you were sleeping with Quinn Barnes."

His jaw tightened.

"Look, you say it to me or I have my friend bring you in for questioning," I snapped. "Were you having an affair with Quinn Barnes?"

Carlyle let out a careful, shaking sigh. "It stopped well before she passed."

I knew that much. "When did it begin?"

Jaw taut, frustration evident through his demeanor, Carlyle walked to his desk and sat in his chair. "Shortly after class began in the fall."

"Why did you break up with her?"

"I didn't." The look he gave me said he found it offensive that I'd even suggest such a thing. "Quinn did. Every time she broke things off, she said it was because she felt guilty."

"Not because you told her you were gonna leave your wife for her and had no plans of actually doing that?"

Carlyle traced his tongue along his teeth. "She said what we were doing was wrong, and she didn't feel right doing that to another woman."

Apparently, he wouldn't answer the original question. "I'm gonna need to talk to her."

His face screwed up in confusion. "I'm sorry?"

"Your wife. The two of you are prime suspects," I said. "You had the most to gain from Quinn's death. You get to conceal your reputation, and your wife gets to keep her cushy life."

"I didn't kill Quinn." He shook his head. "I wasn't even in town when she died. My wife wasn't either. Even so, my wife has far more to gain if she'd just filed for a divorce. The prenup would mean nothing with evidence of an affair."

"You got proof of that? That you weren't in town?"

"Yes. Yes, of course." Sliding his phone from his jacket pocket, he clicked around for a moment. When he handed it over, photos of Carlyle and Cheryl lit up the screen. They were at a resort restaurant, sparkling blue waters drifting behind them. "We were in Florida that entire weekend. Check the timestamps. I swear, we wouldn't have been able to kill her."

"Guess so." I handed him his phone. "But you made sure your buddy Fitz wouldn't open an investigation into Quinn's death."

Tugging at the tie around his neck, he let out another one of those shaking breaths. "He didn't falsify anything. If he believed Quinn was murdered, he would've opened—"

"Bull shit," I snapped. "You begged him not to open a case. You gave him a place to live when he lost his house. He's indebted to you. So even when all the evidence pointed to some sick son of a bitch killing a nineteen-year-old girl you were taking advantage of, he had to choose between being a good man and having a place to live."

"I didn't take advantage of anyone. Quinn was a grown woman—"

"Were you grown at eighteen, Professor?" I grabbed either end of the desk and leaned in. "Was she a *grown woman* eight months before you met her? Did those eight months make her a *grown woman?*"

Teeth tightening to a line, Carlyle leaned back in his seat.

"Yeah. That's what I thought." Straightening, I crossed my arms against my chest. "Did you take drugs with Quinn?"

An eye roll. "No."

"Never?"

"She smoked marijuana in my presence and periodically did ecstasy, but we didn't do them together."

Every word he spoke made me hate him more. "Did you guys have rough sex afterward?"

"I don't see what this has to do with the investigation."

"It'd show me who the son of a bitch was who got her into BDSM, because her bondage equipment was used to tie her up so some sick bastard could shove a fistful of pills down her throat." For the first time through all of this, Carlyle cringed. "So, was it you? Or did someone else show her how to use those things?"

Shutting his eyes, he rubbed the bridge of his nose between his thumb and forefinger. "She was curious. She wanted to try new things."

"So you tied her up and beat her with a paddle?"

He glowered. "Everything we did was—"

"Consensual, right," I said. "Although having sex with someone who's under the influence while you're sober is sexual assault."

Another snort of a laugh. "That wouldn't fly in court."

"That's all you care about, huh?" Narrowing my eyes at him, I tilted my head. "You care more about your colleagues, and your readers, and your wife finding out you're a sadistic predator who takes advantage of young girls, than finding the man who killed your latest prey."

"I'm mourning her death every day." I wished I could say that sounded sincere. "But you come in here accusing me of killing her, and—"

"I *suspected* you of being involved in her death. I accused you of being a pervert and blackmailing your friend to cover up your dirty little secret. But I hope you sleep well tonight knowing that an innocent girl you claimed to care about is dead." Pointing to that book on the shelf behind him, I said, "And I hope you know that's how she saw you. Dr. Jekyll and Mr. Hyde. A good man to most of the world and a monster to anyone who found out who he really was."

Jaw taut, he stayed quiet.

"Have a good night, Professor."

I was at the door when he said, "Wait."

"What?"

"I'd appreciate if you kept what you learned tonight private." Digging in his briefcase for a moment, he pulled out a checkbook. "I'm willing to pay for your discretion."

Something between a scoff and a laugh left me. "Oh my god, you're serious."

"My career is very important to me," he said. "I love my wife. This was a mistake that I wish I could take back."

Sounded eerily similar to someone else I knew.

"Go to hell."

* * *

ALL BUT STOMPING MY WAY OUTSIDE, A MILLION THOUGHTS circled around my mind.

On the way here, it'd all made sense. The theory lined up perfectly.

The creepy professor and best-selling author couldn't have his reputation tarnished by the college girl he was screwing. So when she threatened to come forward, he kills her. He's buddies with the cop who'd be put on the case. As long as he leaves no evidence behind, there won't be an investigation. It all gets written off as an accidental overdose.

But he had an alibi. So did his wife. Timestamped and all.

My entire theory had revolved around finding the mystery man she was dating. It was the most logical. It explained her death better than anything else.

Who else could've had a vendetta against Quinn? Why would anyone want this innocent college girl dead? If not for Steven's accident and hospitalization, I'd explore the possibility that it had something to do with him, maybe that she was having an affair with him as well, but that didn't check out. Even if that were the case, Steven had little to lose if he and Quinn had a relationship. He was unmarried, and although it'd have been inappropriate, there was nothing illegal about the two of them as a couple.

I was back to square one. How the hell was I back to square one?

Every resource available to me was exhausted. There was nowhere else to look, and I was at my wit's damn end.

More so when I walked outside and saw Carlyle's car. Just like he'd said, it was parked before the sign labeled with his name. Examining every inch proved fruitless as well. No scratches. No dings. Nothing to suggest this had been used to plow over a therapist the day prior.

Frustrated, ready to bang my damn head off a wall, I started across the parking lot to my SUV. None of this made any sense. Was I looking at this from the wrong angle? Was it possible that Carlyle was responsible, after all?

Maybe he'd hired a hitman. Was that melodramatic? Possibly, but if Cheryl would get fifty percent of his assets in a divorce, it could make sense. Although, whoever did this, Quinn let inside the house. So it had to have been someone she knew.

Worth exploring, at least. Derek could get a warrant to look through Carlyle's financial records.

Sliding my phone from my hoodie pocket to give him a call, the rev of an engine sounded.

Or rather, the *purr* of an engine.

A headlight shined to my right.

Only fifty yards away.

And getting closer by the second.

I morphed my trot across the mostly vacant parking lot to a sprint. The headlights turned in my direction.

Shit, shit, shit.

Chapter 28

Sprint wasn't the right word. Given my knee, sprinting was out of the question. It was more of a fast, limping waddle.

Headlights rushing closer, I ducked between a cluster of cars.

The roar of a crash sounded, shoving the car at the end into the next. Not enough momentum to push the row of vehicles together. Good thing, too, or I would've gotten sandwiched between them.

Lifting my head just far enough to see the vehicle, heart pounding against my ribs, I watched him gun it in reverse.

Which I thought meant he'd peel tires out of here.

Instead, he put it in drive and slammed on the gas.

I ran.

Not a limping waddle, but a run to the next row. I didn't look behind me, but the clunk and crunch of metal on metal made it clear he was attempting to crush me between those vehicles.

My car was right there, only a dozen yards ahead.

He must've seen me running, because the squeal of tires spinning rang out behind me.

Feet slapping the concrete, so adrenaline filled that I felt no pain, I yanked my gun from my hoodie pocket, aimed in the general direction of the car, and fired. Glass shattered, screaming through the quiet night.

But I must not have hit the driver. As soon as I made it to the driver's side of my car, the black sedan gunned it out of the parking lot.

"Not again, you son of a bitch." I jammed my key into the ignition, turned it over, and pressed on the gas.

He was ahead of me, but not by much. I got a good enough look at him to know that my bullet hit the rear passenger window before he flew onto the country road.

I was only behind him by a few hundred feet, just far enough to miss his plates as he rushed around the bends. But I knew these roads too, and he wasn't getting away from me this time.

Instructing the voice command on my phone to call Derek, I pressed hard on the gas. He answered on the third ring.

"What's going on, kid?"

"I'm chasing him," I said, taillights visible through the foliage some hundred yards ahead. Relaying the route I was onto Derek came next. "This road leads to the highway, but it's five miles or so. If you get a block set up there, you'll get him."

"Hang on." He spoke into his radio, mostly incoherent rambles for a moment.

The road coiled to an S for the next mile, and my car didn't like it, nearly tipping sideways on the first turn. Feeling my tires skid out before gaining traction again, there was no choice in the matter. I had to slow down.

As I did, his taillights faded.

But this road was uphill, winding, and there were no ways off it until the mountaintop. I could catch up on the straightaways.

Or so I hoped.

Gassing it on the next clear patch, Tempest whimpered in the back seat.

"Floor," I told her.

In my rearview, I watched her hop to the floorboards.

That was a neat little trick I'd taught her.

I had a seat belt for her as well, but in an accident, it was very easy for a dog's neck to get caught in that seatbelt and die of suffocation before the driver could get to them. Aside from that, if she was stuck in a leash and we were in a highway accident, I'd have a hell of a time untangling the mess before I could keep the car from getting hit again.

So I had her lie on the floor between the front and back seat. She could get hurt in an accident there too, but it gave her the most stability.

Approaching the next bend in the S, I slammed the brake and cut it with just enough momentum to keep from tipping, swerving into the opposite lane to do so.

The taillights were in my line of vision again.

Ahead was a straightaway to the mountaintop.

Suddenly, he cut the wheel to the right.

Both straight and right led to the highway. He must've been banking on me not knowing that.

Or maybe he was desperate for an escape, no matter how.

This time, he wasn't getting away.

"Alright, I got a couple guys out that way," Derek said. "You still haven't got the plates?"

"You know how it is around these damn bends." I cut to the right. "I'm trying though. I got his rear window."

"You broke his window?"

"I sure did. Shot it, actually."

Derek chuckled. "I didn't hear that."

"I mean, I noticed his rear window was missing. I've still got eyes on him."

"I've got a guy five minutes from you," he said. "We'll get him. But you be careful, kid."

The timing couldn't have been more ironic. When I made it to the foot of the hill, struggling to see on the dim country roads, I was only a few yards away when I realized it wasn't the guy's taillight, but a reflector on a guardrail.

Cutting the wheel to the left, slamming on the brake, I swerved into the opposite lane. My tires spun out, traction lost. Jarred to the left, and then to the right, I fought to regain control.

But before I knew it, there was a tree directly in front of me, and no matter how hard I pressed on the brakes, I didn't have time to stop.

Instinctively, I shut my eyes.

Just as my front end came to a sudden halt.

Body slamming into the steering wheel, my head clunked against the driver's side window.

"Maddie." Derek's voice came from the phone's speaker, now laying on the floor. "Maddie, are you okay?"

"I'll live." Prayed I could say the same for my car. Turning to look in the back seat, wincing at the pain in my shoulder, I checked over Tempest on the floorboards of the back seat. She was panting hard, anxious, but safe. Looking out her window, I watched the red taillights disappear down the road. "I just hit a tree."

"Are you—"

"Yeah, I'm fine, but I don't think my car is. Damn it. Don't let your guys lose him, Derek. I was so close, and now—"

"And now you need to take a breather," he said. "Let me call EMS and get someone out there."

"Don't waste the resources." Finding my phone on the floor, I opened my door. Once I'd hopped out, I let Tempy out and flicked on the flashlight on my phone. "I'll have a friend come get me. Just get that son of a bitch."

* * *

THE DAMAGE WAS BAD. MY ENTIRE FRONT END WAS SMASHED. NOT just the fender, or the bumper, but a solid two feet back.

This car was worth about three grand. I had no doubt that the repairs would cost at least that much. Probably closer to five.

Practically stomping my feet, I called Bentley. He answered on the second ring. "Hey, you."

"Hey. Any chance you could come pick me up?"

"Uh, sure. I thought you had your car."

"I do. And it's wrapped around a tree."

"What?"

Running my fingers through my hair, I rolled my head back and let out a deep breath. "Yeah, not where I saw my night going, either."

After we went back and forth on the "Are you okay?" conversation for several minutes, I sat on the muddy ground with Tempy. Taking a moment to examine her closer, petting her to soothe her fast breaths, I found no signs of injury. She wasn't limping and had no obvious cuts.

Tempy and I were far enough from the road that I wasn't worried for our safety, but I still tucked us as far from the concrete as I could. Made sure to turn the high beams on, too, to hopefully ward off any wildlife in the woods.

Bentley insisted I stay on the phone with him while I waited, so I explained the evening that'd led me here while he drove. It was about a twenty-five minute trip when following the speed limit. Evidently, Bentley did not follow the speed limit, because he arrived in fifteen.

Once Tempy and I climbed into his truck, he spent the next five minutes examining a small cut on my forehead and checking my vitals with the emergency first aid kit he kept on the floorboards. Why the man felt he needed to carry a blood pressure machine was beyond me, but it was endearing.

When I asked if he was done with me, and if we could go home now, he said, "You don't wanna wait for the tow truck?"

"The insurance company said they can't get anyone out here until morning. I already reported it to Derek, so it'll be fine 'til then." At least in the sense that I wouldn't get ticketed for it. "God, this sucks."

Shifting his truck into drive, he looked in both directions before merging onto the roadway. "Insurance is gonna cover it though, right?"

An ironic laugh left me. "I'd be an idiot to pay for full coverage on that thing."

Eyes softening, Bentley frowned. "Shit, I'm sorry. Do you need someone to co-sign a new one for you? I've got good credit."

"That's sweet of you. I'm sure I can figure something out, though." Lips flapping together in a trill, I glanced at him, noting his flannel pajamas. Contrary to his usual sneakers, he wore a pair of old man slippers.

In a different context, I'd tease him about those. "I'm sorry if I woke you."

"You didn't," he said. "Grace is still at that friend's house, so I was bored today, anyway."

Given the puffiness of his eyes, and that half of his face was a bit swollen, as though he'd been sleeping on it, I knew the first half of that was a lie to keep me from feeling guilty. "Still. I appreciate it."

Shooting me a smile, he clicked on his turn signal as we approached the main road. "Anyway. The guy tried to run you over?"

"Yup. In the college parking lot. But I know for damn sure that there are cameras. One of them had to have caught the guy. Derek's working on it."

"Why would he take that risk? He's been cautious until now, right?"

"I guess he thinks I'm getting too close and wanted to get rid of me." Chewing my lip, I turned toward the window. "I'm not. I don't have shit on the guy."

"Maybe you are," he said. "Maybe there's something that's just come to light that's gonna point you to him."

"But I haven't gotten any new evidence since the chaos last night."

"Maybe he thinks you saw him?"

"Nah, his mask never came off."

"Maybe he cut himself in the wood on a thorn or something? Thinks you have his DNA?"

"If he was dumb, I could see that. But it'd be useless unless I had his scent for Tempy to search for."

"Shoe print, maybe?"

"I guess it's possible, but given how organized he is, I guarantee he bought those shoes specifically for last night and burned them as soon as he was done with them."

Bentley exhaled. "I don't know then. You're the detective."

I laughed. "Hey, I welcome another set of eyes. Throw out anything you've got."

"That's about all I can think of." Easing on the brake as we approached a red light, he forced a smile my way. "Was Ox any help?"

This afternoon, Bentley had texted to ask if I wanted anything in particular for dinner. I'd told him not to worry because Ox came over to help me work on the case and had brought food.

Bentley didn't know much about mine and Ox's relationship, but he knew Ox was my ex, and he knew it ended badly. Although I'd never relayed the details, their first meeting had ended with Ox and me in a screaming match. Which didn't paint Ox in a good light.

That forced smile made me wonder, though. Bentley didn't make much of an effort to conceal his contempt for Ox. Now, he was all but gritting his teeth behind that smile.

Was that Bentley's way of asking if the old flame rekindled this afternoon?

To assure him that wasn't the case, I said, "Not really, no."

"Oh?"

"I mean, it was fine, I guess. Mostly just bouncing the same theories back and forth a thousand times. But it got awkward, so I asked him to go home."

"Awkward how?"

Growing quiet, holding his gaze in the glow of the dashboard, I searched for the words. "He wants something I don't."

"He came onto you?"

Was that the right phrasing? That made it out like Ox had forced himself on me. Although he didn't ask for permission first, he didn't shove his tongue down my throat, either.

"There was a kiss. I ended it." Why admitting that felt like admitting I'd cheated was something I'd need to pick apart later. "It's just never gonna work between us. Whatever chance he and I had is long gone, ya know?"

"Why's that?"

Oh boy, the golden question.

I wasn't sure why my cheeks felt hot.

"Because I know where that road leads. It's bumpy, and rough, and it comes to a dead end." My tone was softer now. So were Bentley's eyes. "I don't know. If I'm gonna get back out there, I wanna go down a road that isn't full of potholes and a thousand sharp bends. One that feels safer."

For a moment, Bentley just held my gaze. I wished I could read minds because I thought I knew what he was thinking. I thought he knew what I meant by that. But he didn't lean in to seal the deal.

I wished we weren't both so awkward, specifically when it came to this subject. I wished I were better at talking about my feelings. I wished I could just ask him if we were thinking the same thing.

"Do you think you're ready for that?" Bentley asked. "Getting back out there, I mean?"

Yes. No. Maybe.

I didn't know.

"Are you?" I asked. "It's gotta be harder for you than it is for me, isn't it?"

"I guess." The glow of the red light still shined on his cheek. "Mainly 'cause of Grace. Bella was my world, but she's gone, and I think it's been long enough. Maybe if there was someone Grace liked, and who liked her, and who I liked, I'd be ready to."

Was he talking in code? Was I drawing connections where there weren't any?

I was awful at this. Flirting would be the death of me. I could read people well enough, but with Bentley, it wasn't so easy. He was kind and affectionate with everyone he met. It'd been obvious with Ox. Since he was colder than ice, just the slightest bit of warmth had clarified that he'd wanted more. How could I know if there was any romantic connotation if Bentley didn't make a move?

"I answered. Your turn." Bentley smiled. "Are you ready to get back on the road?"

The light turned green.

That irony wasn't lost on me.

"With the right person," I said. "With someone who wants what I want in life. Someone who respects my career. Someone who likes dogs."

Laughing, he glanced at Tempy in the back seat as he accelerated through the intersection. "You gotta make sure your partner likes dogs, and I've gotta make sure they're cool with a preteen."

"We've each got our hurdles."

"Tempest isn't a hurdle."

"Neither is Grace."

Meeting my gaze, expression tender, he said, "You don't think so?"

"I think any woman would be lucky to have Grace in her life." I paused. "And you're not too bad either."

He laughed. "I hate you."

"You love me."

The look he gave me that time was so damn clear. As if to say, "Yeah, I do. I do love you. So why are we playing this game? Why are we still going back and forth?"

But he didn't. Instead, he said, "As much as it pains me."

To which I laughed and shoved his shoulder. "Go to hell."

"That's where we're both going if you do that again." Chuckling, he yanked the wheel into the right lane, as though I'd made him swerve to the complete opposite side of the road. "Last thing we need is both of our cars totaled."

"You barely touched the yellow lines."

"I *passed* the yellow lines."

"Lies."

"You're the one who's lying."

"Am not!"

Bentley made a *tsk, tsk, tsk,* sound. "Keep telling yourself that."

As my phone dinged, I shot him a universally inappropriate hand signal.

Not sure what I expected the message to be, but it was an email forwarded from Derek.

Not sure how much value this has but check out the notes from 12/8. Stuck out to me when I was leafing through them.

"What is it?" Bentley asked.

"Quinn's records from her sessions with Steven." Scrolling to the one labeled *QuinnBarnes_12/8,* I noted one was an audio recording, another

218

was a transcript with scans of Steven's paper notes. "Do you mind if I play this?"

"Go for it," Bentley said, turning the radio down.

Just as I clicked play, I glanced over Steven's scribbles.

Underlined and circled in red ink, Steven wrote,

Quinn describes him as Dr. Jekyll and Mr. Hyde.

My heart dropped, realizing this was years before she started college.

Chapter 29

"WOULD YOU LIKE TO TALK MORE ABOUT WHAT WE DISCUSSED LAST week, Quinn?" Steven's voice vibrated through the speaker.

Quinn laughed. I couldn't tell if it was uncomfortable or genuine. "Do I have a choice?"

"Hey, I still get paid if we just sit here and make bracelets for the next hour." Steven's tone was softer than when I'd spoken to him. A lot like how Bentley's voice changed when he talked to Grace. "It's up to you, kid."

The rattle of beads sounded in the background. "I mean, everything's fine."

Craning in to listen closer, Bentley pulled off the road into a gas station parking lot. Given the truck's loud rumble obscuring the recording's sound, I appreciated his pulling to a stop.

"Are you sure?" Steven asked. "'Cause the way you said that makes me think it isn't."

Quinn let out a deep breath. "It's just kinda weird, I guess."

"How so?"

"I don't know." She paused. "It isn't that I hate him."

"But you don't like him?"

"I didn't say that."

"Alright. How would you describe how you feel then?"

A long moment of quiet passed, only the ding of plastic hitting plastic as they bound beaded bracelets together. "Sometimes I get sad. And then I get mad. Kinda flips between those two."

"That's the norm when you're mourning."

"I know." Another pause. "It's not like I think Mom moved on too fast or anything. I'm the one who told her to get back out there."

"You want her to be happy."

"I do." Quinn grew silent again. "But I don't get why she had to pick *him*."

"Why do you say that?" Steven asked.

"Because. I don't know. They've only been together for five months. That's, like, half a school year."

"Do you think they're moving too fast?"

"Aren't they? I watch a lot of TV, and couples usually wait a while to move in together. Google says two years. Five months just doesn't feel like long enough."

"Maybe that is a little fast," Steven said. "Have you talked to your mom about it?"

Quinn harumphed. "No."

"Why not?"

"Because she's head over heels for him."

"But she values your opinion, doesn't she?" he asked. "If she knew you didn't like Mark—"

"I didn't say I didn't like him," she said again. "That's not what I mean."

Steven quieted for a few heartbeats, as if to let the conversation temper. "You're right. Those are my words, not yours. What *do* you think of Mark?"

Quinn was silent again. "I think he's using her. Mom was complaining about how hard it is to manage the dealership while working cases, and he stepped right up to take over as manager. Which, okay, fine. He wants to help out. But then he proposes? Not even two weeks later?"

"Do you think that's why he proposed? So he could take over the dealership?"

"Maybe that's not the only reason. But I'm not stupid. The guy was making twenty bucks an hour at a tiny automotive shop. Then he starts dating a widow whose husband owned a car dealership that makes millions in net profit every year. That's anyone's dream opportunity, isn't it?"

"I don't know if I'd say anyone's," Steven said. "But I can see why you'd find that peculiar."

"And she doesn't," Quinn said. "She thinks this guy's a saint."

"Is that all that's bothering you? That you think he's taking advantage of your mom?"

"That's the biggest thing."

"So, what's the small thing?"

A moment of silence. "When Mom isn't around, he's different."

"How so?"

"It's hard to explain." Another long pause, only the clacks of beads tapping together. "Like, when she's there, his voice is soft. Sweet. He has this big smile and he tells jokes, and he laughs all the time.

"But, like, last week, he drove me to school. He was nice and happy when he told Mom he didn't mind. Then we get in the car, and he's a whole different person. My phone was connected to the Bluetooth, and my music was playing. He shut it off and was like, 'I'm so tired of hearing this shit.'

"And then we get to Starbuck's, and he got a black coffee. I ordered my usual, and as we're pulling away from the box, he said something about how my parents spoiled me to let me get a drink with all that in it. It was just a caramel macchiato with extra caramel and extra foam, but he was so mad. I even said I'd pay for it, and he snatched my card out of my hand and said something about that too."

"What'd he say?"

"That 'a teenager doesn't need a damn debit card.' But, like, that's my money. I made it helping Mom with bookkeeping at the dealership. I said that, and he rolled his eyes. We drove in silence the rest of the way. Right after that was when he brought up the whole managing the dealership thing."

"Wow," Steven murmured. "I'd be upset by that too."

"Right? It was mean for no reason. Like he was jealous or something."

"What do you think he's jealous of?"

"I don't know. Maybe because Mom spends so much time with me? Or because my parents have money? And I get it, I guess. I'm sure it sucked growing up without all the opportunities I have, but, like, that's not my fault. And I've never been mean to him, so it was just really rude."

"And you didn't bring this up to your mom?"

"I did, but I don't think I said it right."

"What did you say?"

"That Mark was kinda grumpy when he took me to school." She laughed, with no humor. "I made it sound like he had some road rage."

"And it was a bigger deal than that to you?"

"I think it was a bigger deal altogether, right?" There was genuine questioning in her voice, like she wasn't sure. "I'm not being dramatic for thinking that was, like, really mean?"

"I don't think so," Steven said. "Was that the only time he was like that? Or was it just that one morning?"

"That's when it was the most obvious," Quinn said. "Usually, it's sneakier. Like an eye roll when Mom tells me to grab the laundry she folded, or saying something under his breath when she walks out of the room."

"Wow," Steven said. "That's gotta be really tough. Especially considering how close you were with your dad."

"Yeah." Grief snuck into her voice there. "I've been thinking about that a lot. My dad, he loved reading. His favorite author was Edgar Allan Poe. But he loved sci-fi too. His favorites were Mary Shelley and Robert Louis Stevenson. When I was little, he used to read me *The Strange Case of Dr. Jekyll and Mr. Hyde.* Have you read that?"

"I have. It's a great book."

"It is, but that's who Mark reminds me of. Dr. Jekyll for Mom, and Mr. Hyde for me."

The recording kept going, but my hand was clasped over my mouth in disbelief.

MH. His name was MH in Quinn's contacts, not because his name was Mark Hathway, but because he was Mr. Hyde.

Mark drove a blue sedan, but he owned a car dealership. There were dozens of vehicles at his disposal at any given time.

Stopping the recording, I swiped to my texts with Derek and asked if he could run a check on Mark. Something, anything, that'd confirm he was in this area the day Quinn was killed. Or something that'd connect him to Steven.

"You think it was her stepdad?" Bentley's voice was almost too quiet to hear.

"I don't know, but that's pretty damn suspicious, don't you think?"

"I'd shit myself if my kid said something like that to her therapist about my fiancé," he said, voice still low.

I clicked over to Quinn's contacts, typed the number into mine, and hit the green button.

"Who'd I bitch about my mom's shitty boyfriends to back in the day?"

"Me?"

"Yup. I imagine Quinn bitched to her best friend about Mr. Hyde, too."

Chelsie answered on the third ring. After the greetings, I said, "I just found something odd in Quinn's records. Do you know what Quinn's relationship with her stepfather was like?"

"She tolerated him," Chelsie said. "If that's what you mean."

"Any reason she didn't like him?"

"I mean, outside of him being a general ass?" An awkward half laugh. "Late last year, she got a weird text from him. It said something like, 'can't wait to see you.' He told her it was meant for Evelyn."

"Did Quinn believe that?"

"She didn't bring it up again." Chelsie paused. "Wait. You don't think he hurt her, do you?"

If Quinn found out Mark was having an affair, and she said she was going to tell Evelyn? That was plenty of motive.

"Thanks, Chelsie."

"Wait—"

I ended the call.

"Does she think he did it?" Bentley asked.

"No, didn't cross her mind until I brought it up. But I think he's having an affair, and Quinn found out about it." I dialed Evelyn's number. "Or maybe the bastard's planning to kill his wife, and with Quinn outta the way, he'll get all the life insurance money."

Shaking his head, shocked, Bentley practically held his breath.

"Hello?" Evelyn said in my ear.

"Is Mark home?"

"What?"

"Your husband." My tone sharpened. "Is he home?"

"No. No, he's at the dealership. Why?"

Pointing ahead, I clicked my seatbelt into place. "Get on the highway."

Nodding, Bentley put the truck in drive and hit the gas.

"Where was he last night?"

"I don't understand," Evelyn said. "What're you getting at?"

"Was Mark home last night, Evelyn?" My voice wasn't respectful, and frankly, I didn't care. "Did he come in late?"

She was quiet, thinking. "He said he was at the dealership finishing some paperwork."

I wasn't sure if I was pissed or annoyed that she failed to mention that sooner. "I need you to lock all the doors and get somewhere safe. Somewhere he won't think to look for you."

"I don't understand. What do you mean? What did you find, Maddie?"

"Are you sure Mark was in New York the day Quinn died?"

"You think *Mark* killed Quinn?" Evelyn wasn't defensive, but awestruck. "What? Why?"

"Please, answer the question. Are you certain he was in New York?"

"We left for the airport at the same time on Friday, and... Oh god."

"What?"

"He got back early. He said he upgraded to first class, so he was the first to depart, but I-I don't know. His hair smelled like shampoo when he hugged me, not like he'd just gotten off a flight. He—Oh my god."

"Can you find proof? Can you look through credit card records to see if he spent any money in Pennsylvania that Saturday?"

"I-I can look, but why?" Confusion and heartache laced her voice. "What did you find, Maddie?"

"In those records from Steven, Quinn had called him Mr. Hyde. She considered him a monster. And a few months ago, he sent her a text that was meant for another woman. He told her it was meant for you, but I don't think that was the case."

A long moment of silence.

No doubt about it, that was a lot of heartbreaking information to take in at once. But everything in this moment pointed to Mark. "Evelyn, I need you to lock yourself somewhere safe while you look through those records, alright?"

"Sure." Almost inaudible. "Okay. Thank you."

I hung up.

"You're mad at her?" Bentley asked.

"You aren't?" I shot him a look. "Her daughter didn't trust that man, and she still married him."

"True," Bentley said. "But Quinn clearly didn't want to admit that she didn't like him. She didn't wanna hurt her mom."

"Well, Evelyn should've known. Your kid should come first. If you aren't one hundred percent sure that your boyfriend isn't gonna hurt your baby, they shouldn't make it past the damn door." I pointed ahead. "Make a right."

Chapter 30

As soon as she'd gotten off the phone with Maddie, Evelyn went to the gun safe in her walk-in closet. Her heart was already erratic, but it nearly exploded when she saw her nine-millimeter pistol was gone.

Actually, it wasn't Evelyn's. It'd been David's.

David's pistol was gone.

So was the box of bullets.

The safe was locked when she'd gotten to it, so a random thief hadn't stolen it. Mark had. Mark had David's pistol.

Evelyn hadn't even thought to check the gun safe after Maddie told her that she'd been shot at, nor when she'd been shot. She hadn't thought anything of telling Mark about the details of Maddie's investigation, either. Mark was her husband, her life partner. Why would she have thought to suspect him of anything?

Why had Quinn never told Evelyn she'd viewed Mark as Mr. Hyde?

Evelyn never saw Quinn and Mark as friends, but that had seemed normal. Quinn had been sixteen when Evelyn remarried. It would've been odd for Mark to be overinvolved in Quinn's life. Evelyn thought it was a good thing that Mark wasn't interested in his teenage stepdaughter.

But Quinn told Evelyn everything. Evelyn had thought, at least.

Now, that was far from the truth. Had she known, had Quinn told her she didn't like Mark, she never would've married him.

Shotgun and box of ammunition in hand, Evelyn returned to her bedroom. Once she sat on her bed, she opened her banking application. She and Mark shared a joint account. As grateful as Evelyn was that Mark had insisted on that now, she wanted to bash her head off a wall for not seeing how stupid that was from a financial perspective.

Finding nothing suspicious there, Evelyn went to her credit cards.

And there it was.

The day of Quinn's death, a purchase at the Pittsburgh airport. Mark told Evelyn he didn't make it to Pittsburgh until Monday.

She flipped back a few transactions to the Friday before Quinn's death. Victoria's Secret. A two-hundred-dollar tab at a bar, Evelyn made no attempt to pronounce. Another charge from that Friday, the Friday he claimed to spend resting in the hotel with room service, for almost three-hundred dollars.

If flames could've shot out of Evelyn's eyes and ears, they would've.

The day before her daughter was murdered, Mark took his mistress to get lingerie, to get drunk at a high-end bar, and then to a five-star restaurant. The next day, he took an early flight home. For what? Because Quinn told him she would tell Evelyn about his affair?

He killed her baby to keep his affair secret?

Heart slamming against her ribs, breaths uneven, Evelyn stepped into her slippers, loaded the gun, and jogged out her bedroom door.

Chapter 31

CAREFULLY STEPPING FROM BENTLEY'S TRUCK, DOING MY BEST TO stay quiet, I said, "No matter what you hear, stay put."

"So, if I hear you screaming, 'Help, I'm hit!' I should stay here."

"That's the exception." But I wouldn't say that unless I killed the guy. "Otherwise, stay here with the car off. You see someone run out here, you duck. If he knows you've seen him, he's gonna try to shoot you."

Bentley frowned. "I don't like this."

"You can leave, if you want."

"I'm not leaving, but I don't like it."

Note to self: leave Bentley at home next time.

Patting my thigh, I told Tempest, "Come."

"You don't think it's safe for me, but you think it's safe for her?"

"I think that if I tell her to stay, she will. And I think that once I'm sure he's unarmed, she can detain him until the cops get here. I get my confession, they make the formal arrest, and the case is closed."

Bentley's frown hadn't gone anywhere. "I still don't like this."

"Just stay put. You'll be fine."

"And you?"

"I've got a paramedic waiting for me." With a half-smile, I shut the door and started across the parking lot. Using the vehicles for camouflage, I ducked between them, keeping a mindful eye on the rear exit.

A sign that read *Maintenance* hung over three garage doors, each with windows. Lights shined beyond them. Evening luminance was common for any business, but these were the bold and bright ones. The kind that said someone was inside.

If Mark were only here to finish paperwork, why were the shop lights on?

Carefully approaching those garage doors with Tempy at my side, I held my gun tight in my hand. It held twelve rounds. I'd already used one, and I hadn't loaded more ammunition before Bentley picked me up.

That left eleven.

Usually, I only needed one.

Craning onto my tiptoes, I peeked into the garage. A combination of relief and excitement pulsed through me.

There it was. A black Lincoln. Front end smashed in from the accident. Busted up driver's side mirror. Shattered passenger side rear window.

Sliding out my phone, I swiped to Derek. Eyes peeled in every direction, I whispered a voice note. "Barne's Automotive, get your guys here now. Mark Hathway's the driver. I'm looking at the car right now. I have reason to believe he killed Quinn Barnes. I'm going in to get a confession with Tempest. Bentley's in the parking lot, so if you see a guy in a green pickup outside, don't shoot. He's my ride."

Clicking my phone to silent, I slid to the audio recording application and pressed start.

"Come," I said to Tempest, tiptoeing to the man-door beside the garage door. She followed at my side, panting heavily. "Quiet."

Her panting ceased.

Thankfully, the man-door was unlocked. Turning the handle slowly, I inched inside, gun drawn. I rotated either direction, mindful of any movement. There was none. Ducking low to look beneath the vehicles, again, I found nothing.

With caution, steps as silent as a cat's, I listened closely.

Almost inaudible, a voice sounded in the distance. Mark? Was he on the phone?

It came from my right.

Chill creeping up my spine, I stalked slowly toward that door. Gun held out before me, the quiet clink of Tempy's claws on the concrete drowned out the voice in the distance.

Continuing ahead through the cracked doorway, the hinges remained silent. The scent of rubber invaded my nostrils, and I focused on it. Grounding techniques, like paying attention to every sense your body picked up on, was the best way to stay calm in times of crisis. Although this wasn't a crisis yet, if I was correct, I was approaching one.

Breaths slow and steady, the echo of the voice heightened in volume. It could've been because I was getting closer, or because the grounding technique was doing its job. However, it was still incomprehensible. There wasn't a way for me to be sure it was Mark at all.

It had to have been. Right? He had all the means and motive to have been responsible for everything.

Unless it was an employee. But what would an employee have to gain from Quinn's death?

All questions left my mind as I inched down the hall. Because the closer I got, the clearer the sound became.

Not one voice, but two.

Mark Hathway and Evelyn Barnes.

"Lie to me one more time!" Her tone was like acid. "One more time, Mark!"

"I'm not—"

Boom!

Trekking down the polished cement toward the sound of their voices, pain dulled with adrenaline, I cursed myself.

Calling Evelyn had been a mistake. I'd needed confirmation. Proof. Without some type of tangible evidence that Mark had been in Pennsylvania the day of Quinn's murder, I had nothing to use against him.

Now, there was plenty of proof. Steven's records would speak volumes in a courtroom, and the car was all we needed for an arrest.

Maybe not an arrest for Quinn's murder, but he was going away for the attempted murder of Steven Benedict. Hopefully, they'd throw the book at him and hit him with two counts of attempted murder for shooting me last night and attempting to run me over tonight. Not to mention all the vehicles he'd driven into in the college parking lot.

All of that would be for nothing if Evelyn had just shot him.

The flash of the gunshot had come from a door on my left. Arriving there, Tempest and I ducked inside.

"Lie to me again." Evelyn's tone was somewhere between infuriated and heartbroken. "And the next one's going through your gut."

"You're out of your damn mind, Evvie!" Mark screamed. "Put the gun down. We can talk."

Adjoining rooms. Their voices carried from the right.

Tiptoeing, struggling to see in the light of the moon and the dim glow cast from the glass door in the corner, I took in one more deep breath. Exhaling slowly from my nose when I reached the door, I told Tempy, "Stay," making sure she was tucked away from the entry.

She sat still and panted up at me.

I lifted a finger over my lips.

Tempy quieted.

Damn, I loved this dog.

I tipped my head around the glass door that separated this space—a breakroom, I imagined—from the manager's office.

On the other side of the glass, beyond the desk, stood Mark. His arm was outstretched, gun in hand. Behind him, in an open cabinet, was a safe. Also open. A duffle bag sat on the tabletop, overflowing with cash.

A hole the size of a cantaloupe was blown through the wall straight ahead, which I imagined was why Mark hadn't fired his gun. While his was a pistol, Evelyn stood with a shotgun perched on her shoulder. Looked like she had a solid shot lined up, but with a gun like that, she didn't need perfect aim.

"Yeah. Let's *talk*, Mark." Evelyn's voice was rougher than a jagged piece of shattered glass. "Let's talk about why you were in Pittsburgh the day Quinn died."

"That's not true—"

"My credit card statement's the liar, then?" she snapped. "My apologies. I guess I'm gonna have to call and complain about the charges at Victoria's Secret from the day before too, won't I?"

I began inching open the glass door. Neither of them seemed to notice. I lined up my shot at Mark's forearm. Not an easy shot to make, and I typically aimed for the shoulder. But I didn't have that option here.

Uncomfortably licking his lips, Mark shook his head. "Our card must've been stolen—"

"Ah, yeah, that makes perfect sense. Why didn't I think of that? That explains why you're emptying my safe and aiming a gun at me too, doesn't it, Mark?"

"You just shot at me!"

"You wanna see me shoot at you?" She repositioned the shotgun on her shoulder. "This is the last time I'm going to say it. Tell me what the hell you did to Quinn."

"Nothing! I didn't—"

Boom!

The flash of gunfire lit up the room.

Drywall rained from above.

"Answer the—"

Another boom, this one from Mark's gun.

I pulled the trigger.

Chapter 32

But I'd moved my barrel.

Instead of hitting Mark in the arm like I would've liked to, I shot at the vase before him on the desk. As it shattered, shards of glass exploded in all directions.

Screaming, Mark dropped the pistol. He stumbled backwards. Blood drained down his arm.

Fingers crossed that wasn't from my bullet, 'cause I really didn't wanna go to jail tonight.

Thankfully, Evelyn bolted across the room and snatched the gun off the floor.

"Get him," I told Tempest.

She sprinted past me to Mark. When within a foot of him, she jumped. Tackling him to the ground with a clunk, Mark squealed again.

I jogged that way, gun centered on his face when I made it to his side. "Long time no see."

"Son of a bitch!" He rolled his head from side to side in agony, sobbing. Only then did I see why. A shard of glass at least four inches long protruded from his bicep.

Tempest snarled in his face.

"Grow some balls," I said. "I didn't cry when you shot me."

"I didn't shoot anyone!" Was he weeping or hyperventilating? I couldn't tell. "Get this thing off me!"

Part of me considered shooting him for calling Tempy a *thing*.

Evelyn lifted her foot and slammed it onto his bleeding arm, shoving the glass so far it surely came out the other side. Again, Mark wept his misery. Evelyn said, "You just tried to shoot me, asshole."

"Gaslighting at its finest," I said.

"I didn't do anything! Call an ambulance!"

They were already on the way, but Mark didn't need to know that.

"So, you text Quinn the message that was meant for your mistress," I began. "She's a smart girl. Does her own research. Finds the evidence she needs. But she's not sure what she's gonna do with it."

"No," he sobbed. "No, I didn't—"

"Shut up. I'm talking," I snapped. "Quinn has evidence that you're cheating on Evelyn. Maybe she told you she'd keep it quiet. But the guilt's eating at her. So she takes up therapy again, with the same therapist she had when you started seeing Evelyn. This guy already knows the type of piece of shit you are."

"I don't know what you're talking—"

Evelyn lifted her foot and thrust it into his bleeding arm again. I wished I could thank her for that. "She said *shut up*."

Sobbing, he rolled his head away from Tempest, eyes sealed shut.

"Quinn called you the Saturday of her death," I said. "You told me it was because she'd lost her keys, but that wasn't it at all, was it, Mark?" He only wept. "She was going to tell Evelyn. She was gonna tell Evelyn *everything*. That she always suspected you married her for her money. So you could get out of your shit job at that shit shop. So you weren't a poor, useless—"

"Shut up!"

I laughed. "That's what it's all about, huh? Money. You're a washed up peaked-in-high-school nobody without Evelyn. Quinn told you that, didn't she? When she found out you were screwing around on her mom, she called you every awful thing you know you are—"

"Shut—"

Evelyn thrust her foot into his wound again. His cry was more of a scream now.

"And you were so mad that the spoiled little brat saw you for what you are. You started planning. You knew the cops were dumb enough to believe she was nothing more than a party girl. All you had to do was tie her down, sit on her chest, and pour those pills down her throat. That's what you did, right? You pried her lips open, dumped that ecstasy down her throat, and tied her to her bed, didn't you? What else did you do to her while she was tied to that bed? Did you spread her legs and—"

"No." His eyes opened to the size of moons. "I'd never want that little whore. Just like her professor didn't."

There it was. He may not have realized it, but he was seconds from giving himself away.

"Call her a whore one more time," Evelyn began.

"What was going through your head?" I knew this was awful for Evelyn to have to think about, but she was too adrenaline-filled to realize what I was doing. "How did it feel? When you were in the next room, hearing her scream for help, begging for her mom, were you getting off on it?"

He narrowed his gaze, as though he found that offensive. "She was gagged."

And there it was.

Mark didn't say, *Yes, I killed Quinn Barnes.* But he may as well have. With all the physical evidence, that would stand in court.

"How could you?" Evelyn sobbed. "She was a kid. She was my baby!"

"She was a little bitch!" Mark's eyes were as lethal as a blade. "She wasn't the precious little angel you thought she was."

Even with a beast of a German shepherd snarling above him, even with two guns aimed between his eyes, Mark had the audacity to blame that nineteen-year-old girl. Staring down at him, seeing that shift in his demeanor, comparing the way he looked now to the docile man I'd met earlier in the week, I understood that line Quinn had underlined in red pen.

O my poor old Henry Jekyll, if I ever read Satan's signature upon a face, it is on that of your new friend.

Quinn had annotated, *Even when you look him in the eye, Mr. Utterson, you can't see him for who he is. Why does no one see him for who he is?*

Now, I saw exactly what that young girl had. There was a devil in his gaze.

The only other time I'd seen a pair of eyes like Mark Hathway's, a ski mask veiled them. Those were dark, and Mark's were light but the ferocity, the devil like hatred, was blood curdling.

Mark Hathway may have killed for financial gain and the security of his social status, but there was little difference between him and the Country Killer.

"Shut your mouth," Evelyn said through gritted teeth. "Say another word about my daughter, and it'll be the last word you speak."

Not that I blamed her, but it didn't sound like she was bluffing. Her finger was eerily close to that trigger.

Barrel aimed very close to Tempy's face, I noted.

"Your little junky slut of a—"

Evelyn raised the gun.

I tackled her sideways.

Just as the *boom* sounded.

Landing on the sparkling cement, agony ripped up my leg, then through my arm. I struggled to grab the gun from Evelyn's hand. She shouted some profanities that didn't register. May as well have been, "Let me at 'em!"

She released when I said, "Quinn wouldn't want you in prison and that son of a bitch walking away the victim!"

When she stopped fighting, heaving in breaths as she collapsed to her ass, I flicked on the safety. "Alright?"

Face scrunched up in a combination of heartache and fury, she nodded.

Just as I kicked the gun away, Tempest yelped.

Pain stretched up my leg, slowing me as Mark scrambled to his feet, grabbed the duffle from the table, and bolted to the door.

Chapter 33

Come hell or highwater, Mark wasn't leaving this car dealership unless he was in cuffs. I may've been slower due to my knee, but I was no snail. He wasn't getting away from me this time.

Struggling to my feet, I ran after Mark with my gun in hand. After a tap on my hip, Tempest was at my side.

The bang of a door broke through the silence. Jogging as fast as I could, ignoring the pain, I focused on my other senses, listening closely for the sound of a vehicle. I didn't hear one, not yet, but I had no doubt Mark had a pair of keys in that bag.

Tempy looked up at me for direction. Much like Evelyn a few moments prior, her expression screamed, *Let me at 'em.* Noting her pace decelerating every few steps, my heart hurt.

Being the good girl she'd become, Tempest was holding back. I'd given the command to stay at my side. But she could catch up before Mark had time to get to a car. And she wanted to. That bastard had just hit her to free himself.

Tempy was out for blood now.

Knowing she trusted me as her handler now brought me immeasurable joy. We'd worked so hard to get here, and I wasn't sure if I'd ever been so proud. But when I looked down at her, I saw Bear for a heartbeat. Terror tore through me at the thought of losing her like I'd lost him.

But like me, Tempest had a job. It was bred into her DNA to work. Keeping her from her duty wasn't fair.

I just had to remind myself that Mark wasn't armed.

"Get him," I said.

Brown eyes lighting with excitement, Tempest barreled down the hall and cut a sharp right. She was out of sight in a blink.

Every second she was out of my field of vision burned something deep in my chest, making me run faster than I knew I should have. Heart drumming, all other sensations faded. All I could hear was my blood rushing through my veins. All I could see was the direction Tempy had run. Everything else blurred into nothingness. Even my limbs were numb, like I existed as pure energy darting down that hall after my dog.

An ear-piercing scream.

A snarl.

"Son of a bitch!"

She got him.

When we got home, she was getting all her favorite treats.

Rounding the bend, red *Exit* light glowing at the end of the hall, red and blue lights shining through the glass. Sirens sang like a hallelujah chorus.

On the floor, only a few feet before the door, Tempy had Mark by his ankle. Blood pooled beneath him. Sobbing, he yanked against her grasp. For most, I would've told them that the harder they pulled, the more it'd hurt.

For killing his own stepdaughter, Mark deserved every ounce of misery.

The door swung inward.

"Put the gun down!" a voice said, flashlight aimed at me. It dulled the rest of him, but I imagined he had a gun on me, too. "On the ground, *now!*"

Holding my arms in the air, I said, "I'm the one who called. Just let me—"

"On the ground!"

Well, I'm getting there, pal.

"I'm gonna put the gun down first." Aiming it at the concrete, I lowered it to the cement. "And then I'm gonna stand with my hands up at my sides because I have an injured knee, and I can't kneel easily. Is that okay?"

A few seconds of quiet passed, like he was trying to connect the dots. His voice wasn't familiar, so if he knew me, I didn't know him. "Castle? Madison Castle?"

"Yes, sir." Straightening, I held either hand up at my side. "And my dog's got your killer there. Can I tell her to release?"

The aim of the flashlight, and presumably the gun, turned on Mark in the center of the hallway. "I've got him. Give her the word."

"Free him," I told Tempest. She released. "Come."

She bolted to me, wagging her tail and smiling widely, blood pouring from her sparkly canines.

"Lay down." She did. "Stay." She didn't move, just panted up at me, licking crimson from her lips before smiling again. It was hard not to laugh. "Good girl."

Chapter 34

MARK HATHWAY GLARED AT ME FROM THE GURNEY. AS THEY loaded him into the back of the ambulance, cuffed to the rails, I smiled. Waving my fingertips, I watched his glare deepen.

After they'd read Mark his Miranda rights and put him in cuffs, Evelyn and I gave our statements. We left out the part where Evelyn attempted to shoot Mark. While Derek was speaking to her, I took a second to examine Tempest. She was fine, but I still planned to take her to the vet on Monday morning.

While I squatted away from the crowd, I trimmed Mark's confession, cutting the part where Evelyn's gun fired, and the part where she threatened to shoot him. It was down to a thirty second clip by the time I was done, mostly of me insisting I'd known what he'd done, and that snippet where he admitted to gagging her.

Was it questionable to cover Evelyn's ass? Sure. But she was writing my check, and I needed that money. Aside from my personal gain, Evelyn had done nothing wrong. She'd learned that her husband murdered her child. I would've tried to blow his brains out, too.

The jacked-up Lincoln in the garage had been enough evidence for Derek to make an arrest for aggravated vehicular assault. He expected to tack on an attempted murder charge once he spoke with the judge. After

241

I sent him the confession, Derek said he was certain it was enough to charge Mark with Quinn's murder. Once ballistics collected enough evidence from last night's shooting in the woods, paired with my bullet wound, Derek believed the district attorney would hit Mark with assault with a deadly weapon and an *additional* attempted murder charge.

This wasn't a victory. The true victory would've been if Quinn were safe in her dorm tonight. But watching that ambulance pull from the lot provided a sense of respite. Victory was best, but justice was a close second.

"Excuse me." Detective Fitz's voice caught my attention. "Do you have a minute, Castle?"

Tempy growled at my side.

I shot her a look.

Almost seeming to grumble, she sat. As if to say, *Fine, I'll shut up, but I don't like him, so keep your guard up.*

I tucked my arms across my chest. "What is it?"

Fitz scratched his head, uncomfortable. "Look, I wanted to apologize."

"I don't accept it." I nodded across the lot to Evelyn, who was still speaking with an officer. "That lady's owed it more than I am, though. Try giving it to her."

"I will." He stowed his hands in his pockets. "And I understand why you're upset. There was clearly more to this case than I realized."

"You did realize," I shot back. "You knew your buddy was screwing her. To protect him, you almost let a young girl's murderer get away. As a result, he attempted to kill three more innocent people. Do you think he would've done that if there were an ongoing formal investigation? Or do you think he stalked me, and shot at me, and ran over Steven Benedict because he thought no one would care?"

Fitz slouched, avoiding my gaze. "I see now what you did."

"Please answer the question, Detective." Propping my hands on my hips, I stepped forward. "Do you think he would've attempted to kill you the way he attempted to kill me? Or do you think he thought no one would care if the poor, lower class, washed up P.I. ended up dead?"

"I don't think that about you. You're a hero, Castle."

"*He* thought that about me," I said. "Just like he thought no one would care about Quinn because she had a history with casual drug use. And you played right into it, because you don't care about people who live certain lifestyles or fit into certain demographics. It was *your* biases that nearly let a man get away with tying an innocent girl to her bed, force feeding her drugs, and letting her die in misery."

Shame shined in his eyes. "It wasn't a bias—"

"Yes, it was. And all to protect your friend. What'd he do for you? Let you live in his mansion while you drank all your money away? Or maybe you gambled it away?" One of those struck a nerve, judging by the way Fitz's shoulders curled inward. "That's your cross to bear, Detective. Hopefully, you'll think about the consequences before you allow yourself to be manipulated again by a murderer and a grown man who likes to sleep with little girls."

"Hang on just a minute now," he began, but I'd already turned away. "She was an adult, Castle."

I shot him a hand signal that showed my disgust. Regardless of whether it was legal for Professor Carlyle to screw his eighteen-year-old student didn't make it acceptable.

Only then did I see Bentley waiting on the other side of the blockade. I could practically see his heart getting ready to slam from his chest. Tense, eyes wide, he searched the crowd.

With a wave to catch his gaze, I walked that way. When he saw me, his posture relaxed. His deep breathing formed a cloud in the chilled spring evening.

"Sorry I'm just finding you," I said once within hearing distance. "I had to talk to the medics, and then I had to send Derek my evidence, and I kinda forgot you were here."

"I'm gonna try to not be offended by that." A half smile. "Are you okay?"

"We're fine. No new bullet wounds or anything. I'm gonna be a while though. I probably have to go to the station. There are a million reports to file."

"I can take you, if you want."

"I can't tell you how much I appreciate that." I smiled back. "But I'll manage."

"I don't mind."

"I mind. You've done enough for me this week. Please, go home. Get some sleep."

Bentley's expression was torn. Like he wanted to say I was right, but he also didn't want me to think he was abandoning me here. "It's not a big deal. I can wait."

"The bags under your eyes say otherwise. But"—I held out Tempy's leash—"would you mind taking her home for me? She's gotta be exhausted. And she took a hit from the guy."

"Aww." He squatted to look her over. "Want me to just keep an eye on her? You can take her when you get home?"

"That's perfect."

"Will do then." Taking the leash, he guided her beneath the barrier. "And if you need a ride, just call me."

"That won't be necessary," Evelyn said on my left, walking toward me. "I'll make sure she gets home in one piece."

Bentley looked at her, then at me as if to say, *Do you trust her?*

"Bentley, this is Evelyn Barnes. She hired me for this case. Evelyn, this is my friend Bentley. I totaled my car chasing Mark tonight and Bentley came to pick me up."

"Must be fate," Evelyn said. "You needed a new one."

Bentley chuckled.

I glowered.

Evelyn managed what she could of a smile. "I was hoping you'd let me take you to get something to eat before we head to the police station. I wanted to go over everything with you."

Certainly wasn't turning down a free meal.

* * *

EVELYN AND I HAD DRIVEN IN SILENCE TO THE NEAREST DINER. Aside from both ordering a coffee, we'd been quiet since sitting down as well.

There was no emotion on Evelyn's face. It was all settling in, I supposed. When she got home, when she walked past her daughter's room, when she saw Mark's things hanging in her closet, I imagined she would fall apart. In this moment, though, she was numb.

"I should've known," she said eventually.

"You shouldn't have had to suspect your husband."

"No, but I'm a lawyer. I know when people lie. I don't know why I didn't see it with Mark." Swirling her spoon through her coffee, she toyed mindlessly with the empty sugar packet in her free hand. "I should've found it suspicious that he was there when I got off my flight."

"Should've, could've, would've. Nothing you can do about it now." As frustrated as I was with her for not realizing it, after seeing that shift in Mark's demeanor, I understood. "Evelyn, you're a victim in all this too. Mark's a psychopath. He manipulated you from the beginning."

She snorted a laugh. "That's exactly why I should've known."

"Lawyers aren't psychiatrists," I said. "Who does best with a jury? Attractive, charismatic, psychopaths. The Marks of the world. And the smart ones no one knows about until they've done something horrendous."

"Quinn did." She said that so quietly, I almost didn't hear it. "Quinn knew."

"Did she tell you?" I asked, mostly for the sake of conversation, but also curiosity. "Did she ever say to you, 'Mom, I don't trust Mark. I think he's after your money.' Or 'I think Mark's gonna kill me.'"

Evelyn rolled her eyes. "If she had, I would've divorced him."

"Did she ever say *anything* that made you question him?"

"A few times when she was in high school, she mentioned that he'd never replace her dad. She called Mark a dick once or twice, but nothing that stood out." Evelyn chewed her lip. "I brought that man into our house. If Quinn had told me, I would've ended it. She came first. She *always* came first. I never would've put her at risk."

"Then you need to stop blaming yourself."

"How?" She finally looked up from her coffee. "How am I supposed to look in the mirror after this?"

"You just do," I said. "There're always things left unspoken when you lose someone. But one thing you can be grateful for is that you and Quinn didn't leave things off on a bad note. Quinn died knowing you loved her. When she was dying, she managed to write you a message on the window, probably using her nose as a pencil, just so you knew she was thinking about you. That she was loving *you* in her final moments. That's more than most of us can say for those we've lost."

Evelyn studied me for a few heartbeats, blinking at tears. "You don't think she blamed me when she was dying?"

"No. I think she was pissed you wouldn't know the bastard's dirty little secrets," I said. "The fact that you would've left him if you'd known how Quinn felt speaks volumes."

"It doesn't mean a damn thing to her in the grave."

Evelyn had every right to feel her feelings in this situation. But as someone whose mom brought shitty men into my house and forced me to eat dinner with them, maybe I could give her some solace right now.

"One of my mom's boyfriends came into my bedroom when I was sleeping one night. I think I was around thirteen," I said. "He didn't get the opportunity to touch me. I kneed him in the balls so hard, he couldn't walk. Guess who went to school with a black eye the next day?"

Evelyn's fallen mouth and wide eyes told me she didn't expect that trauma dump.

"I'm just saying. Coming from someone who had a horrible mother, none of this is your fault. Had Quinn come to you, had she told you how much she hated him, only for you to blame her, then it'd be your fault. But she was trying to protect you. She wanted you to be happy. It's not your fault she's gone. It's not your fault that you didn't know your husband was a psychopath. You were a heartbroken, single mom. A sweet guy came in and swooped you off your feet. The way narcissists do. He made sure you only ever saw Dr. Jekyll. He hid Mr. Hyde in a closet, and he only let him out when he knew you weren't looking. You can't blame yourself for not having eyes on the back of your head."

Again, she was quiet for a few. Just when she opened her mouth to speak, the server set our plates in front of us. We both said our thanks. When I began cutting my waffle, Evelyn didn't move a finger.

With the maple syrup coated goodness in my mouth, I felt Evelyn's eyes on me. Between chews, I said, "What?"

"Who was he?"

"Who was who?"

"The married man," Evelyn said. "You found him, didn't you?"

Swallowing, I covered my mouth. "You're not gonna shoot him, are you?"

Evelyn laughed. "No."

"Carlyle Moore. Quinn's English Literature professor," I said. "I have a recording of our encounter. I'll send it to you."

"I'd appreciate that. And you don't think he had anything to do with this?"

"No, Quinn had ended things with him. My guess is when she found out Mark was having an affair. I think realizing the pain that would put you through is what made her rethink sleeping with a married man. He also has a sound alibi," I said. "But he is a piece of shit, and I'd like to punch him."

That got another chuckle out of Evelyn. "How old is he?"

"Approaching sixty?" I couldn't stop my cringe. "I don't care if she was legal. They met when she was eighteen. He's a damn predator, and I'm gonna make sure he loses the job that gives him access to young girls."

"I'd like to be the one to tell his wife, if you don't mind."

"Sure. Just let me know when so I can blast his ass online. Colleges like to sweep things like this under the rug to protect their reputations. I'm gonna make sure every university in the country knows who this man is."

"If he sues for slander, you call me." Evelyn sipped her coffee. "I'll cover the case pro-bono."

"You've got yourself a deal," I said.

"While we're on the topic of finances"—Evelyn dug in her purse for her checkbook and scribbled on one of them—"I believe this covers your services."

When she slid the check across the table, I had to stare at it for a solid minute before it registered.

$15,000.00

"That's more than I expected," I said.

"You did more than I expected."

Picking it up, staring at the numbers, I laughed. "You're serious."

"I am."

"It's not gonna bounce?"

"It will not."

"This isn't a mistake?"

Sighing, Evelyn lifted her fork and sliced into her sausage patty. "You believed me when no one else did. You took a bullet to find my daughter's killer." She paused. "Also, you kept me out of jail."

All things considered, it was logical. She was right. I had done those things. And I didn't like handouts, but I knew Evelyn's wallet wouldn't suffer for this. I needed it, considering my totaled car.

"Eh." Stowing the check in my hoodie pocket, I smiled. "The bullet went through me. I didn't really *take* a bullet."

"One way or the other, you deserve this." Evelyn gulped her water that time. "And please, for the love of god, use it to buy a new pair of shoes."

That wasn't a bad idea. But I thought back to what Bentley had said the other night.

First thing on the list was health insurance.

Chapter 35

Once we finished eating, Evelyn and I went to the state police department to give our formal statements. I turned over all the evidence I'd gathered throughout my investigation. And just as we were walking to Evelyn's car, as ironic as the timing was, I got a phone call from Alice Benedict.

Steven had woken. He wasn't his best, but they expected a full recovery after extensive physical rehabilitation. Despite his condition, he asked Alice to speak to me. Of course, I went back into the police station to let Derek hear the conversation. Evelyn waited outside.

Steven explained that he'd seen the driver who hit him. As we'd suspected, it was Mark Hathway. Steven admitted that he didn't have substantial evidence that Mark had hurt Quinn, but Quinn had known about Mark's affair and debated in length whether she should tell Evelyn. The other woman Mark was seeing lived in New York, was barely twenty-five, and was unlikely to cross Evelyn's path.

That affair was why Quinn returned to therapy, and why she eventually broke things off with Carlyle. Not only did she feel guilt for being the other woman, but she slowly noticed the patterns of abuse from men like Carlyle and Mark. Although Quinn felt neither she nor Mark's mistress were innocent in the matter, both Carlyle and Mark exploited young girls who were too naive to realize what they were to them.

Steven recognized that and was prepared to testify against Mark Hathway in court.

Once that was established, Steven wanted to speak to Evelyn. I gave them some space, trying not to pry as she dabbed at her teary eyes. I hoped Steven was telling her how much Quinn loved her. Given the softness of her demeanor when she handed me my phone, I assumed that was the case.

"I'm sorry again for your loss, Evelyn," I said. "But I hope you find some comfort knowing that her killer's behind bars."

"Don't know if I'd call it comfort. Maybe more like relief." With a deep breath, she nodded to her car. "Now come on."

"I'm just gonna call an Uber," I said. "You go home. Get some rest."

"I'm not taking you home." Evelyn unlocked her car doors. "And I'm not arguing with you. Just get in the car."

"You're not gonna shoot me for ruining your marriage, are you?"

An eye roll. "Get in the damn car, Madison."

"You didn't answer my question."

"They took my guns." She waved toward the police station. "Now let's go."

MORNING SUN REFLECTING FROM THE WINDSHIELDS BLINDED ME AS we pulled into the lot of Barne's Automotive. The many cruisers and ambulances that'd been here last night had cleared out. Any evidence that remained of Mark's arrest was long gone.

I was still unsure of why we were here, but every time I'd asked for an explanation, Evelyn turned up the music. When we rolled to a stop by the rear door, she told me to get out. I did. She told me to stay put, went inside, came out a moment or two later, and waved for me to follow her. Again, I did.

Weaving through the maze of vehicles, Evelyn stopped at a Subaru

Impreza hatchback. Purple vinyl wrap that twinkled like diamonds in the sun encased it. White butterfly decals accentuated both the left and right side, wrapping onto the hood. The rear end was coated in bumper stickers. Adorable, paisley printed covers lined the seats.

Evelyn made a vague gesture to the car that looked like it'd climbed out of a five-year-old's fantasy. "Do you want it?"

I would've been a liar if I said I wasn't tempted. It was far from professional, but something about it made me giddy. "How much do you want?"

"Just pay for the title transfer." Crossing her arms, she leaned against it. "A college kid traded it in. We only paid a grand or two for it once the paperwork was done. It's only got sixty thousand miles. Runs well. All wheel drive. And it'd cost me thousands to get this decorative wrap off and repaint. The interior's a pig sty. Burn holes on the seats, writing on the ceiling, pop stains. And stains from other mysterious liquids I don't wanna know about. The guys in the shop were pissed Mark accepted a trade in for it at all. All the cosmetic stuff is gonna make it a bitch to sell. So do you want it?"

For free? Evelyn wanted to give me a car for *free*? "Are you serious?"

"Look, you solved my kid's murder and totaled your own car. If you were working for a company or the government, they'd cover the cost of a new vehicle. But you do this on your own for pennies because you got screwed trying to catch a murderer the cops and FBI couldn't. Just like you caught a murderer they couldn't last night." Evelyn's tone was flat, face emotionless. "And if I'm being honest, I have an absurd amount of money and belongings that I don't need and no one to share them with anymore. I feel like shit, and I wanna do something good for someone. You seem like the kind of person who's worked your ass off time and time again, and life's slapped you in the face for it. You deserve some good karma. So, do you want it or not?"

I blinked hard, staring at her, and then at the car.

Was this what people meant when they said luck was finally on their side? Couldn't think of a time when I'd had much of that. And here a giant chunk of it was.

No, a purple car covered with butterflies was not the ideal ride for a private investigator. In fairness, my rumbling SUV hadn't been either. Neither were discreet.

But how the hell could I turn down a free car? Especially a free car that was so damn cute?

"You're sure?" I asked.

"Is that a yes?"

"You've already given me a lot of money, and I don't want to take advantage of you, but if you're sure—"

"Let's go do the paperwork."

* * *

THE DRIVE HOME DIDN'T FEEL REAL. MAYBE THE SLEEP deprivation was to blame for that. Could've been a mild concussion from the accident last night, too.

Or maybe it was the fact that there was a GPS on my dashboard, my phone played music via Bluetooth, and there wasn't a spring jutting into the side of my thigh.

It was an average vehicle, nothing extravagant, but it felt fancy compared to the SUV that was almost as old as me. And the funny thing was, as I drove it, a vague memory from my childhood floated back to me.

When I'd been around five, Mom's license was suspended for a D.U.I.. She'd thrown a fit about how she needed a car to get to work. Dad worked in construction, meaning he'd made more than she had at the gas station. So he'd saved up and got her a minivan. It wasn't extravagant either, but it was better than his lemon.

On the way home from the store one day, Mom had nodded off behind the wheel. From the back seat, I'd screamed for her to wake up as we swerved off the road. She didn't. Not until the car slammed into a telephone pole. Neither of us had been hurt, but the minivan was done for.

When the cops came, they'd arrested Mom for another D.U.I. and called my dad. He'd picked me up at the police station. On the drive back to the trailer park, I'd said, "Daddy, why didn't you give Mommy this car?"

He'd asked what I meant.

I'd said, "Because she breaks everything. You shoulda gave her this one and kept the nice one."

In the rearview, I'd seen heartache in his eyes. "You're too young to worry about this shit, kid."

"But why?" I'd insisted. "Now the good car's gone. Why didn't you keep the good one?"

"Because a half-decent man doesn't let his girl drive his kid around in a car that isn't safe," he'd said. "If she would've wrecked this one, you guys might've ended up in the hospital. It sucks that it's gone, but you're okay because you were in the good car, and that's all that matters."

Once, when my brake line had gone out in the SUV, I'd barely made it to Ox's condo. I'd asked him to co-sign for me so I could get a new used car. Ox's counteroffer had been *loaning* me the money to fix the brake line.

I'd thought about that conversation with my dad that day, but I'd pushed it to the back of my mind. *Ox is a good man*, I'd told myself. *It's not a big deal. I'll get the brake line fixed, and I'll save up on my own to get a new car eventually.*

Last night, Bentley had offered to co-sign for me to get a new car.

Now, he didn't need to, but that memory gave me confidence in ending that kiss with Ox. And in a future with my best friend.

Soaring down the highway, I played with the acceleration to get a feel for how it handled. There was something about the way the seat cradled my body that took pressure off my knee, although that could've been because pressing on the brakes didn't feel like a workout. The back had plenty of space for Tempy.

For the first time in my life, I was driving a nice car, and it was mine.

I couldn't believe it was mine.

I couldn't believe I had a check for fifteen grand in my pocket and another five in the bank.

As I pulled into the trailer park, the oddest sensation hit me. Like an all-encompassing bubble of contentment wrapped itself around me, whispering, *This is your life.*

By no means was it a dream, but it was becoming less of a hellscape by the second. I'd started over with nothing. There was no way for me to guesstimate where life would lead me. But it brought me home, and as much as I'd resented it when everything fell apart, for the first time, it felt like I'd rebuilt from the shambles.

Shifting into park in my driveway, I took in my trailer. Rust coated the siding where it hadn't fallen off entirely. Weeds claimed the flower beds. The handrail lining the stairs wobbled in the wind.

But it was mine. Just like this reliable, pretty car was mine. Once I handed Greg his check, that piece of shit tin can was mine. Not Ox's. Not my mom's.

No one would be able to kick me out. No one could derail my life again. Sure, the trailer needed some work, but now that I had an extra four hundred bucks a month that had been going toward paying it off, I could fix it up. Maybe I'd paint it purple too.

Stepping from my car, I clicked the key fob to lock it. It was a small thing, but it made me smile. So did the automatic start I'd just realized it featured.

When I made it to Bentley's door, I tapped on the frame. Tempy erupted in barks on the other end. Bentley said something to her that I didn't catch. A few minutes later, the door swung inward.

He was still in the pajamas he'd been wearing last night. The brown curls around his face were a knotted mop, but something about his sleepy brown eyes made my heart skip a beat. "You look way too happy for eight in the morning."

"'Cause I am. Look." I pointed to my driveway. "Look what I got."

Still half asleep, he squinted that direction. Then his eyes widened. A laugh escaped him. "That's yours?"

"It is."

"I like the butterflies." Stifling a yawn, still in his slippers, he walked past me off the stairs. "Ooh, it's got a bike rack."

"And a GPS." Tempy howled inside, so I tossed Bentley the keys. "I'm gonna go grab her."

Another vague nod, still trying to blink himself awake.

Tempy's crate was in the living room, so it only took me a minute to let her out and give her some affection. I told her it was time to go outside, and she waited for me to clip her leash to her harness.

Once we were in the yard, Bentley surveyed every inch of my car.

"The wrap job is pretty well done." Then he straightened, expression stone-cold serious. "But how many miles is on it?"

"Sixty thousand."

"When was it inspected?"

"Last month."

"Is there a spare?"

"What?"

"A spare tire." He furrowed his brows. "Maddie, please don't tell me you bought a car and didn't check that it had a spare tire."

Oops. "I did not do that."

Bentley frowned. "Why didn't you call me? I might not look like it, but I'm good at haggling. I could've gotten them to come down *and* made sure they gave you a spare."

"I don't think you could've."

"Are you questioning my haggling skills?"

"I'm sure you're an excellent haggler." Smiling, I guided Tempest to the car. "But you couldn't have gotten it any lower than what I paid for it."

"And what'd you pay for it?"

"Nothing." My smile grew. "Evelyn gave it to me."

Bentley was less bubbly in the mornings, it seemed, because his face was still screwed up in disbelief. "You're kidding."

"I am not."

"She gave you this car."

"I paid for the title transfer, but yep," I said, giving Tempest a head scratch when she sat at my side. "Wanna go for a ride? I'll tell you about it on the way. Coffee's on me."

"Sure." Bentley stifled another yawn. "But I gotta pick up Grace at ten."

"We can pick her up in this, if that's okay," I said. "I kinda wanted to take her with me somewhere today, anyway."

"What for?"

I smirked. "It's a surprise."

Chapter 36

"The whole thing's insane." Bentley leaned back in his seat, whooshing some hair from his face. "All night, I tried to wrap my head around it, and I just can't. How could anyone do something like that?"

I was just as stunned by the findings of the investigation initially, but now, it'd settled in.

"I don't get it either, but it's not like it's the first time a parent has hurt their kid," I said. "We both know that."

"Yeah, but our parents hit us in a blind rage. Usually 'cause they were drunk or high." He passed Tempest, who sat on the concrete beneath the patio table, a hunk of banana from his fruit bowl. "This guy premeditated murdering his stepdaughter. Just because she was gonna tell her mom about his affair."

"I think it was to protect his reputation, too. Narcissistic psychopaths will do any and everything to make sure they look good."

"That's even worse." Bentley's face was a little green at the idea. "This is the shit that makes me scared to date. You think you know some-one, and then they kill your damn kid."

I wasn't sure why that made my stomach churn. Coulda been at the thought of someone hurting Grace, or at the thought of Bentley getting a girlfriend. The former was obviously worse than the latter, but neither were comforting.

"If you bring a narcissistic psychopath into Grace's life, and the bitch tries to hurt her, we've got that shovel in your shed."

He laughed, shaking his head. "I don't wanna bring anyone new into her life."

"Never?" I asked. "I thought you said you were ready to get back on the road with the right person."

The corners of Bentley's eyes wrinkled, and a hint of a smile touched the edges of his lips. "Yeah. With the right person."

That look said it all.

Or at least, that's what I would've said if I wasn't so close to the situation. But I knew what I wanted, and maybe I was drawing conclusions where there were none. Maybe I was seeing what I wanted to see.

"For what it's worth, I think I'm ready to get back on the road, too." Reaching across the table for the sugar packets, I smiled. "With the right person."

His smile was as genuine as mine, and all doubt vanished.

We were on the same page. We wanted the same thing.

And then he said, "But I think I need to drive slow. Like, *really* slow. The way old people drive after church on Sundays. Ya go too fast when you've been off the road for a while, and something's gonna go wrong. And I don't want that. I wanna take good care of the car I get in with the right person."

Chest warming, my stomach flipped.

We did want the same things, but whatever was budding between us mattered too much to rush into. "That makes sense. Because if you rush, whenever you get to a tight bend, you're gonna fly off the road."

"And then everyone inside gets hurt. Nobody wants that."

"'Course not. I wanna take care of my new car. And the people in it."

His eyes flicked over me, smile inching higher. "So we're on the same page."

"I think we are."

* * *

BOTH EXHAUSTED, WHEN BENTLEY AND I FINISHED OUR COFFEES, we got two more for the road. The drive to Grace's friend's house was almost thirty minutes according to the GPS, but it took us closer to forty-five. We drove through backroads with the windows down, breathing in the smell of the spring flowers, stopping to watch the deer scamper across the road, singing to throwbacks Bentley played on my phone, and laughing at how horribly we both sang.

That sensation of comfort that'd come over me this morning transformed into joy as we drove those winding trails. Being with Bentley was the most freeing feeling in the world, regardless of context. With him, I let my brain shut off and focused solely on the moment I was in.

When we arrived at Grace's friend's house, and she came outside in her pajamas, brown hair tied into a messy bun atop her head, the cackle she gave my new car only made that sprout of joy within me grow taller. "*This* is your car?"

"You don't like it?" I waved over it, as though presenting a prize. "It's a work of art."

"Is it though?"

"Don't try to be cool for them," Bentley said, waving goodbye to the parents with Grace's friend on the porch. "You love purple."

"I do love purple, but butterflies? On a car? C'mon, Maddie."

"Hey, butterflies are pretty," I said.

"It looks like one of those battery-powered Jeeps for kids."

"And ya know what?" I opened her car door and gestured inside. "Five-year-old me would think I'm the coolest person in the world for owning a car like this."

"Would thirteen-year-old you?" Grace asked, sliding into the back with Tempy.

"Absolutely not." I sat in the driver's seat. "Thirteen-year-old Maddie was *so* not like other girls."

"I see what you're getting at." Grace laughed. "And it's not that I don't like it 'cause it's girly. I don't like it because the butterflies look tacky."

"Have you seen her house?" Bentley hooked a thumb in my direction as he sat in the passenger seat. "Tacky is Maddie's taste."

Narrowing my gaze, smiling, I said, "For that, I might reconsider getting you your surprise."

Chuckling, he apologized.

"You got him a surprise too?" Grace sat forward between the seats. "Can you tell me?"

"You can help me pick it out, if you want," I said. "That's where I'm going now."

"But he's here."

"She's dropping me off at the house and then taking you," Bentley said. "Unless you wanna be surprised, too."

"Nope, I'm gonna pick it out." She grinned at me in the rearview. "Thanks for letting me, Maddie."

"Any time, kid."

*　*　*

So, we did just that.

After dropping Bentley off at home with Tempy, Grace and I headed to the nearest shopping mall. In the car, I told Grace about my plan to get Bentley a new dining table. A good one, the kind that'd stand up to the many meals he'd serve at it. Grace got a little dewy-eyed at that, saying, "That's way too nice of you."

"Your dad does a lot for me," I said. "I got more than I was planning to from this case, so I can swing it. And he deserves it."

"He's gonna tell you he doesn't deserve that much, you know."

"And he's gonna have to suck it up, because I'm gonna 'lose'"—I held up air quotes—"the receipt."

Grace laughed. "Good idea."

"I thought so."

"Is that the only reason, though?"

"Is what the only reason?"

"Buying him this. Is it only because he does a lot for you, and you wanna return the favor?" She paused for dramatic emphasis, not continuing until I glanced from the road to her. "Or is it something else?"

It wasn't because I was interested in a relationship with Bentley. Buying him a new table really was because he deserved it and I had the money. Even if that weren't the case, I wouldn't be the one to tell Grace that.

"Friends do nice things for each other," I said. "That's all this is."

"It's not because you're in love with him?"

"No, Grace, I'm not in love with him." Although, I might've been falling.

"I don't believe you. And I don't believe him when he says so either," she said. "Why are you both lying to yourselves? It's so stupid. You're together all the time, anyway. Just kiss already."

"No one's lying to anyone."

"Even *that's* a lie, and you know it."

Chuckling, I glanced from the road to her. "Why are you so insistent about us getting together, kid? You've only known me a couple months."

"But he's known you forever, and he loves you. I think he's always loved you," she said. "He's been lonely for too long. His whole life is about me. And I love him for that, but I'm gonna be eighteen in a few years. I'll go to college, and he'll be even lonelier than he is now."

"It's sweet that you're worried about him like that," I said. "But he'll be okay without you."

"Yeah, he'll *survive*, but he won't be *happy*," Grace said. "And he deserves to be happy. When you're around, he is. He's happier than he's been since my mom died. No one makes him as happy as you do."

That wasn't true. Grace made him happier than anything. But I saw the point she was making. "And I can do that as his friend." I shot her a smile. "You don't need to be in a relationship to be happy."

She quieted for a few seconds. When I looked over, she was frowning.

"What's the matter?"

"That's really all you see him as?" she asked. "Because I know he sees you as more, and if there's no chance, you should tell him so."

Damn. The tone changed quickly.

"It's not fair to string him along," Grace continued. "Friend zoning him isn't—"

"Alright, hang on a second," I said. "I'm not stringing anyone along. Stringing him along would be if I said I was in love with him one day and then blew him off the next. Being friends with someone doesn't require a platonic declaration, either. Contrary to what you might hear on TV, the friend zone isn't real. It's just something guys say when their friend of the opposite gender isn't interested in what they want. And I didn't say I wasn't interested in something like that *ever*. I said the reason I'm getting him this table is because he does a lot for me, and because I have the money right now."

The faintest hint of a smile edged up her lips. "But you might be interested in that one day? Is that what you're saying?"

I laughed. "Listen, you let me and your dad figure out what we wanna do in that department. No one needs you to play matchmaker."

"Fine. I'll stop," she said. "But are you saying you might wanna be with him one day?"

"I'm saying that the friend zone isn't real, and me and Bentley will decide if we want more than friendship when the time is right for us, and that right now, we're happy as friends. Okay?"

The biggest smile stretched across her lips. "Okay."

* * *

GRACE PICKED OUT A FARMHOUSE TABLE WITH DISTRESSED WHITE legs, a deep mahogany finish, and a drop leaf for when they had guests. It was beautiful, but not what I thought Bentley would like. I'd suggested the mid-century modern glass top table instead, saying it'd match their coffee and end tables.

Grace had said, "Dad doesn't like those. He says they're a bitch to clean. Mom picked those out. He likes this rustic stuff."

After reminding her not to cuss, I said, "The farmhouse table it is then."

Once the employees loaded the boxes into the back of my car, just barely squeezing it in, we headed home. We considered telling Bentley to go to the bedroom so he wouldn't see us unload it and set it up in the kitchen, but my knee wasn't its best.

So when we arrived, we told Bentley to come out and lug it into the house. The packaging didn't say what it was. He accused us of filling a box with bricks as he got his dolly from the garage and struggled it into the house for us.

While he did that, I walked to the trailer whose backyard bordered mine. Trekking through the mud, I bent to give Duke a pat on the head. Holding out a piece of kibble from my pocket, I told him to give me paw. When he did, I rewarded him with a handful.

Avoiding the landmines that coated Greg's yard, I scrubbed my sneakers on his pavers as a gentle reminder that he needed to clean up after his dog. Using the rickety wooden railing for stability, I climbed to his porch and knocked a few times.

He opened it in his usual glory—boxers and a stained white tank top—a moment later. Speaking through the cigarette perched between his lips, Greg said, "I didn't forget about that broken window lock. I'm coming by tomorrow to take care of it."

"Great. But that's not why I'm here." I held out the check. "Just don't cash it 'til tomorrow, so it clears my account first. I just did the mobile deposit thing, so it might take a few."

He looked down, then arched a brow at me. "You're paying off the trailer?"

"Sure am," I said. "Now it's just lot rent, right?"

"And utilities," he said, eyeing it a moment longer. "Well, damn, kid, good for you."

"Thanks. I'm still expecting you to make the repairs you promised me, though."

"Yeah, yeah." Coughing, he pulled the cigarette from his lips. "We can do the title transfer one day this week."

"You know where to find me." Walking off the porch, I smiled over my shoulder. "And thanks for selling her to me."

"So, you like it now, huh?" Greg asked. "Once upon a time you couldn't wait to get outta this place."

Bentley yelled from the porch, "Son of a bitch!"

"Stop being a baby," Grace said. "There's hardly any blood."

Laughing, I nodded that direction. "Home's who you're with, ya know?"

He eyed me for a minute, then his smile grew so wide, if I didn't know better I would've thought he'd just confiscated a bag of weed off a few teenagers. "It sure is, kid."

* * *

AFTER IT WAS IN THE KITCHEN, WE BANISHED BENTLEY TO THE bedroom and got to work. Assembly took us about half an hour. Standing neatly in the center of the dining area, all six chairs positioned carefully around it, Grace and I took a moment to admire our hard work. Then she gasped, nearly giving me a heart attack.

"What?" I asked. "What's the matter?"

"These!" Grace ran to the island, dug around in the drawer, and came back a moment later with a table runner and matching place mats. "This is what it's missing."

Once that teal piece of fabric was draped over the center, place mats resting before each chair, the new furniture looked like it was right where it belonged. Now that Grace mentioned it, I saw what she meant about Bentley's style. A dainty mirror with distressed shutters hung on the wall behind the table, little panels of wood dividing the glass into sections. Just last week, he'd installed a white subway tile backsplash and floating shelves above the counters that matched the mahogany finish.

The table, and those teal place mats, brought the whole room together.

"What do you think?" Grace asked.

"I think he's gonna love it," I said. "Go get him."

Giddy with excitement, she bounced past me toward his bedroom. Chatter sounded from that direction.

The pitter patter of claws on the floor clicked as Tempest came into view. I thought she was excited to see me, but the little maniac was ecstatic over the bubble wrap from the packaging. Taking it in her jaws, she shook her head back and forth, wagging her tail with each pop.

Coming from the hall, Bentley was first. Grace walked behind him with her hands over his eyes. Tripping over Tempest, he muttered a curse. "You're gonna get us both mauled."

"She doesn't care," Grace said.

That was true. Tempy was too concerned with popping every bubble to mind that Bentley had nearly pummeled her.

Waving her off, Bentley said, "Can I open my eyes yet?"

"Just a few more steps." Grace guided him forward, stepping carefully around the mounds of packing material scattered about. "Right about here."

She dropped her hands to her sides.

And Bentley's jaw hit the floor. Stepping forward to examine it closer, he laughed. "You got me a table?"

"Grace picked it out." I smiled. "But you won't let me buy you the ingredients for all the meals you cook for us, and it's about time I brought something to the table. Or the table itself."

"That was the lamest joke you've ever told," Grace said.

I stuck my tongue out at her.

Grace laughed.

Bentley stepped closer, warm smile spreading across his cheeks as he stroked a finger down the top. "And it's the real thing."

"Not that cheap pressed stuff." My smile widened. "Do you like it?"

"It's amazing. How much was it?"

"None of your business."

"It had to have been at least a grand." He reached into his back pocket for his phone. "What's your Venmo?"

It was three grand, actually. "It was 'you're out of your damn mind if you think I'm gonna let you pay me for a gift.' And fifty-six cents."

"A gift is a new jacket."

"Or a new table."

"Maddie, I can't accept—"

"You can, and you will." Snatching the phone from his hand, I pulled out a chair. "Sit. See how comfy the seats are."

"Yeah, we paid extra for the butt cushions," Grace said, skipping past him to the chair on my left. "Seriously, it's so nice. Oh, and look. See the leaf? It collapses below into the table. So it doesn't have to take up all that space in the closet anymore. It's perfect. Isn't it perfect?"

Bentley's eyes were full of joy, laced with guilt. Giving gifts was his preference, not receiving. I didn't like taking handouts either, but he forced me to every time he fed me, or took Tempest out for me, or helped me down the porch stairs when my knee was bad.

"You do everything for everyone else," I said. "You deserve something nice for yourself."

He was still smiling, but it was an awkward one. "Can you afford this?"

"Evelyn gave me that car, *and* twenty grand. So yes, I can. And I'm not taking no for an answer. You're gonna take this table, and you're gonna like it." I paused. "Well, if you don't like it, we can go pick out a new one, but putting it together was hell, so you're gonna do that part by yourself."

He opened his arms and wrapped them around me. Hugging me tight, he kissed the top of my head. "Thank you."

I could say, "Thank *you*," but he was probably tired of hearing that. Instead, I went with, "You're welcome." Craning up to look at him, chin against his chest, I embraced the hug for as long as he'd allow it. "So what's for lunch?"

Laughing, he tugged away and started to the fridge. "I've got some ribs thawing for dinner, but how about chicken wraps for now?"

"Ugh, we had chicken wraps on Tuesday," Grace said. "Can you make that homemade pizza?"

"I don't think we have sauce."

"Can we order a pizza, then?"

"We ordered pizza on Monday. Let's not eat out twice in a week."

"Maddie can buy it. She's rich now."

"Twenty grand isn't rich," Bentley said before I could. "No, we'll make something. How about…"

He proceeded to offer a dozen suggestions, all of which Grace protested. And it was a simple thing, a silly thing, really, but hearing them bicker, pulling on the toy Tempy brought me, watching Bentley dab some marinara sauce he'd decided was a decent substitute onto Grace's nose, was the sweetest feeling.

I didn't know what came next. Maybe in five years, Bentley would have that piece of land he was saving up for. Maybe he'd have a happily ever after with someone else by then.

Or maybe we'd be a couple, trying to figure out how both of our trailers would fit on that piece of land. Maybe we'd be arguing over which one we should live in. Maybe we'd both have a ring on a special finger.

Or maybe I was getting way ahead of myself.

One way or another, for the first time in my life, it felt like I was exactly where I was meant to be.

* * *

Maddie's story continues in **Hunting Grounds**, now available for pre-order here:

https://www.amazon.com/dp/B0BY38PCX9

Want a free copy of the Maddie Castle prequel novella? Sign up for the L.T. Ryan reader newsletter and download a free copy today:

https://liquidmind.media/maddie-castle-newsletter-signup-1/

Also by L.T. RYAN

Click on a series name or title for more information

Ripple Effect

Blowback

Take Down

Deep State

Rachel Hatch Series

Drift

Downburst

Fever Burn

Smoke Signal

Firewalk

Whitewater

Aftershock

Whirlwind

Tsunami (2022)

Mitch Tanner Series

The Depth of Darkness

Into The Darkness

Deliver Us From Darkness

Book 4 (2022)

Cassie Quinn Series

Path of Bones

Whisper of Bones

Symphony of Bones

Etched in Shadow

Concealed in Shadow (2022)

Blake Brier Series

Unmasked

Unleashed

Uncharted

Drawpoint

Contrail

Book 6 (2022)

Affliction Z Series

Affliction Z: Patient Zero

Affliction Z: Abandoned Hope

Affliction Z: Descended in Blood

Affliction Z : Fractured Part 1

Affliction Z: Fractured Part 2 (Fall 2021)

About the Author

L.T. Ryan is a *USA Today* and international bestselling author. The new age of publishing offered L.T. the opportunity to blend his passions for creating, marketing, and technology to reach audiences with his popular Jack Noble series.

Living in central Virginia with his wife, the youngest of his three daughters, and their three dogs, L.T. enjoys staring out his window at the trees and mountains while he should be writing, as well as reading, hiking, running, and playing with gadgets. See what he's up to at http://ltryan.com.

Social Medial Links:

- Instagram: https://www.instagram.com/ltryanauthor/
- Facebook: https://www.facebook.com/LTRyanAuthor
- Twitter: https://twitter.com/LTRyanWrites
- Goodreads: http://www.goodreads.com/author/show/6151659.L_T_Ryan